Praises for Love Tag

"It has been a very long time since I've lost myself so completely in a novel. Shianna is a brilliant writer, a masterful weaver of words. His characters are blood-and-bones real. There is not a false note between the covers of his beautifully crafted book."

Esther Luttrell, author of *Murder in the Movies*

"*Love Tag* is a page turner. As a family copes with friendships, sexual exploits, adoption, temptation, marital strife, and faith, we identify with their love, sadness, anger, disappointment, and hope. I want a sequel!"

Lorraine Harris, author of *The Casserole Parade*

"Peter Shianna weaves an engaging tale of deceit, betrayal and pride. Right from the beginning, the reader is deftly brought into the lives of a family in crisis. *Love Tag*'s intriguing cast of characters, and their journeys, kept me turning the pages to the very end."

Lois Podoshen, Essayist

Also by Peter Shianna

Take Off: A Time for War, A Time for Love

See www.petershianna.com for more information.

LOVE TAG

A Novel

Peter Shianna

Fireside Publishing Company
Lady Lake, Florida

Published by
Fireside Publications
1004 San Felipe Lane
Lady Lake, Florida 32159
www.firesidepubs.com

Printed in the United States of America by
SPS Publications
POB 787
Eustis, Florida 32727
www.SPSpublications.com

This is a work of fiction. Names, characters, places, businesses and incidents are either the product of the author's imagination or are used fictitiously, and any resemblance to actual persons living or dead, events, places of business or locales is entirely fictitious.

PEPSI and PEPSI-COLA are registered trademarks of PepsiCo, Inc.

ISBN: 978-1-935517-50-4

This book is for

Loretta "Lori" Johnson Shianna

Lover, wife, friend.

Thank you!

Ray Andrews for your questions and comments, especially on structure, all of which were helpful.

Chris Coward for your astute line editing and deft touch. I find it difficult to express the depth of my gratitude.

Mary Lois Sanders for your general editing. Your tone-perfect ear remains unsurpassed.

Joan West, editor and publisher, for your gentle nudging and patience, and for catching things no one else did. Wine at Pizza Hut? The very idea!

LOVE TAG

Chapter One

Wade Lankar. The only person in the world who could pollute this special day.

Phil Tag ground his teeth and glanced around the auditorium. He would not allow the presence of Lankar to spoil the graduation ceremony.

David graduating from high school. Major, major victory. A year late but a big win.

Ellen sat on Phil's right in her butter-colored linen dress, as beautiful today as she was thirty years ago. Her auburn hair and summer complexion complemented her dress so perfectly that Phil couldn't resist squeezing her hand and brushing her thigh. Her White Linen perfume teased him every time he leaned against her.

Jessica sat on Phil's left. Discreetly flirtatious, she was the object of admiring appraisals from boys who weren't at all in her league. At home it had taken her a few minutes longer than the rest of them to get ready before she finally appeared in a white print dress, navy heels and matching purse, carrying an overnight bag for yet another sleepover. How lovely she had become at seventeen! No wonder the wannabe studs had begun coming around. *Well, let there be no mistake, boys: her Old Man's eyes'll be wide open.*

"DAVID TAG."

David strode across the stage to accept his diploma. Ellen squeezed Phil's hand. "If you don't stop beaming like that," she whispered, "they'll have to give everyone sunglasses."

He gripped her hand and took a deep breath to quell the surge in his chest. David outwardly epitomized the All-American

Boy: tall, athletic, a ready and winning smile. By lifting weights in moderation, he had given his body definition without developing rigid, bulging muscles. He waved his diploma and proceeded to his chair on the side of the auditorium, a walking commercial for confidence.

Hold it together, son. Be a winner.

The usual congratulations, handshakes and jostling among the new graduates followed the ceremony. Several of David's friends from his original graduating class had attended. Knowing there were parties planned and that David would want to leave soon, Phil motioned him aside and led him to the car, along with Ellen and Jessica. Phil opened the trunk of the Cadillac to display four Cragar S/S mag wheels for David's Camaro.

"Wow! The ones I wanted, Dad! How'd you know?"

"I have my sources. We couldn't agree on one gift, so we have something for you at home. Wouldn't fit in the trunk."

"And you won't know what it is till you get home," Ellen said.

David made a menacing face and shook his fist. Everyone laughed and took turns with the camera.

"We know you want to get to your party," Phil said. He shook David's hand and hugged him. "Have a good time and be careful."

After David left, Phil, Ellen and Jessica were getting into the car when a voice behind them said, "Hello, Tag. Did they give you a real diploma or a blank?"

Phil knew the voice. His fists tightened as he wheeled around to face the speaker, a large man with a toothy smile and bulging midsection.

"Hello, Wade. What brings you here?"

"Daughter of one of my VPs graduated." Wade Lankar thrust his hand out. Phil shook his head and did not extend his hand. Lankar drew back. The smile left his face. He snorted and turned away. "Still a loser."

Jessica watched the man walk away. "Who was that, Dad? Why wouldn't you shake hands?"

"How long have you known he was here?" Ellen asked.

"Let's get Jessica to her party."

"Who is he, Dad? What's going on?"

Ellen frowned and motioned for Jessica to drop it, and they all got into the car. After they dropped Jessica off, Ellen broke the silence. "How long?"

"What's the difference?"

"I think you know."

"From day one."

"Thanks a lot."

"There was no reason to concern you."

"Thirty years is a long time. Don't you think you should let it go?"

"I'm not stalking the jerk. But I haven't forgiven him, either."

"Obsessing like this and keeping it to yourself all these years doesn't sound healthy to me."

"Come on, El. Don't get spooky."

"Me get spooky?"

"It's not all in the past. For the last seven years, he's blocked me from doing business with Lars Borglund."

"He works for Borglund?"

"Executive VP. Number two guy in the food chain."

"And you just couldn't bring yourself to mention that, either."

"Honey, please. How often do I talk business at home? I don't want you to worry about Lankar."

Ellen closed her eyes for a moment. Then, staring straight ahead, she said nothing the rest of the way home.

Chapter Two

From Phil's vantage point on the forty-second floor of the IDS Tower in downtown Minneapolis, the jets approaching Minneapolis-St. Paul International from the west appeared to fly at eye level. It was a perceptual sleight of hand so realistic that Phil could almost smell the exhaust fumes as the planes made their final approaches to runways one-one left and one-one right.

He fought the urge to drive to Flying Cloud Airport, where he hangared his Cessna 182. Maybe do some touch and go's for an hour. No, there wasn't enough time. Besides, why put more hours on a plane up for sale? God, he hated to sell it. He'd rather cut off a thumb, but he just couldn't afford a plane right now.

Turning from the window and going to his desk, Phil recalled the real estate broker's glowing description of the view from the Normandale Lake office building in Bloomington. The young broker's enthusiasm had overcome Phil's misgivings, and he and Marty had taken an option on space, but … Bloomington? Sure, the IDS Tower was expensive. Of course it was. But in terms of class and prestige, it beat hands down anything Bloomington or any other suburb had to offer. How do you put a price on image? Marty was right, though. Cost aside, most of their employees lived south of town, and it was getting more difficult to keep them because of the commute to the city.

A rap on his open door and his partner strode into the room. Marty Goldman always looked taller than his five-ten and younger than his forty years. Was it his boyish face and tousle of sandy hair? To top it off, inexpensive suits looked great on his athletic frame. Go figure.

"*¿Qué tal, Felipe?* Barnhill has a great column today on

software. Thought you might want to read it."

"To improve my mind?"

"As good a reason as any."

They both laughed. Barney Barnhill wrote a newspaper column on computers that Marty never missed and Phil never read. Barnhill seemed to know everything about computers and everyone in the Twin-Cities' computer world.

Marty's expression turned puckish. "The price keeps going up."

"You're serious? I thought we agreed—"

"Estamos de acuerdo. We agree. Just kidding. How is it with Borglund?"

"I sent him a copy of my article on estate taxes. He wrote me a nice note."

Marty's expression fell somewhere between skepticism and pity. "This correspondence approach isn't you, Phil. You go for it, and it's there or it isn't. How many articles have you sent the guy? You trying to destroy our postage budget?"

"Trust me, Marty. I'm going to tap into Borglund's billion if it kills me."

"Still trying to get around his main man?"

"Did I tell you I ran into him at the graduation?" Except for Ellen, Marty was the only other person who knew about Phil's connection with Borglund's executive VP, Wade Lankar.

"Ha! Bet that was interesting."

"Biggest jerk who ever walked the planet."

"You've got to pull off an end run or give it up." Marty walked out shaking his head.

One of Phil's earlier articles on taxes had elicited a complimentary letter from Lars Borglund. But so far, the man had referred every request for an appointment to Lankar. Which was the same as throwing them into a shredder.

At five-thirty Marty returned to Phil's office. "Care for a quick refreshment?"

They went upstairs to the Windows On Minnesota Restaurant and took a small table by a north window. Shadows reached out over the traffic backing up on Hennepin Avenue. Nicollet Island squatted in the distance, where the Mississippi surged around it and cascaded over the falls before ducking beneath the Third Avenue bridge. Riverplace and St. Anthony Main crowded the Pillsbury warehouses.

"What's on your mind, my friend?"

"Nada. I wanted to buy you a drink."

"Thanks. What else?"

Marty ran his hand through his unruly hair. "I wanted to pry you out of the office. Just in case nobody mentioned it, today is Friday. Even galley slaves get a break on Friday night."

"And?" Phil smiled and waited.

Marty shifted in his chair and fidgeted with a small placard that extolled the qualities of Ron Rico rum. "You used to get to the office by seven. Now it's six. You used to knock off by six. No more. And all day Saturday. And night appointments. We'll pull out of this slump without giving the undertakers more business. Or do you want to own the world?"

"Got a ton of things in motion. Need to stay on top."

Marty shrugged. "How's David doing?"

"We keep our fingers crossed and take it one day at a time. He just got a part-time job with UPS. The way Jessica takes everything to heart, we worry as much about her."

"Kids are pretty tough."

"You sound like Ellen."

The cocktail waitress brought their drinks, a martini for Marty, Scotch rocks for Phil. The woman had long, firm legs and a winsome smile. Phil sipped his Scotch and watched her glide away.

"Te gusta," Marty said. "You like her."

"I'm observing, not lusting."

"Your ice cubes melt from observation?"

Phil laughed. Marty always gave him a lift, no matter what. He sipped his Scotch. "Got a big weekend planned?"

"A great one! We're flying up to Gull Lake to meet Ed and Julie Larson for brunch tomorrow. On Sunday we all fly to South Dakota. They're open-pitting a steer on the airport grounds at Watertown."

Marty, bless him, worked as hard as Phil, played even harder and could have a great time right up to the poorhouse door.

He, too, was doing it on savings. The Spanish interjections got tedious at times, sure. But how could you fault a guy for such a minor thing when he made you laugh every day? Because of his Spanish mother, his love of Hispanic culture and of fishing off Baja California, he for years had made annual five-figure contributions to a Mexican historical society.

"Ever regret leaving the law?" Marty said.

"I use my legal training every day."

"Happily?"

"Is this an inquisition, my *amigo friendo?"*

"Okay, okay. But I remember the time you thought about selling out and going to the University. The first symptom was sweatshop hours. If you want out, all I ask is enough lead time."

"Out of the question unless the U quintuples the pay. And you know I wouldn't leave you twisting."

"These days a teacher's salary looks pretty good."

"Ha! You're right. But we'll be okay. Your casualty carriers can't cut prices forever. I've got Bridger on an expense-cutting mission on the TPA side. Life sales are up."

"Keegan called again. He'd like to meet with you. He did a hundred thousand in life premium last year. Plus other stuff."

"I'm sure he's a nice guy, Marty, but he's in the family market and as big as he'll ever get. We need to stick to business and estate planning, the big tickets."

"Overrides on a hundred thou would help pay the light bill."

"We need to stay pure. Otherwise, we become just another good insurance agency and third party administrator, not the best. We're homerun hitters, not squeeze bunters."

"Okay, but it wouldn't take much to send our cash flow over a waterfall. A couple of out-of-the-ordinary splashes and there it goes. I'm telling you, Phil, we're up against it."

"It's going to turn, I can feel it. We'll be golden. And our image will be intact. Winners. Grand slam winners."

Marty smiled and shook his head. "When you get right down to it, the problem hasn't changed for years. We spend money faster than we make it."

On the following Tuesday, after reading a card that had come in a *personal and confidential* envelope, Phil hurried to

Marty's office and handed him the card. Marty read it and let out a whoop. He threw his arm around Phil's neck.

"A dinner party at Borglund's. Damn, man, you did it!"

"My foot's in the door, Marty!"

"You can bet he's checked you out six days from Sunday. Now comes the final exam."

"Top of the heap, kings of the hill, partner. That's us!"

Back in his office a few minutes later, Phil leaned over his desk. Getting only a piece of Borglund's business would be a coup that would make them a ton of money and give them the kind of local prestige that most guys only dreamed about. That was better than the money. Teaching at the law school could never match the money or the rush the business provided when things clicked. Oh, sure, there were other rewards in teaching. Ellen would welcome a change. That's why she was getting her degree. She wanted them to teach and take summers off. He wanted it, too, but not yet. This unfinished business with Lankar was far too important. After years of doubt and frustration, the decision to come to Minnesota had turned out right. Maybe he'd take the airplane off the market.

"Look out!"

Phil's father hit the brakes. The seat belt dug into Phil's belly as the red Corvette convertible cut them off and angled into the last space behind the backstop. Phil unbuckled and shoved the door open.

"Let it go, Phillip," his father said. "Don't ask for trouble your first day of practice. I'll park down the line."

The car door squeaked and rattled when Phil slammed it. "That's our spot!" he said to the driver of the Corvette.

The sun gleamed on the straight blond hair of the young man who emerged from the Corvette. Tall and big-boned, he wore white baseball pants and a gray sweatshirt with blue sleeves and the words "Marquette University Athletic Dept." across the front. He leveled his gaze at Phil. "Got a problem, kid?" He looked past Phil and smirked. Phil turned and glanced over his shoulder. His father stood next to the car, his work pants dirty, his blue shirt sweaty. Nobody stayed clean working at Bucyrus-Erie.

"Put up or shut up, kid."

"Let it go, Phillip."

Albert Tag got behind the wheel and put the car in gear. With white smoke pouring from its tail pipe, the blue Ford crept down the left field foul line. The Corvette guy faked several coughs before he turned his back on Phil and headed for the diamond. Phil clenched his teeth and strode to the first base side of the infield. His car was in the shop getting a used radiator, so he'd had to hitch a ride with his father to his first practice with the Marquette University team. Bad enough not to show up in his own wheels; now this. He would have ridden with Lou Romano, who had played with Phil in high school and was the only other player Phil knew on the Marquette team. But Romano's girlfriend had borrowed his car for a run to Madison.

Romano was swinging a bat near the first base dugout.

"Who's the blond Babe Ruth?" Phil asked him with a nod at third base, where a knot of players stood talking. "The one with the beer gut."

"The big guy? Wade Lankar. Transfer student. Pitcher. Throws bullets."

A week later the team played its first intra-squad game. About twenty people occupied the bleachers, many of them old retired guys. A group of four young girls, probably high school kids, sat directly behind the freshmen dugout, their every word audible to the players. Phil smiled at their incessant chatter. They talked, shouted at individual players and giggled without seeming to take a breath. Their appraisals of the players—which ones were cute and which ones weren't—made up most of their conversation.

"Ball three," the umpire called.

"What the hell's Lankar doing?" Romano said to no one in particular. "All of a sudden he can't find the plate with a map."

Phil swung his bat to loosen up. "He's walking Huber on purpose. He'll pitch around Wojcik, too. He wants me. Why not?

He's already struck me out twice."

"What is it with you two?" Romano said. "You've had a feud going from day one. It's only a practice game, for crying out loud." Romano looked across the infield and laughed. "Look at Coach Shitsel. Doesn't know whether to cuss or go blind."

With every ball Lankar threw, Shitsel shook his head and kicked the dirt. Phil smiled. Lankar was Shitsel's ace. The Varsity wasn't supposed to let the freshmen get many runners on base. Maybe a scratch hit here and there, and maybe a walk or two, but Lankar was throwing like a Little Leaguer. It was obvious to everyone.

"Ball four!"

Lankar also walked the next hitter on four pitches that came nowhere near the plate. Coach Shitsel called time and went to the mound. When Shitsel returned to the dugout on the third base side, Phil swung his bat a few times, stepped into the box, and pulled his cap down on his forehead. A good showing might get him on the team as a freshman. That meant a shot at a full scholarship next year, and four years of college ball just might get him drafted by the pro's. All he had ever wanted to do since he was five years old was play baseball. He was good and getting better. The scouts had shown interest, but his father had persuaded him to get his education. By the time he finally applied to Marquette, all they could offer him was a partial ride and maybe a better deal next year if he performed. He could begin right now to make that happen.

He leveled the bat over the plate and focused on Lankar. It was two on, two out, Varsity up two-zip. When Lankar went into a full windup and threw a fastball strike, the runners advanced to second and third. It was clear that Lankar couldn't have cared less. Working quickly, he wound up again and threw another fastball strike that said, "Tag, I can take you out with nothing but heat. No curves, just heat."

Phil stepped out, leaned over and rubbed dirt on his sweaty hands and on the bat handle Lankar threw a heavy ball that was more than just fast; it moved up and in on the fists. He also had a wicked curve that broke so sharply it could freeze a hitter in his jock strap. As he straightened to get back in the box, Phil heard one of the girls behind the dugout shout, "Nice buns, batter! Hit one a mile!" Phil glanced at the mound. Lankar glared at the girls, then turned to Phil.

"Get back in there, Tag. So I can strike your Polack ass out."

Phil stepped into the box and dug in. He was guessing fastball all the way. Lankar delivered his third pitch, a fat-city fastball, belt-high and riding up. Phil got all of it and took it downtown. The ball catapulted into the power alley in right center, shot over the 370 sign on the chain-link fence, and disappeared.

Phil loped around the bases with no outward show of emotion, but when he reached home, he jumped on the plate with both feet and glanced at the mound. Lankar spat tobacco juice and pursed his lips. A moment later, just as all the attaboys and high fives were winding down, one of the girls called out, "Hey, bacon-butt. Let's see another pitch like that. Homeruns are fun." All the girls giggled. They giggled and hooted more when Lankar flipped them the bird.

Three days later they faced each other again Lankar threw two junk curves wide of the plate before coming in with a fastball. Phil flung his arm up to protect his head and tried to twist away from the pitch. He knew before he hit the ground, knew even before he dropped the bat, knew from the sound and the pain and the vile taste in his mouth that his elbow was broken.

"Hot dog me again sometime, Tag, you Polack prick."

Chapter Three

"And then there's Tag," Ted Lucas said. He threw an empty Budweiser can, his sixth or seventh, into a trash can. "By-product of a good night in Minnesota. Correction. By-product of a *bad* night in Minnesota."

Everybody looked at David and laughed. Beads of sweat gathered on David's forehead. He swallowed against the constriction in his throat, the pumping in his chest. Lucas made people laugh when he was sober. Put a few beers in him at a party, and he became the comic stud of the senior class, complete with mean streak.

Finally, David smiled at Lucas, puckered his lips, parted them with a light smacking sound and winked. Lucas's taunting smile vanished. David turned his back on the new laughter and left the room. In the kitchen he leaned over the sink, shaking, his breathing ragged. He gripped the edge of the counter. Lucas's taunt had alluded to *A Farewell to Arms*, which the English class had discussed just before finals. Catherine is about to die and Lieutenant Henry thinks, "What reason is there for her to die? There's just a child that has to be born, the by-product of good nights in Milan. It makes trouble and is born and then you look after it and get fond of it maybe."

Why would anyone call a baby a by-product? The whole room had seemed to close in on him when Mrs. Turner asked the class what the passage said about Hemingway's philosophy.

"Mind if I join you?" Pam Linder said from the doorway. She looked kind of uncertain, like maybe she thought she was intruding.

David waved her in. *What a rack.*

"I could sure go for a soda," she said, with no detectable emphasis on soda. "How about you?"

"Sure."

He dug into the ice in the red Igloo cooler on the counter next to the sink, fished out two cans of Pepsi, and set them on the counter. He shook his hand.

"Man, that's cold!" He blew on his hand and wiped it across his pants.

Pam took a Pepsi and popped it. "Ted's crude. And a bore."

"Yeah, well, I guess we're in the minority on that. You having a good time?"

"I'm getting partied out. You?"

He shrugged. It was the third party in a row since graduation. Pam's easy smile brightened her whole face, and her blue eyes sparkled even when she wasn't smiling. He'd always liked her, though he'd never had the courage to ask her out.

"Want to go for a ride?"

"Okay," she said.

They headed for the back door. Ted Lucas appeared in the archway to the family room.

"Gonna get a little, Tag? Bet you'll have to show him how, Pammy baby."

David whirled around and slammed the heel of his fist against the fridge. A green magnet and sheet of yellow notepaper fell to the floor.

"Go to hell, Lucas!" Pam said. "Let's go, David. Too dirtballish in here."

"Just remember what it's there for, Davie," Lucas said in a syrupy voice.

David took a step toward Lucas. Pam held his arm and tugged. "Don't, David. Please."

Lucas leaned forward with clenched fists. "One of these days I'm going to waste you, Tag."

Pam pulled David to the door. They walked through spring damp grass to David's Camaro. Inside the car the soda can slipped from David's hand and spilled on his crotch.

"Aw, shit!"

He rose off the seat, pushed the door open and swung to the

ground. The night air hit the wetness and made it even colder. He pressed his handkerchief into the seat and hoped the Pepsi wouldn't leave a stain. Then he tried to soak the moisture out of his pants. Pam giggled.

"Jeez, you're a big help," he said with a laugh. She had such a neat personality.

He started the engine. Pam's hand lay on the ridge of the bucket seat, her knuckles touching his outer thigh.

They wound through the dark streets of Wayzata to Highway 12 and went east. At I-494 David headed north at sixty miles an hour. He accelerated to seventy, then eighty. The Camaro roared past the Highway 55 interchange at eighty-five with the cool air howling through the open windows.

"The cops'll be out, won't they?" Pam said.

David took the Camaro to ninety. Pam removed her hand from the edge of his seat. The speedometer registered ninety-five.

David held it just under a hundred. They hurtled into the darkness. Speed. The one thing he still enjoyed with confidence.

"Look out!"

Lights and reflectors filled the windshield, but what was her problem? He saw the semi-truck three hundred feet ahead. David whipped left. The Camaro's tail slid to the right. It went around the semi with room to spare, straightened, fishtailed twice, and left the truck behind.

"Take me back right now! Are you crazy?"

She hunched into the corner of her seat tight against the door and probably wouldn't put her hand back where it touched his leg. What was the big deal? He'd seen the truck. How couldn't he? It was lit up like a carnival, and whipping around semis like that was fun. No sense taking a ride any longer, though, because Pam was royally pissed, so he drove back to the party.

"Maybe Lucas is right, you bastard!" she said just before she slammed the car door.

David winced. No one should call anyone that.

Everyone had gone to bed by the time David got home.

He took an apple from the fridge and made his way in the dark to his upstairs bedroom, closed the door and flicked on the light. He still had his birthday and graduation gifts in his bedroom. A complete set of Titleist DCI irons, four Taylor Made metals and a blue and tan Titleist bag stood against his dresser. Just the set he'd wanted for a long time. It must have cost a mint. And on top of the golf stuff and sport wheels for the Camaro, they'd given him a used set of *The Story of Civilization* by Will and Ariel Durant, which he couldn't wait to begin reading. Yeah, it was a birthday and graduation deal, but they'd overdone it just the same.

He looked at a card on the dresser. His eyes watered and it took him a few moments to figure out exactly what it said: "Here's to many birdies for an eagle of a son. Love, Mom and Dad."

He sat on the bed. It was so quiet, like he was the last person in the world; the way it had seemed all night, in spite of all the hammered people around him. Being sober in a crowd of drunks will do it every time.

He noticed the walnut slab with the laser-carved inscription Jessica had given him after his birthday dinner. It was easy to read because he had read it earlier.

To make a happy fireside
To weens and wife,
That's the true pathos and sublime
Of human life.
Robert Burns

How'd she find things like this? He read it again. He wasn't big on poetry, but the four lines hit him somewhere between his heart and gut.

They'd all spent so much. Too much. He closed his eyes and dropped back on the bed with his arm across his face.

A few minutes later, he set the alarm for six, switched off the light and lay in the darkness. He had an important appointment in the morning, an appointment he wasn't certain he should keep. He had the right, but was it right?

Chapter Four

David parked on the street instead of in the lot so the Camaro wouldn't get dinged. One of his dad's habits. He didn't turn off the ignition right away, so the wipers kept squeegeeing across the windshield. He peered down the rain-slicked avenue. He had thought about this for so long.

The wipers stopped upright when he turned the key. He swung from the Camaro and dashed across the street and down the sidewalk in long, leaping strides to avoid the puddles. Rain peppered his face. He misjudged a puddle. Cold water squished into his left Docksider and sent him dancing.

Moments later, his chest heaving, he leaned against a counter in the office of the Children's Refuge Association of Minnesota.

A tall woman in a blue dress approached the counter. "May I help you?"

"Does Mrs. Pederson work here? I mean, I have an appointment."

"Hang on a minute." She disappeared behind an orange divider and returned with a pretty woman with light blue eyes, wire-framed glasses and sandy hair pulled back into a bun.

"Hi, David. I'm Greta Pederson." She thrust out her hand and smiled up at him. She was five-five at most, her hand puppy-belly warm. Too friendly, though. Probably another phony.

"Let's go back to a conference room." She hurried down a hallway. "Is it still raining? Lord knows we've had enough. Then again, maybe He doesn't. Probably delegates it all to Mother Nature and hasn't the slightest clue. Ha! Bet she does all the work."

What the hell?

"Here we are. Coffee?"

"No, thanks."

She sat at a small table and motioned him to have a seat. "Good. Stunts your growth. See what it did to me?" She rolled her eyes, and a sound between a giggle and a laugh burst from her. Her blue shirt strained at the center button. Coffee hadn't stunted everything.

"Don't drink the stuff myself, actually," she said. "Tastes awful, don't you think? If it tasted like the grounds smell in the can, I'd drink a lake of it. Kind of like pipe tobacco. Ever smoke a pipe?"

He stammered something unintelligible.

She leaned toward him, elbows on the table, fingers knitted beneath her chin. "So you've decided to find your birth parents. Little scary, isn't it?"

He nodded.

"You've come to the right bounty hunter. If I can't find 'em, they ain't findable."

She giggled in a breathy way that gave him a rise and kind of made him want to laugh. But the thought of all the other social workers and psychologists his parents had taken him to put a brake on that impulse. Bunch of con artists. Maybe not on the surface, or to begin with, but sooner or later they all tried to con you into doing their stuff. So you played along with their game and in the end conned them. Most of the time they didn't even know it, or didn't let on, because if they did they'd be admitting they'd lost, and nobody needed failed cases.

"Let me answer a few questions in advance," Greta said. "Number one, how long does it take? My search rarely takes more than six months. Usually less. Number two, what's my success rate? Better than ninety percent if they still live in the state. Three, cost. Based on your ability to pay. We'll talk about that later, so don't worry about it in the meantime. Four, how do birth parents react? Varies all over the place, from elation to anger."

Jeez, what is she, a CPA? Everything is one, two, three.

"Let me tell you their legal options. One, they can agree to see you. Two, provide you with current non-identifying information, and not see you. Three, refuse to see you and refuse to give information." She leaned back and smiled. "You knew most of that, right?"

She seemed straight. Just kind of weird, maybe? "Where do you start? I mean, it's got to be tough to find somebody after nineteen years."

She smiled and shook her head.

"How long do you think it'll take?"

"Bet you a beer I find your birth mother in two months. Ha! I wouldn't have to pay off for two years anyway, when you're legal."

"What happens next?"

She opened a manila folder. "First, here's some literature for you to read." She laid two pamphlets on the table. They were loaded with print. David flinched.

"Something wrong?"

"No."

Greta hesitated a moment before resuming. "Second, complete this genetic search form before you leave. See me if you have any questions. Third, don't sign the form. Think about it for a week. Then sign it or tear it up. Okay?"

"I'll sign it."

As if from nowhere, she brought out a playing card and placed it on the table. It was the five of hearts. "This is you," she said, touching the lone heart in the center. She pointed to the two hearts at the top of the card. "You know and love these two hearts. Do you want to know the other two?"

Greta put the card aside. "Take the week, David. The world won't end in the meantime. If it does, I'll owe you a beer."

She laughed, and this time he almost laughed, too. She pushed her chair back and stood. "Fourth, don't call me for status reports. I'll call you. Do call me if you want to talk."

His puzzlement must have shown.

"I've seen it all, David. From every side and angle. Let me know if you want to talk."

David picked up the two pamphlets. "Do I have to read this stuff?"

"Yep. They'll help you—Is there a problem reading them?"

"I'm not exactly crazy about a lot of reading. Unless it's history. For some reason, I like reading history."

Greta came around the table and laid her hand on David's shoulder. "May I ask a personal question?"

"Sure."

"Are you dyslexic?"

David nodded.

She squeezed his shoulder lightly. "So am I, David. Bummer, huh? But, hey. Could be worse. We could have permanent bad breath. Let's compare notes and talk about it one of these days, okay?"

He nodded again.

She opened the door. "Do you lift weights?"

"Yeah, some."

"Good for you." She smiled, led him to the lobby, and pointed him to the exit.

David hurried to his car, where he turned his attention to the form. The questions read like gibberish. He pulled the two summaries from the folder she had given him. One was titled "Post Adoption Rights of Birth Parents and Children," and the other, "Birth Record Statutes (Summarized) After May 17, 1970." More gobbledygook. Mrs. Turner would have a ball with this stuff in English class. She was totally funny when she got her hands on something like this. Give her anything written by the government, and she'd have the whole class howling in two minutes.

Something sour seeped into the back of his mouth. Maybe this wasn't the right thing to do. But didn't Dad always say not to just let things happen? Make things happen, he said. Good things.

Yeah, but someone had decided she was better off without him, so why risk facing her? To be lied to? Or worse, maybe, to hear the truth? He folded the papers and stuffed them into the back pocket of his Guess jeans. Maybe it would be better for Greta Pederson to find someone else's parents. Someone who maybe needed it more.

* * *

Greta watched David through the window as he ran through the rain to his car. Good-looking kid; boyish and athletic, with that winsome dimple in his left cheek that popped into prominence whenever he smiled. He probably charmed the girls right out of their socks. Panties? She flushed and turned from the window.

Chapter Five

Phil angled his newspaper to see David better while pretending to read. Why was David up so early? And why so fidgety? The stubble on his face didn't hide his good looks, but why did young guys feel they had to have a three-day beard? Gillette would go broke if everyone emulated today's athletes and entertainers. David's rusty blond growth barely showed, even now with the morning sun slanting through the alcove windows. But why have it at all? Did the girls like it? A macho thing?

Ellen leaned against the counter that separated the breakfast nook from the kitchen, her coffee cup poised in midair. Her short auburn hair caught the light, her chin and nose profiled against the white Amana fridge.

"The Twins are hanging tough," Phil said. David closed his eyes and pressed his fingers to his forehead. Good, he was listening. Maybe he'd rise to the bait on the next cast. He was up early for some reason.

"Hard to believe," Phil continued, "Minnesota in a dogfight with Chicago and Detroit. Too bad Kansas City is stuck in the basement. Be nice to see a couple of have-nots hold their own against the big-money teams." Phil smiled behind the newspaper. David was forever accusing him of getting off on any noun with the word ball attached to it.

Phil held the paper aside and poked a corner of rye toast into a fried egg, one of the two he allowed himself each week. David couldn't stand the sight of eggs sunny side up. He called them embryo slimes.

"Want a bite?" Phil asked. David grimaced. Ellen frowned. Okay, bad taste. *Mea culpa.*

David's untouched Honey Nut Cheerios floated in a soggy mass in the blue bowl Ellen had made years ago during her ceramics period. David sat up straight, took a deep breath and said, "I'm finding my birth parents."

Ellen returned Phil's look, but her expression told him nothing, not a hint. He let the newspaper fall to the table.

"I've like, y'know, thought about it a lot and it's—I know you wonder why, but it's something I want to do."

"Like to talk about it?" Ellen said with a smile in her eyes, those dark eyes that sparkled and crinkled at the corners like no others in the world.

"I guess so. It's been on my mind for a couple years, maybe longer, so I hope you won't get mad or anything. I've already met with a social worker."

Phil shifted in his chair and pushed away the plate with the half-eaten egg.

"We won't get upset, Davie," Ellen said. When David winced at the diminutive, she quickly added, "It's cool you're telling us."

"I don't want you to think I'm unhappy or anything. You're my real parents, and I'd never in a zillion years want to change that. But I'm curious, and want them to know I'm okay."

"Can we help?" Ellen said.

David scratched behind his ear and ran his hand over his short mop of uncombed hair. The dimple in his left cheek came and went. He shrugged. "Need to check it out, think about it some more."

"Are you sure you want to do this, son?" Phil instantly regretted the faint, unintended note of challenge in his voice.

"I said I've thought about it, Dad."

"Okay."

David pushed back from the table. He carried his bowl and spoon to the sink, rinsed them and put them into the dishwasher. He opened the fridge and peered inside. "Hey, who ate the last apple?"

Ellen snapped her fingers. "I knew I forgot something. I'll pick some up on the way home."

"Gotta pick up Wagner and get some things done," David

said, and headed for the door to the garage.

"Just a minute, young man," Ellen said with mock severity. Fists on hips, shoulders squared, she waited. David started to roll his eyes before catching himself, though his pained expression probably wasn't entirely feigned. Bending down from his six-two height, he hugged Ellen to complete the ritual, seldom used for years now, that had begun so long ago when he was little more than a toddler. Ellen hugged him back. "Have a good day, babe," she said.

David made his escape.

Phil drank the last of his cold coffee. To sweeten the bitter aftertaste, he took a sip of orange juice. The garage door rolled up, followed by the muffled roar of the Camaro's engine.

Ellen emptied her coffee down the drain, ran fresh water into the heavy beige mug and poured it into the Hotshot instant coffee maker.

"Maybe we should talk this over," Phil said.

She contemplated him for a long, vacant moment before turning to the Hotshot. When the water boiled, she scooped instant coffee into the mug and added the boiling water. The aroma of fresh coffee curled into the air. "I don't think we should feel threatened," she said. "He might forget all about it in a week or two. No big deal if he doesn't. His openness was a big piece of his putting Humpty Dumpty back together again."

"Or another dose of impulsiveness."

She sat down across the table from him. "Honey, he didn't get up this early by coincidence. He wanted to catch you before you left. He needs support, not second-guessing."

"If he wants to do it, shouldn't he do it on his own?"

"Three years we hung in there with him. Did it take too much?"

"Don't start imagining things, El."

"I'm not."

"Why don't I cancel my first appointment? So we can talk."

She shook her head in a way that made her lustrous hair fly. "I have to finish my term paper after mass."

Something told him to press. But maybe she was right. His day was jammed, and so was hers. Every day was jammed. She wouldn't skip daily mass. Take an Act of Congress for that. Besides, her lips had that pouty look that meant her mind was made up.

He stood, snugged his tie and slipped into his suit coat, a navy Hickey-Freeman he had bought on sale and was wearing for the first time. Only one out of three suits ever felt this good, regardless of price.

"Tonight," he said.

"Have a good day."

He kissed her.

"Don't be upset," she said. "Just go with the flow."

"Good morning," Jessica said. She curled into a chair across from Phil. "Why was David up so early?"

"He and Wagner have something going on," Ellen said. "Hungry?"

"Uh-uh. I'm going to shower." She yawned and slouched off the chair.

"You should eat something. Breakfast is important."

"Oh, Mom, you know I don't like to eat in the morning."

Ellen started to say something but apparently thought better of it. She turned to Phil after Jessica disappeared up the stairs. "I hope David's project doesn't affect Jessica. She doesn't need that again."

"We don't either. Let's keep our antennas up. Gotta run."

Phil ducked into the half-bath next to the mudroom to brush his teeth one last time before leaving for the office. When he finished, he checked himself in the mirror. His face was still smooth, but maybe a straw hat for golfing was a good idea to keep the sun off. Maybe get one of those rakish Australian ones like old Greg Norman's. How many rounds this year? Three? Four, if he was lucky? There never seemed to be time for golf anymore. Whatever happened to Norman? Did he still play?

He stepped out to the patio. A few dandelions poked their heads through the greenbrown grass, and trees that had leafed out overnight quivered in the light breeze that scuffed patches of Wayzata Bay. Seven sailboats floated across the gray water in every direction. Across the bay to the right, Breezy Point and Cedar Point spread wide and low in the water. Gray's Bay lay invisible in a thick web of fog two miles straight ahead.

The view equaled any other on Lake Minnetonka's one hundred miles of jagged shoreline. Yet, as much as Phil loved the water, he could never quite dispel a nagging sense of fiscal and egotistical absurdity that attached to living on a lake and owning a cabin on another lake up north, to say nothing of four power boats, two here and two at the cabin. How could you possibly justify that many? Practically a small navy. Plus an airplane. The nuns always said material things couldn't bring happiness. Were they right? Probably. On the other hand, the stuff didn't exactly bring unhappiness, either. Wasn't happiness a matter of attitude, regardless of possessions? Couldn't a poor man and a rich man have equally good or rotten attitudes? Be equally arrogant or humble? Attitude aside, didn't the one with the most toys win?

In the garage, he pressed the button to open the second stall door. Ellen had long ago commandeered the first stall for loading kids and unloading groceries. The third housed David's Camaro, the fourth everything from powered lawn equipment to snowmobiles.

The gray Cadillac DTS howled to life. Great car, the Cadillac. More practical than a Corvette or Mercedes SL 550. Less expensive, too. None of that had had much to do with his decision to buy it, but if you're going to rationalize, why not do it respectably? No sense tying today's decisions to a rebuttal of fantasies you had at eighteen. *Eighteen. Where have twenty-nine years gone?*

And how often had Ellen criticized sports cars and middle-aged men who drove them? She hadn't been subtle in her opposition to a sports car.

Commuters by now no doubt had begun to clog Highway 12 into downtown Minneapolis, a problem he never faced when he left home by six. Marty was right about moving the office to Bloomington. It would cut expenses and be easier on everybody. God knew they had to cut somewhere. The business was bleeding. Who knew what would happen if things didn't work out with Borglund? Downsize the business? The street would pick up on that in no time. Drop out of the country club? Sell the house? How do you show your face after that? And now David wanted to complicate things by dredging up the past. Maybe some kids should find their birth parents, but not David. Not with his problems. Not now. What would it accomplish? Nothing, except to confuse the kid. Or worse. And maybe Jessica, too.

Phil turned a corner and headed for the ramp to Highway 12. He gripped the wheel and jammed the accelerator to the floor. The DTS fishtailed over the asphalt, its tires screaming to achieve parity with the racing engine.

The bells of St. Bernadette tolled overhead. In the church rectory, Ellen listened to Father Banning's sales pitch. Forty-five and too handsome to be a priest, he leaned forward with his elbows on his desk.

"I really need your leadership on this, Ellen. And your organizational skills."

Ellen's shoulders slumped. "All right, Father. But please don't expect me to take on anything else. Not until I finish school."

"Busy people always get things done." He came around his desk and led her to the door, where he took her hand in his. "Thank you, Ellen. I can't tell you how much I appreciate you."

She felt her eyes widen ever so slightly when he gently squeezed her hand just before releasing it. His hand touched the small of her back when she stepped through the door. In addition to directing the Parish Nurse program and serving on the Parish Council, she now found herself in charge of the Spring Bazaar, the biggest annual fund raiser for St. Bernadette parish. She had no idea where she would find the time.

Chapter Six

"He needs to find himself, Phil."

"Isn't college ideal for that?"

Ellen didn't answer. She faced straight ahead as Phil turned into the sloping driveway of the Wayzata Country Club. They joined Don and Carlene Boyd on the tennis courts.

Thirty minutes later, squinting against the western sun, Phil watched Ellen's ball land deep in the backcourt, inches short of the base line. How she loved doing that! She could hit those shots, like flat lobs, all day long and not make a mistake.

"Deuce!"

It was the same on the golf course. Down the middle, not long, but always in play.Too late, he reacted to the ball coming at him. It caromed off the edge of his racquet.

"Should've had that, Tag," Ellen said. She winked and added, "Tough shot." And to Don, "Nice shot!"

They tried to play doubles at least once a week during the short summers. Phil could never generate the intensity for doubles that he did for singles, but that was no excuse for sloppiness. A sensuous hint of a breeze flowed through his sweat-dampened shirt. He licked the saltiness at the corners of his mouth. Perspiration beaded his forehead and stung his eyes.

Ellen had the legs of a thirty-year-old: long, firm and smooth. Few would guess her to be nearly fifty. The pleated white peplum danced and rippled against her tan legs with every move. Men on doubt elbowed one another at the sight of her, with lascivious under-their-breath remarks. Probably flirted with her too, and that was okay. Good for her ego and libido.

Ellen hit a beautiful drop shot to make it ad out. On Carlene's next serve, Phil lashed a cross-court shot that caught the tape and rolled over for match point, a lucky shot to end his otherwise lackluster performance. As it did whenever he rotated the elbow with force, a stab of pain reminded him of his old baseball injury.

"Hey, great game! See you at the bar," Don said. He hated to lose, but rarely allowed his displeasure to show.

"Let's go to the boat," Carlene said. "It's too nice to go inside."

They drove the short distance to the Boyds' home on the lake and had drinks on their new Trojan cruiser, a white and gold beauty that must have set them back a quarter of a mil. Dozens of boats gleamed in the sun on Brown's Bay. Beyond, on the open water of Lake Minnetonka, countless sail and powerboats created a medley of motion on the dusk-darkening water. The air teetered on the edge of chilliness.

"Is David all squared away for school?" Don asked.

"I understand you had to return your car to the dealer again," Ellen said.

Phil caught Don's look. "He's been accepted by the U and by Loras, a small school in Iowa," he said to smooth the awkwardness.

Later, Ellen said nothing in the car until they were nearly home. "Don Boyd's big nose matches his mouth."

"He didn't mean anything. And he's not exactly a stranger, honey."

"All the more reason for him to know better. David isn't ready for college. May never be."

"There's no reason for him not to go, El."

"He couldn't cope right now. I hope he works for a year first."

"Should be the greatest time of his life. Football games, parties, girls. Independence."

"Has it ever crossed your mind he might be scared to death?" She shifted in her seat and looked squarely at Phil. "He's an alcoholic, for God's sake! How can you talk about parties? Where's your brain?"

Phil pulled into the driveway too fast and had to hit the

brakes.

"It's *his* life," Ellen said.

"Of course it is. But what's wrong with a little direction?"

"You mean *control.* You and Don Boyd can both go to hell!" She swung from the car, slammed the door, and ran into the house.

Phil pressed the remote to open the garage door. He closed his eyes and stroked his forehead. Ellen seldom lost her temper and virtually never swore. They couldn't put life on hold, could they? David was nineteen. He had to learn how to live his own life. They all had to forge ahead. Things would work out. They'd make them work out. They couldn't play defense forever.

Cool and clean smelling, the night air evoked a crisp image of autumn, Phil's favorite season. The familiar, haunting cry of a loon came from the lake beyond the open bedroom window. Moonlight poured through the sheers and filled the room with the glowing grayness of an old black and white movie.

"We've got to let him find his way, Phil."

The pleasant autumnal feeling vanished. Phil drew the sheet up and folded his arms over his chest.

"He needs more time to mature. More time to gain confidence."

"I still believe college would do that. Might get him off this birth parent kick, too."

"Don't you think you're over-reacting to that?"

"I don't want him to get hurt, El."

"He might have a real need. Totally apart from us."

"Dangerous combination, curiosity and immaturity."

"What about unsatisfied curiosity?"

The sheers billowed, suddenly pregnant by the night breeze off the lake. Their own self-perceptions to the contrary, how fetching pregnant women always looked to him! Because they looked so soft, so fulfilled, so complete? Or because he had never made one that way?

Ellen rolled onto her side and brought her face close to his.

Her breath was warm, her White Linen perfume still fragrant.

"Know what?" she said, a note of mischief in her voice. "I'm kind of curious about them myself."

"Sure. We could all go to the movies together."

Ellen fell back on her pillow. "Can't I share my feelings with you?"

He braced on an elbow and curled his arm around her. "I'm sorry. It was a bad deflective joke."

"We're not in sync anymore."

"I'm really sorry I made light of it, El. It was dumb. Let's not fight."

"You seem so disconnected from us. Not engaged. Is everything okay at the office? I mean, any new bad news?"

"Everything's fine." A wave of fatigue engulfed him. It was nearly midnight. Five in the morning would arrive before it was welcome. "Okay if we talk tomorrow, El? I'm totally wiped out."

She rolled away from him. "If we ignore it, maybe it'll go away?"

"Nobody's ignoring anything."

"Could've fooled me."

A minute later she rose up and punched her pillow, an invitation, he knew, for him to say something. But anything he'd say wouldn't be right, and he was so tired, so damnably tired, that he just lay still and listened to the old grandfather clock tick-tocking in the hall. He reached over and touched her shoulder. She jerked away. Seconds later, she threw the covers back, swung her feet to the floor and hurried from the room.

Sleep would be elusive tonight. For reasons other than a concern for David's well-being, did he object to David's locating his birth parents? No. Did he find it threatening? No. Maybe in a year or two it would be just the ticket. Right now David and Ellen were still healing. They had borne the brunt of David's meltdown with alcohol and drugs because, right or wrong, the business had absorbed much of Phil's attention. Ellen hadn't had that escape. That's when she began to immerse herself even more heavily in church work. He had never made the connection before. He had assumed her work for the parish was religiously inspired, but perhaps it was as much therapeutic as it was spiritual.

Phil rolled off the bed. The air streaming through the window had gotten chilly. He wended his way through the moonlit room, down the hallway to one of the spare bedrooms and lay beside her.

"Come back to bed, honey."

"I'm fine here."

He draped his arm over her and nuzzled her cheek. Her skin was as smooth and tight as ever.

"Love you, El."

"I love you, too."

He kissed her cheek. She put her fingertips to his temple. He shifted his weight so that he could reach her lips with his.

"Just hold me," she said, and so he did, the ridges of her shoulder blades moving when she moved, her slender back so arousing to his touch. So clean of line when young, so unconditional, so much of a headlong rush into the unknown, how could love become so complex? Shouldn't it get easier to communicate? Shouldn't a lot of things get easier? Maybe they were out of sync. No, it couldn't be. They'd always been in lockstep, had always been of one mind and heart.

Phil gazed through the window of the tiny married student housing apartment at the heavy snow swirling in a strong wind. Nearly midnight. She should have been home thirty minutes ago. Traffic at this hour might be crawling, but the hospital wasn't that far away, only fourteen blocks. He reached into the compact fridge under the countertop next to the range and grabbed an apple, a firm Red Delicious. The first bite told him it was perfect. Ellen had a knack for selecting the best apples to feed his boundless appetite for them. On the rare occasion she got fooled and the apples turned out woody or not sweet enough, she would march right back to the market and demand an exchange or her money back. They would urge her to sample one, and as often as not would throw in several extras. She sometimes even got a free bag for her inconvenience, which made Phil shake his head in proud wonderment.

Setting the apple on the counter, he pulled on his boots and parka and charged out the door and into the howling wind.

Knowing the route Ellen always took, He trudged through the already calf-deep snow and watched for the old brown Chevy she called Susie. Drifting snow clogged the streets. The few cars moving were overlaid with snow, which made them hard to identify, but he'd recognize Susie. The huge red Christmas bow Ellen had attached to the antenna would make it a sure thing if it hadn't blown off.

Were it not for his concern for Ellen, the snow swirling in the hazy glow of the street lights and neon signs would have created a sense of excitement and wonder. By the time he had slogged six blocks without seeing her, though, his concern had morphed into fear. What if she'd had an accident? What if she were stuck on that lonely stretch of road that ran along the cemetery? Or what if—What was that ruckus up ahead?

A skinny guy was screaming at a car angled in the middle of the narrow street lined on both sides by parked cars. Another man tried to calm him down. The car in the street was Susie. Though not visible through the snow on the windows, Ellen had to be in the car, so the guy was cursing Ellen. Another car had crumpled into Susie's back bumper.

"What's going on?" Phil asked.

The screamer turned. He was a kid about eighteen, maybe less. "None o' yer damn business!"

"Come on, son," the other man said. "Just back off and we'll get this taken care of." He put his hand on the kid's arm.

"Git yer hands off me!" He kicked ~~Betsy's~~ Susie's door and yelled, "Damn women drivers anyway."

Phil shoved the kid hard. He windmilled backward and fell down.

"That's my wife in the car. You got a problem, you talk to me."

The kid struggled to his feet and lunged at Phil, who blocked his punch and pinned him against the car. "Mister, you do that again, you're going to get duked. Now calm down!"

The kid tried to kick Phil but was too pinned to get any leverage. "You son of a bitch!" he said. Then he lowered his his head and began to cry silently.

Phil released him and turned to the other man, who looked relieved.

"I live over there," the man said, pointing to a small house across the street. "Heard a crash and came out to see. This guy was on a tear by the time I got here. I don't blame your wife for staying in the car."

Phil put his face close to the car window and wiped away the snow. Ellen was sitting up, her eyes closed and her hands over her ears. He tapped the window. When Ellen saw him, her eyes widened and she unlocked the door. Leaning into the car, Phil embraced her. "It's okay, honey. It's okay. Just sit tight till I get some information, and we'll go home. You okay?" She nodded vigorously.

He got the older man's name and address, took down the license number of the kid's car and asked him his name. No answer.

"Have it your way," Phil said. He went to the kid's car, an old yellow Dodge about as beat-up as Susie. He opened the door and took the keys from the ignition. "I'm calling the police." To the man: "May I use your phone?"

Before the man could respond, the kid said, "Please mister. She was stopped in the middle of the street. I couldn't see her till it was too late. We don't have no insurance or nothin'. I'll pay for your damage."

Going to the back of the car, Phil inspected the bumper. The Dodge had shoved it in against the trunk deck, but the trunk still opened okay when he inserted his key. The Dodge had suffered more damage. One more ding in Susie wouldn't matter much.

"This your car?" Phil asked.

The kid shook his head. "My mom's. She was laid off a while back. I work second shift at the truck stop in Caledonia. I'm sorry I ran into your wife, I really am. I'll pay for your car somehow."

"How old are you? You had anything to drink?"

"No, sir, not a drop. I'm sixteen. You can check at the truck stop. I just got off an hour ago. Took me all this time to get this far."

Phil handed the kid's car keys to him. "You don't have to pay for anything. But the next time you want to yell at someone, think twice about it. Now go home."

The kid ran his sleeve across his eyes and headed for his car. A moment later, he turned around in a driveway and drove off.

"Thanks," Phil said to the other man. "You'd better get inside." The man crossed the street to his home. Phil opened the car door.

"Slide over, El. We're going home."

The look on her face in the dim light was an admixture of emotions. Was she going to cry? Laugh? Be angry?

"Honey, what's wrong?"

A smile tugged at the corner of her mouth. "We can't go home."

Nonplussed, he said nothing.

"Susie's out of gas."

The whole scenario came to him in a nanosecond: his hurried trip to the bookstore shortly before Ellen had to leave for work that afternoon; her reminder that the car was on empty, would he throw a couple dollars' worth in; the hassle at the book store; his rush to get back so she wouldn't be late; his failure to stop for gas.

"Oh, God, El, I'm so sorry."

"It's okay. More than okay, 'cause I get about fifty martyr buttons. But don't for one minute think I'm waiting here while you get gas. I'm going along, Tageroo. Too many crazies around here."

He leaned into the car and kissed her. "Do you know how much I love you? More than I could tell you in ten lifetimes."

They tromped off through deep and blowing snow in search of a gas station.

He buried his face in her hair. "Let's go to our bed."

She lay still for several seconds before she sat up. "You've always been so protective of David," she said, "even if you won't admit it. He's an adult now. Can't you understand it's time to give him some room? Let him make his own decisions?"

"Would that make you happy?"

"It would give *him* some *confidence.* You were married and on your own at his age. Don't you even begin to see the incongruity?"

"Okay. I'll take a swing at it. Right now, I'm so beat I could sleep for a week." He knew his words were a mistake. Ellen started to say something, but instead she swung her feet to the floor. They returned to their bed and waited for sleep.

Chapter Seven

David followed Greta Pederson to the same conference room they had used previously.

"What's on your mind, young man?"

He shrugged.

"Hey, you called me," she said.

"Yeah."

"Want a soda?"

"No, thanks."

She leaned back in her chair, took off her glasses and propped her feet on a chair next to her. She looked tired.

"How're things at home?"

"Okay."

"Shared any more of this with your mom and dad?"

He shook his head, not really sure why he had come to see her.

Greta broke into a smile that said, Okay, you called and wanted to talk, but now you don't, or don't know how to begin, and that's okay. She was so cool that way.

"Look," she said, "it's Friday, it's three-thirty and I could use a beer. How about it?"

A blockage filled his throat, but he nodded his acceptance.

They met at Smooch's, a sports bar just down the street from Greta's office, and found an empty booth way in the back. Greta ordered a beer. David ordered a Pepsi from a cute waitress who smiled at him. When the drinks arrived a few minutes later, the beer came in a frosted mug and looked like the best thing in the world.

"Here's to you, Mr. Tag." She drank a third of her beer in

one long pull. "So what's on your mind?"

"My dad isn't too crazy about me looking for my birth parents. I think maybe he's right. I mean, they didn't want me then, so why should I find them now?"

"I don't know, why should you?"

He slumped back against the booth partition. "Why are you asking all these questions? I need answers, not questions."

"Because I make the rules," she said with a giggle. "So why should you want to find them? Other than to piss off your dad?"

That struck his funny bone. His laughing set hers off. When they stopped, it didn't seem funny anymore.

"I don't know if that's a good reason. There's a lot of tension at our place and I'm adding to it. My dad's working like a slave. But it's more than that. Everyone's uptight, and I don't know why."

"Number one, mister, you have a right to find them. Number two, your father has to respect that. Number three, he'll come around."

"Number four, how do you know? You've never even met him."

"You're nineteen, David. An adult."

The waitress swayed past and looked at David from the corner of her eye. She had a swing in her hips, a slight bow in her legs. Greta ordered another beer. The girl looked nice walking away, too.

"Your eye contact is terrible. By the way, do you carry condoms?"

"What?"

"Condoms. Rubbers. Do you keep them on you?"

"No."

"What happens when you make a baby? Marry the girl? Pay for an abortion? Tell her to put it up for adoption? How about AIDS?"

"Screw you!"

"That activity explains why we're here in the first place, mister."

"It's private. And you're assuming I'm … out having sex."

Her lips formed an O without sound. David's hands trembled. It was none of her business.

"It's okay, David, it's okay. I'm sorry." She covered his hands with hers. "I'm sorry I said those things, really sorry."

"It's all right. Jeez, sometimes I think girls are so great I can hardly stand it, know what I mean? For three years, I had them hanging on me, but now that I'm.... Most of the time I can't figure them out at all, and they mess me up. I used to have confidence. Not anymore. And with herpes and all the other stuff...."

Her beer arrived. David looked down at the table, then at the waitress. "I'll have a beer, too."

The waitress smiled at him and hesitated. She glanced over her shoulder towards the front of the restaurant, but she didn't card him. Greta frowned and started to say something. David cut her off. "How can you give all this advice? I mean, so you're a social worker. Big deal. That doesn't mean you know what it's like."

"What what's like?"

"How my father feels, for one thing."

"Well, sweetheart, for your information, I have two adopted daughters, eleven and thirteen. The thirteen-year-old—she was three when I got her—is getting real curious about her biological parents. So I can relate to your father. And your birth mother, too. Because I had a kid when I was seventeen. Got knocked up by the sweetest talking guitar player you ever saw. By the time I found out I was pregnant, his gig was up and he was strumming his strings who knows where."

She took a big drink of beer and ran the back of her hand over her mouth. The waitress brought David's beer. Greta looked at the beer and frowned. "I was in high school," she said. "My mother insisted on an abortion because she didn't want to be embarrassed. She was a widow, but she had more money than Rockefeller—still does—and could have taken care of it, no problem. But that was a life in me. I'd made a mistake, but the life in my belly wasn't a mistake. That kid—a boy, as it turned out—didn't know or care if I was married or single or swinging on a trapeze in the circus. All he cared about was getting out and seeing the world. They call it life.

"My mother wouldn't hear of it. Told me to get an abortion or get out. I got out. I could take care of myself. Problem was, what about the baby? Bring him up on welfare? Not my kid. I put him up for adoption so he'd have a good life, a chance to be something when he grew up."

"How old is he now?"

"Seventeen, almost eighteen. Nearly as old as you."

"Okay, Mrs. Pederson—"

"We're not in the office, David. You can call me Greta."

"Okay, whatever. So maybe you can relate to my parents, but don't try to tell me how I feel."

"Now you've thrown the switch, baby. Because *I'm* adopted. My mother couldn't get pregnant for seven years after she married, so she and my daddy adopted me. Everything was hunky-dory for two years. Then she had three babies in four years. She probably would have had three more at the rate she was going, if my dad hadn't died. As I've said, David, I've seen it all, from every side. Why do you think I'm in this crazy business? It's a magnet and I'm a pile of metal shavings. Let's have one more. Soda for you."

He insisted on ordering a beer. She looked angry and said she wouldn't pay for it but said nothing to the waitress.

She was divorced, had settled for a GED and managed to get a B.S. and M.S. from the University of Minnesota in social work, had worked her present job for six years. They had another beer.

When they left, she said she worried about his driving home. She insisted that he sit with her in her car, a battered Chevy with a torn bench seat. The beer had practically wiped him out. Before he knew it, he was lying across her lap and nearly falling asleep. Or maybe he did fall asleep. After a while he came out of it, his face buried in her lap. She seemed kind of nervous. "Let's go back inside, David. You need some cold water."

In Smooch's rest room he splashed cold water in his face. *Almost hammered on three lousy beers.* He spent twenty minutes in the rest room before returning to his car.

"Are you sure you're okay to drive?" she asked. "I can't believe I allowed you to drink with me. Stupid. Crazy stupid. We are going to stay right here until I'm convinced you're sober."

She stayed with him another thirty minutes until he finally persuaded her he could drive okay. He knew he wasn't drunk. That wasn't the problem at all. All the way home, higher and higher waves of an endless black sea rolled over him, engulfed him, dragged him down, smothered him.

Chapter Eight

Ellen heard David in the garage and sensed that something was wrong even before he entered the house. Seconds later she smelled the alcohol.

"Davie—"

"Let me alone, Mom!" He tried to slide past her to the stairs. Ellen threw her arms around him and held him. He stopped struggling, clung to her and began to cry.

Phil had gone down to the dock for a few minutes before it would be time to leave for the long-awaited Borglund dinner party. Praying that he would stay there a little longer, Ellen managed to get David to a sofa in the family room, where she sat and held him.

"Why, honey? Why?"

"I—don't know—Mom—I don't—know." He couldn't stop sobbing.

Before Ellen could say anything else, Jessica bounced down the stairs.

"What's wrong?" she said, just as she caught the look on Ellen's face and wrinkled her nose. "Oh."

Phil entered the room from the patio. He approached the sofa and stopped abruptly. "Tell me what happened, David."

David broke free and ran from the room to the foot of the stairs. He stumbled on the second step, regained his balance, and climbed out of sight.

"Daddy, how could you? Can't you—" Jessica turned and ran after David.

Ellen gazed at Phil in the quiet of day's end. She knew what was going through his mind, knew the decision he had to make. He found a number in his pocket planner, went to the phone and dialed. "Hello, this is Phil Tag. May I speak to Mr. Borglund, please?" It took only a moment for Borglund to get on the line. "Mr. Borglund, Phil Tag. I regret having to call you so late, but my wife and I won't be able to make it tonight." Phil listened for a few seconds. "I appreciate your concern. Our apologies to you and Mrs. Borglund." He hung up and leaned against the bookcase next to the phone.

Ellen waited for him. She needed him to hold her, to reassure her that the whole world wasn't ripping apart. He embraced her.

"Go to him, Phil. He needs you."

He trudged up the stairs. Passing the hallway bathroom, he heard a sound. He stopped and put his head to the door. Jessica was gagging or vomiting. He rapped on the door. "Are you okay?" He tried to open the door. It was locked. "I said, are you okay?"

"I'm just fine, Daddy. I'm really okay."

Phil closed his eyes for a moment before proceeding to David's bedroom door, which was also locked. Phil knocked, waited and knocked again. "Please let me in, son."

Silence.

"I'm not angry."

"Let me alone."

"Please open the door."

"No."

Phil took a deep breath, backed away from the door and retraced his steps down the hallway. The bathroom door was open. He went to Jessica's room. She lay face-up on her bed with radio earphones on, her feet twitching. Bending over and kissing her on the cheek, he lifted the earphone away from her ear and said, "It'll be okay, honey. Love you." Jessica closed her eyes tightly.

Downstairs, Ellen hung up the phone just as Phil came into the kitchen.

"Who was that?" Phil said.

"Pat Bristol, Renaissance Center. She can't come tonight, but in the morning." Ellen picked up the phone again. Phil put his hand on her arm. "Who are you calling now?"

"Father Banning."

"We can handle this."

"Father helped David so much last time. And David really likes him. We need all the help we can get, Phil."

"Fine. Call him. I won't be here. I'm going for a walk."

"Phil, please…."

"I'm taking a walk."

"Okay, I won't call him."

"Hell, go ahead and call him. Talk to him all night. I'm taking a walk."

He walked on Ferndale to Grove and took Lake Street until he came to the old renovated depot. He dropped onto a faded bench and gazed out across Wayzata Bay, a small piece of Lake Minnetonka that from the air reminded him of the head and beak of a misshapen bird. The village of Woodland lay hidden in the trees on the far shore. The channel veered to the right of Breezy Point, and Spirit Island poked above the water line in the middle. A vague swampy odor drifted off the water and blended with the dry, pungent smells of old creosote, rusty steel and the weathered platform timbers of the depot.

Why did Ellen put so much stock in outsiders? Was it something in her nurse's training? For someone who expected David to be self-reliant, she sure seemed to rely on others, especially Father Banning. *The hell with Father Banning.*

The sun had the look of congealing blood as it slumped into a stack of stratocumulus clouds on the horizon. Higher clouds, awash in red and pink and persimmon, would give way to magenta, violet and black. Always black in the end.

The air cooled Phil's face. Children played in the middle distance behind him. What beauty the world held. What ugliness. God could have done better, should have done better. Had complete power, complete knowledge. Used the power, not the knowledge. Not all of it. Couldn't have. The world was too messed up to think otherwise.

He reached down and pried a loose nail from between the platform planking. His father, that gentle, unassuming man, used to take him walking on the Soo Line right of way in South Milwaukee. Once, Phil had spied a large-headed nail with embossed numbers on the head. “That’s a date nail,” his father explained. “When they replace a section of ties, they drive in a date nail. The number is the year.” Each time they walked, they looked for a nail with Phil’s birth year on it. They finally found one and pried it out. Phil still had it.

How much did the fact that David was adopted have to do with it? David and Jessica had always known they were adopted. Ellen had begun to communicate that to them with a lovely little singsong melody when they were infants so that it would never come as a surprise to them.

Would Phil have searched for his birth parents had he been adopted? Sure. Would it have been major surgery on a serious wound, or balm on a scratched curiosity? The latter. Curiosity. A lifelong strength and weakness. Yes, he’d want to find his birth parents simply because he’d want to know. But he wouldn’t particularly care if his father were a garbage collector or a CEO, his mother a barmaid or a brain surgeon. So what? He was who he was, and what he was. How could new information change that?

His own parents were gone. So what if someone other than your nurturing parents gave you life? The bonding took place after you were born, didn’t it? Of course it did. Why, then, this trace of chalk in his iron ingot of certainty?

Only crimson reflections on hovering clouds remained of the sun. The air had cooled, the bay had taken on the dullness of dusk. Here and there small fish flipped against the surface of the flat gray water to create fleeting disturbances in their watery universe. Did a higher intelligence view human thrashings that way—distant, fleeting, random, without meaning?

David once said, “I was born unlucky, Dad.” The words had seared Phil’s heart. They still did every time he recalled them, which was often. And what about Jessica? Every time David got off track, so did Jessica by running and working out and eating barely enough to stay alive.

“And that’s all I know right now,” Ellen said to Father Banning in the family room.

"Lapses are to be expected. You have to move forward. God has a way of providing sufficient grace."

"Come on, Father. Give me a break. That might be true in the long run. I'm not so sure how it works day to day."

"Shall we pray?"

She rolled her head. "I feel like throwing something through a window, damn it! He's been through so much. God can't want this. And I can't understand why He allows it."

Father Banning crossed over to her. He put his hands on her shoulders. "What do you want me to do?"

"Please talk to him. He's upstairs."

The priest inched closer to her. Ellen pressed her hands against his chest in a way that made him stop. "Please go up."

He took a deep breath, nodded and turned to the stairs.

"Third door on the right," Ellen said.

The priest took the stairs two at a time. Ellen hurried to the kitchen and began making a pot of tea. The priest joined her a few minutes later.

"He wouldn't open the door. Try to bring him to the rectory tomorrow."

"All right. If he'll come."

"Are you okay?"

"I need to be alone now, Father. I'd offer you tea, but I need to be alone. Thank you for coming. I really shouldn't have called you. Phil'll be back shortly."

He approached her with outstretched arms, as if to embrace her.

"Please, Father. I want to be alone."

"Certainly."

The priest did nothing to mask his disappointment when Ellen showed him to the door.

"All right then," Phil said, "don't tell me who got it for you. And maybe you don't know why you drank it. But how can I help if you won't open up?"

"It's not your problem, Dad."

"Don't give me that line. While you live in this house, it is my problem."

"Then maybe I should move out."

"You're staying right here, and you're going to let us help."

"I wouldn't want to take you away from your work."

Phil felt his fists tighten. He counted to three. "Cheap shot, David. You're not a victim unless you choose to be."

"Why do you always have to try to fix everything, Dad? I have to do it. Just tell me you're on my side."

"Oh Christ! Do I have to tell you the grass gets wet when it rains?"

"Could we talk tomorrow? I'm wiped out and need to think through some things, know what I mean?"

"All right. You do your thinking. Tomorrow we talk. I want to know how you got the booze. It's your deal, but I want answers."

"You've got to let him handle it, Phil," Ellen said, her voice disembodied in the darkness of their bedroom in the moonless night.

"And if he can't?"

"Then he can't. It's up to him."

"That's cold."

"Good thing you have your own business. You couldn't work for anyone else. Know why? Because you wouldn't be calling the shots. Do you have to be the same with David? He's an adult. If you keep this up, you'll alienate him completely. Or make him dependent on you. *That's* cold."

"So why'd you bring in Father Banning? I can't help, but he can? You're talking from both sides, El. Doesn't make sense and I don't like it. Which way do you want it?"

She didn't answer right away. The only sound came from the clock in the hallway.

"Okay, that was a mistake. It's just that—when you left, I—it was a mistake. You're right. I've already called Renaissance Center and told them to work with David, that we won't be directly involved. I'll try to get David to see Father, but I won't go along."

The pendulum clock went about its business in the hall. It sounded particularly raucous tonight. Phil threw the covers off, slid off the bed and went to the window. "All right. It's his deal. As of right now, I'm out of it. I'll be there for him, but I won't stick my nose in. I still don't buy the alcoholism-is-a-disease malarkey. A hell of a lot of people with cancer would gladly trade places with the drunks of the world."

"That's unfair and insensitive."

"You can decide to drink or not drink."

"Can't you just love him?"

"Oh, come on, El."

"He needs us to love him enough to let him find his own way. If we don't, we'll end up not loving each other."

Phil returned to the bed and climbed in. "I don't see the logic."

"Love in a family isn't a bunch of separate ponds. It's a chain of lakes fed by a common stream. When the flow is cut off we all dry up."

How do you respond to that? He found her hand beneath the covers and said nothing.

Chapter Nine

Following lunch with a client at La Belle Vie, Phil crossed Hennepin Avenue to the Walker Art Center. Maybe the Walker would help him digest an expensive meal. La Belle Vie had never been cheap, but now the city should require the place to attach financing options to the menu.

Inside the Walker, he came to an area devoted to an artist with an apparent obsession for tools. One display consisted of a workbench and numerous hammers, screwdrivers, pliers and wrenches, all spray-painted with dull orange primer. Phil shook his head in disgust and turned away, only to be confronted by a row of garden and farm artifacts leaning against a section of barn wall. Rakes, pitchforks, hoes, shovels—all painted gray and highlighted in orange. There was an old-fashioned water pump painted bright yellow. A horse-drawn harrow in brown. An ice auger in blue enamel. A green drill and bit.

Irony heaped upon irony. With minimum imagination and effort, some self-styled artist had received a prominent showing in a respectable gallery by simply spray-painting useful articles that represented inventiveness in their creation and hard labor in their in their use. Fraudulent works that required neither inventiveness nor hard work; artifacts appropriate for gracing a curio shop on the interstate, but in an art center that took itself seriously? He left with no intention of returning.

"You trying to corner the life insurance market, or hitting on the cleaning lady?

Marty stopped pacing Phil's office and slumped into a chair. His charcoal-blue suit looked rumpled. He looked fresh.

"It's Friday, it's six-thirty, you've been here twelve hours. Ellen kick you out?"

"She should have done that a long time ago when I hooked up with you."

"That's what worries me. She gets mad at you, and she might come after me with a club. How's David doing?"

"Still has the job at UPS loading trucks. Seems to like it. I'm trying to stay out of the mix. Every time I get involved, we argue. You know how much better Ellen is with that kind of stuff, so it's for the best."

"Look, we're going up to Madden's this weekend. Why don't you join us? They have openings."

"Sounds great. Let me call Ellen. You taking Sarah and Steve?"

"It's their trip."

"Good. Give me Madden's reservation number. I'll call you later at home."

Marty went to his office for the number. "By the way," he said when he returned, "did you read where Lars Borglund donated thirty million to a Lutheran seminary?"

"Whoa! I knew he was into religion, but thirty big ones?"

"Yeah, in the newspaper this morning. Two years ago he gave fifteen million to the law school at the U. He could give a hundred mil and not put a dent in his wallet," Marty said with a laugh.

"Maybe I should have Ellen call him. They'd be on the same frequency."

Marty laughed when he saw it was a joke, then looked at Phil closely. "She's really getting into the religion thing?"

"I think I notice it more," Phil said. He dropped into a secretarial chair and locked his fingers behind his head. "It was always church two, three times a week, even when I was in college. The daily thing began when David was in the hole. Went to church and pulled into herself. Protection through self-containment, maybe. Then she got into committee work like an unpublished professor. Good works, you know? Offer up the hardships. Guess she could be doing worse things with her time. Father Banning seems to play a big role in everything."

"The women always seem to carry the load at home. Let me know about this weekend. Be a good break for both of you."

"Okay." Marty didn't like to pry, and Phil had told him more than he had wanted to hear.

Phil didn't call Ellen from the office. Instead, as soon as he got home he said, "Let's go away for the weekend. Up to Madden's. It's so beautiful there."

"It's too expensive. And there's so much we need to do around here."

"Let's go anyway."

Worry furrowed her face.

"It'll work out, honey," he said and put his arms around her. "It'll do us good to get away."

"Would be nice."

"Done deal!"

To Phil's surprise, David and Jessica agreed to go, and even showed enthusiasm. David got on the phone and lined up someone to work for him at UPS on Saturday. Then Phil and David packed and got the fishing tackle and golf clubs together while Ellen and Jessica began packing their things. They voted unanimously for flying their plane instead of driving. Phil called Flight Service and got a forecast of perfect weather. They would depart from Flying Cloud at eight-thirty in the morning.

They took off on runway three-six into a five-knot wind and climbed over Starring Lake with the sun still an orange blob beneath their right wing. He didn't do much flying anymore, hadn't for three years now. That didn't eliminate the high cost of owning a plane, and he knew he had to sell it. So far, no one had turned up with the cash. A deal with Borglund would have solved the problem, but that wasn't going to happen. Marty was right. They were good at making money but better at spending it.

Ninety minutes later they landed on the grass strip and put their luggage in Madden's white van for the short ride to the lodge. It was too early to check in when they got there, so the adults decided on nine holes of golf before lunch, while the young ones went for a pontoon boat ride. A lazy afternoon of shuffleboard and shopping followed lunch.

Cocktails at six, dinner at seven. Video games, an indoor pool and saunas beckoned the teenagers. Phil and Ellen agreed to meet the Goldmans in the lounge at nine.

"It was cool in the dining room," Ellen said back in their room. "I'm going to put on slacks." She dropped her skirt to the floor, revealing her pantyhose and lace panties.

"You look great that way."

"Lecher."

"Even lecherous lawyers need love." He smiled and winked. "Cuddle up with me."

"Just for a few minutes."

He held her close and buried his face in the lustrous dark hair at her neck. Everything was critical in the early stages with Ellen. Nothing different should happen, nothing spontaneous. She expected a set pattern that began with his lightly massaging her ankles, and moving up behind her knees. From there she wanted him to caress the small of her back and her shoulder blades at length before progressing to breasts and belly and thighs, and only then would she welcome his touch down *there*. Consummation would follow in the missionary position. Anything out of sequence ran the risk of turning her off.

They kissed. He staved off the urgency. Ellen's body felt strangely new to him. It seemed forever since they had made love.

"It's been so long!" Ellen whispered, as if reflecting his thoughts.

Afterward, they lay in each other's arms until they felt chilled.

"They'll think we got lost," Ellen said, glancing at her watch. "Lord, it's five to nine!" She rolled off the bed.

"Who cares? I'll just tell Marty I got laid."

She threw a pillow at him, a playful toss with a serious look.

"Not a word to Marty. Promise."

"You know me better than that."

In the main lodge, Phil, in spite of his best efforts, laughed before Marty finished saying, "Smile if you played kissy-face."

Ellen's frown and a sharp elbow to his ribs were his recompense.

"Don't knock it, Ellen," Liz said. "This one slept for an hour."

"In preparation for truly daring exploits later!" Marty said.

Ellen and Phil called it quits at midnight. They knew Marty and Liz would go strong until the place closed.

"That blonde in the bar really had it for you," Ellen said when they were in bed. "Glares weren't enough."

"Meaning?"

"When you went to the john, I took her aside and told her to get lost."

"I wondered why she suddenly ignored me. It's hard to be humble when a strange blonde likes your body, even if she's tipsy and plain."

"Plain? She was homely. And weak. Caved in like a heavy cake."

"I didn't encourage her at all, El."

"I know you didn't."

Something in her voice told him there was more.

"I didn't appreciate you and Marty making a joke of you-know-what."

"He caught me off guard, El. You know how Marty makes me laugh. He was only teasing."

"What we do behind closed doors is private. And sacred."

Phil closed his eyes and ran his hand over them and through his hair. Yes, their lovemaking was private. No, it wasn't trivial or something to make light of. Of course not. But did it have to be as high-minded and solitary as a statue in a dark church? Or was he out of touch with her feelings, "out of sync"?

When had this kind of tension begun? Would it continue? How long, into old-age? When had it started? How could it have been so much simpler years ago and become so complicated? He found other women attractive. Sure, he did. But he wanted no other woman in his life. How then could the only woman in his life be so maddening? Or was he the problem? Maybe he was Phil the Maddening. How could you know? Go to a counselor? David had gone to a dozen of them for his issues, and none of them had done a spit of good, so scratch that.

Chapter Ten

After noon mass at St. Olaf's, which he attended occasionally during the week, Phil went to the pastor's office. He had made an appointment, but the priest hadn't yet arrived from the sacristy.

"Mr. Tag? I'm Father Wark," the priest said when he bustled into the room. He was a tall and powerfully built man of sixty with a shock of free-spirited white hair. "Please have a chair. Coffee?"

"No, thanks, Father. I won't take much of your time. I've been coming to St. Olaf for a long time and wanted to meet you. Have you ever wanted to be anything other than a priest?"

The priest stared at Phil for a long moment, apparently taken aback by the abrupt, out-of-nowhere question from a man he'd never met before. He nodded slightly and said, "Before or after my ordination?"

"After."

"Not for a long time. I was zealous and idealistic. And I began increasingly to fall back on Carlyle's directive to 'Find your work and do it.' But for years I had two recurring fantasies. One had me in a monastery, away from the pressures of parish work. I'm too old now. It's a rigorous life." The priest leaned forward and twisted out of his black suit coat, which he laid across a small file cabinet. "I also wanted to be a narcotics agent. Wanted to nail drug dealers and send them to prison forever. Surprised?"

"To say the least."

"But I'm still here and probably will be until they haul me off to a retirement villa. Why? Who knows? Inertia. Fear of the unknown. Work that needs doing. The narc dream had a lot of pipe in it." He laughed as if at a funny memory. "How seriously would anyone take an agent with a tag like Wark the Narc?"

Phil laughed with the priest. "What kept you from the monastery?"

"Let me answer your question with one of my own. What would I have accomplished? I still would have had myself to contend with."

"I don't follow you."

"Let's take a run at it. "Are you sure you won't have some coffee?"

Phil declined with a wave of his hand.

"Emotional equilibrium—happiness, if you will—is mostly attitude," the priest said. "Victor Franckl said it best when he wrote, 'The last of the human freedoms is to choose one's attitude in any given set of circumstances.' In my single state, that's bedrock."

"But it's different in a marital state?"

"I would think a spouse so intrinsically constitutes part of the circumstance that she becomes part of the attitude, so to speak. Another stratum in the sediment, if you will."

"No offense, Father, but I didn't come here for marriage counseling." The priest said nothing, so Phil continued. "If attitude is bedrock, where does God come in?"

"God is the molten core, the gravitational pull that holds it all together. Without him, there is no bedrock, only whirling debris."

"Interesting analogy, Father. You've given me some things to think about. Unfortunately, I have an appointment. Many thanks for your time." He stood, shook the priest's hand and strode for the door, where he stopped. "You didn't mention Holy Orders as a reason for not becoming a narc. Aren't they forever?"

"Dispensation is possible."

"Unlike matrimony."

"For good reasons."

"Run a couple past me."

Father Wark stroked his chin and tilted his head back. "For

one thing, there's another person involved. And possibly children."

"So the sacrament of matrimony isn't inherently permanent? I always thought the rules surrounding the sacraments flowed from their essence. You're telling me that practical considerations supersede sacramental substance?"

"No. The nature of marriage goes all the way back to the Commandments. However, we must always be mindful of practical considerations and responsibilities."

"We digress."

The priest stroked his chin again. Was it a thought-inducing mannerism or just an old habit?

"Perhaps we could talk again sometime, Father. I've enjoyed it."

"Are you at a crossroad, Mr. Tag? If you are, I'm willing to listen."

"Am I at a crossroad? At times, I think I've been at a crossroad all my life. Aren't we all? Maybe on another occasion. Thanks again."

Phil and Marty sat across the conference table from the Minnesota Pioneer Mercantile Bank loan officer, Bob Landry, who had done everything possible to maintain an upbeat atmosphere.

"We value your business," he said, "and want to keep you as clients for a long time."

"But this is the end of the line on our line of credit," Marty said.

"Yeah, but you guys always come through. As your cash flow increases, you'll have a new line within the year."

When they walked across the lobby leaving the bank, Marty gave Phil an elbow in the ribs and laughed. "They have a lot of confidence in us all right. I guess the lien on everything we own is just in case their faith gets shaky."

In spite of the knot in his stomach, Phil laughed, too. What would he do without Marty Goldman?

* * *

Surrounded by the clatter and bustle of the Panakoken Restaurant, Ellen pushed her coffee cup away and waited for Joan Jeske to respond.

"Okay, smooth talker, count me in. I'm as crazy as you are. Any idea how much work Spring Bazaar involves? Does Father Banning cast a spell over you, or what?"

"No, I'm merely crazy."

"Isn't he a good-looking devil, though? I'll bet he wasn't always celibate—if he is now. Bet he's well-endowed, too."

Ellen laughed. "Jo, when did you get so religiously randy?"

"It's never crossed your mind? Not once?" Her smile was wicked.

"Well, thoughts do pop up. But no, I don't think of him that way. Going full speed helps keep my mind off other things."

"Oh, you're no fun," Jo said with a laugh. "A little wickedness can't hurt, keeps our clergy employed. Oh, well, I can see you're not going to cooperate. Any idea yet why David stumbled?"

"He's totally tight-lipped. And of course Phil wants to fix everything. He means well, but—anyway, you know the story."

"Maybe it's tied in some way with his search."

"I hope he finds them and gets it out of his system. I worry more about Jessica. She's so sensitive about everything."

"Is she eating all right?"

"Most of the time. Runs on the edge, though, and needs close monitoring."

"Not to be insensitive, but let's split a piece of chocolate cake. For therapeutic reasons."

"You're on."

Chapter Eleven

David turned off the radio and eased the Camaro into the Lund Supermarket parking lot. Tom Wagner, on time for maybe the second time in his life, waved to David from a space in the back.

Wagner threw his canvas athletic bag into the back seat and climbed in. "All right! You got the sheepskin covers in blue." He clicked on the radio.

"You're five seconds late with the radio. You slipping, or what?"

"Hey, dude, I'm now a laid back high school grad. Get your final grades?"

"Yeah. Everything's bad," David said. "They can't take back the diploma."

"Decent! Me, too. What now, big guy?"

David shrugged. Wagner also had had to repeat his junior year, and their senior year had been in doubt up to the last minute.

"Slow down, dude," Wagner said. "Isn't that Pam Linder?"

She carried a maroon duffel bag and a racquet in a black cover. Her short white skirt rippled against her golden thighs.

Wagner bent forward until his forehead practically touched the windshield. "What a body! Would I like to get in her pants, or what?"

"Quit dreaming."

Wagner leaned out the window. "Hey, Pam! Want a lift?"

"Whose car is it, Wagner?"

David angled to the curb. Wagner jumped out.

"Going to the club?" He flipped the seatback forward.

"Uh-huh. I'm meeting Angie. Hi, David."

Wagner climbed back into the car. "You and Angie wanna play some doubles?"

"Sure."

David, at the edge of Pam and Wagner's conversation, drove in silence. Pam had to be totally ticked at him for the wild ride on graduation night. Maybe she had a right to be. They all liked to hang out at the country club in the morning before the old people swarmed all over the place, especially the three zillion women who had taken up golf this summer. They hadn't overrun the swimming pool and Jacuzzi yet. Not in the morning, at least.

David and Angie played against Pam and Wagner. David couldn't get his game together. Nothing went right. He kept double-faulting and hitting the ball onto the adjoining court, and couldn't even return Pam's weak second serve.

The ruffled panties Pam wore beneath her tennis skirt didn't make concentrating easy. Neither did the habit she had on her serve of tucking the second ball under the panties where it bulged out and revealed part of her left cheek. Or when she missed a shot said things like "Oh, screw!" or "Suck!" that distracted him like crazy and made him weak in the knees. He didn't have the courage to ask her out. She'd probably tell him to get lost, and not only because of the ride that night. Oh, the crap he'd pulled for three years.

David wiped the sweat from his eyes. Some ride, those three years. Phone calls day and night, parties and girls, mostly scumbag broads, but easy and willing and who cared in all that haze? Class clown and surface confidence galore, riding cool as midnight through a sun-blazed black sky. But God, all the other crap, too.

"David!"

He'd seen the ball coming but couldn't react. He looked over his shoulder. The ball spun into the corner where the fences met and made him think of a prison.

"Jeez, David! Now it's set point," Angie said.

Big-ass deal.

On the next serve Wagner smashed one at the net. The ball hummed between David's legs. A few inches higher and the family jewels would have been history. Wagner tried to keep a straight face but couldn't. He turned away and broke into a laugh. Pam giggled.

"I'm going to the Jacuzzi," David said. "Don't feel good, y'know? Sorry." He wasn't ticked at Wagner, really wasn't. Just didn't feel like playing anymore.

He gathered his towel, watch and wallet, and hurried to the bathhouse adjoining the pool and Jacuzzi. He lowered himself into the hot water until it rose over his upper lip. The thought of the tennis ball he'd seen but couldn't react to recalled the dream he'd had more than once. In the dream he was naked, except for a holstered revolver, when suddenly other people appeared, far away at first, but he sensed they were mean and that they meant to hurt him. In an instant they were closer, men and women, and he drew his gun as they closed in. He tried to fire. It wouldn't fire. He began to run, turning often to shoot at them, but the gun wouldn't fire. Every time, just as the attackers grabbed him, he woke up.

The bubbling Jacuzzi water touched his nostrils. He took a deep breath and slipped under. It would be so easy. And so cowardly and stupid and so many other things that he couldn't even think of, or begin to put in words if he could think of them.

He'd read about a man who captured anacondas. He grabbed them by the head as they lay on a limb over a jungle stream and wrestled them in the water. The snake, coiled around the man, would weaken first. The man, still gripping the head, would rise to the surface, and helpers in the boat would put the snake into a burlap bag. But if the snake ever got a tail-hold on an underwater root or limb, it was all over for the man because the snake would have the leverage to hold him under.

Something gripped David's arm.

Snake!

He broke the water's surface, thrashing and choking.

"You okay?" Pam asked.

David ran his hands over his face and tossed his hair back. "Yeah, sure. Just trying to hold my breath as long as I could, y'know?"

He gulped air and swallowed. Blinking water from his eyes, he stared at Pam kneeling at the edge of the Jacuzzi in a yellow two-piece swimsuit. She leaned over. Her breasts spilled nearly free, their tan giving way to a delicate creamy color. Her nipples weren't quite visible, but the circles around them were. She saw where he was looking but made no effort to cover herself.

"Mind if I come in?" she asked.

"C'mon."

She touched his shoulder for balance and stepped into the water.

"Where's Angie and Wagner?"

"Swimming."

"Want to join them?"

"Mmm. This feels nice," she said.

David wanted to stay in the Jacuzzi alone with Pam. But what would he say? What would they talk about? How could he—? "Too hot," he said. "Let's go to the pool." He climbed out of the Jacuzzi. She followed him.

After the Jacuzzi, the pool felt icy until they began playing underwater tag. Wagner tagged Pam, who in turn lunged for David. He twisted to get away, slipped and foundered, which allowed Pam to catch up. They became entangled beneath the surface. She grasped him between the legs and squeezed. He sucked in water and popped to the surface hacking and gasping.

"David's it! David's it!" Pam shouted.

In the car later he still felt her touching him but decided for the umpteenth time that it must have been accidental.

"Angie's hot," Wagner said. "She rubbed her boobs against my arm three times."

"Aw, hell, Wags. That doesn't prove squat. She probably didn't even know it."

"Didn't know it? No way! Are you kidding? They always know. If you had a set of knockers, wouldn't you know? I keep telling you. Someday you'll believe me."

David slowed the Camaro to the speed limit.

"Look, Tag," Wagner said, "you know when you're in a crowd how you're aware of people touching you and pressing against you? You always know if it's an elbow or shoulder or what, and you know which part of your body they're touching, right? And can't you usually keep from touching if you want to?

“Same thing with the babes. Why would it be any different? They can dip and weave and slide through a crowd, hunch their shoulders and cross their arms in front, and guess what? They never brush their rack against anyone. Or they can rub them across every guy in titty range, like they can’t help it because it’s so crowded. Yeah, right. You think they don’t know? Hah! Wake up, dork!”

David laughed. “‘Titty range’? Wagner, you are totally weird.”

“You know I’m right, man. Hey, just let me off at the corner. I gotta swing into Lund’s to pick up some stuff.”

David waved goodbye and pulled into traffic. A block away, he snapped the clutch, rammed it to the floor and shoved the stick into second.

They do know, they always know, wouldn’t you? Yes yes jesus yes!

Chapter Twelve

"Thanks, Karen," Phil said to the attractive young woman handing him a thick file across his paper-strewn desk.

"You're certainly welcome."

She lingered when he turned his attention back to his desk. He looked up. "Is there anything else?"

"I like your suit."

"Thank you."

He returned his gaze once more to his desk, again conscious of a slight hesitation in the woman's departure. New to the firm and eager to please, she apparently possessed an ambitious libido. Her legs demanded attention as she dallied her way to the door. Well, the best way to handle the situation was to ignore it.

Phil pressed the intercom.

"Ruth, when you get a moment, could you come in, please? My computer's hung up in outer space."

His assistant entered his office trying not to smile. "Any idea which galaxy?"

"Haven't the slightest."

She broke into a broad smile, sat in his chair and clicked his mouse several times.

"Good grief, how did you manage this?" She clicked away, laughing under her breath and shaking her head. "Did you download anything recently?"

"Nope."

"Are you sure?"

"Well, there was this email about a fantasy baseball program that caught my eye. It was hyperlinked and …but I got out of it as soon as they began asking for a bunch of personal information.

"Looks like they imbedded something. This might take a while."

"I've got to see Marty on a few things. I'll be back." He retrieved two manila folders from his desk and left. After visiting with Marty, he proceeded to one of the vending machines in the cafeteria, where he bought a soda for himself and one for Ruth before returning to his office.

"There you are, back on planet earth," Ruth said. "Anything else?"

"If smugness were money, your name'd be Gates. Like a soda?"

"Then I'd quit and who would get you unlost?"

"Maybe you should get lost before I forget to say how much I appreciate your help."

"Oh, don't mention it," she said with mock condescension. She took the soda and departed. Phil laughed under his breath and shook his head. He wouldn't trade Ruth and her healthy irreverence for anything. He paid her more than he had to, and she was worth every cent. He crossed the room to the window. Low cumulous clouds, their massive cauliflower heads gleaming in the sun, floated in serene arrogance across a pale blue sky. He wheeled around and reached for the intercom.

"Ruth, please cancel my appointments for the rest of the day. Reschedule them the best you can. Thanks." Her silence shouted her disbelief. "I've got to get out of here for a while," he said with a conviction that belied the lameness of his excuse.

Unable to recall the last time he had spontaneously taken time off, he strode to his car with a sense of truant anticipation. He took off his coat and tie, draped the tie over the rearview mirror, hung the coat on the back seat hook and unbuttoned his shirt. He drove to the Foshay Tower, luckily found a parking space nearby and hurried to the shoeshine stand in the first floor lobby. His shoes didn't need shining, but he wanted to get them shined anyway. There used to be seven or eight bootblacks. Now there was one, the only one Phil had ever allowed to work on his shoes: an old black man by the name of Lester Wilking who had been there for nearly fifty years. When Lester retired or died, the tower would undoubtedly dispense with the shoeshine stand altogether.

"Good afternoon, Lester. Got time to squeeze in a good shine?"

The old man laid a newspaper aside, smiled broadly and eased his way down from the elevated chair. "Good afternoon, Mr. Tag. How you been?"

"Not bad. Any good news in the paper?" Phil climbed into the chair Lester had vacated.

"Well, now, the thing about of it is, it all depends how you look at it. You read the paper and you think it's all bad. You think people are nothing but scoundrels and scalawags. Ain't true."

"Better make it a quick shine, Lester. I need time to get to Louie's."

Lester broke into a high-pitched laugh that never failed to give Phil a lift. It had become a standing joke between them that Phil would go to another shoeshine stand in the Greyhound terminal to get Lester's mistakes fixed. Lester gave the best shine in the world, and Phil enjoyed talking with him. He was wise beyond all appearances and a good man—a good man who happened to enjoy Canadian Club, a bottle of which Phil always gave him between Christmas and New Year.

"Louie asked me last week who was shining my shoes these days. Said they were in such bad shape, he was going to have to up his price."

Lester laughed again. "Thing about of it is," he said, still laughing, "old Louie don't know bad leather from good vinyl. You send him over here and I'll teach him how to shine shoes, all right. He won't ever go back to Greyhound, for sure."

Phil laughed and tried to think of another acquaintance whose company he enjoyed more. Only Marty's. That's why he always paid Lester exactly double the going charge for a shine.

When he returned to his car, he drove south on I-35 to I-435. Fifteen minutes later, the matronly hostess at the Hotel Sofitel's La Terrasse Café showed him to an outdoor table. He ordered a St. Pauli Girl beer.

"Ice cold," he said to the hunky waitress in peasant garb.

He ate a hard roll with sweet butter, a spinach salad and a mushroom quiche, followed by coffee and a huge slice of cheesecake.

After lunch he drove to the Lake of the Isles. Of the dozens, maybe hundreds, of lakes in the Twin-Cities, he liked Lake of the Isles the most, but he hadn't walked around the lake for years. The profusion of joggers, hand-in-hand lovers, and elderly people astonished him. How did so many find the time? Did they do this every day?

"Sir, could you tell me the time?"

At first he didn't realize the girl was talking to him. "Two-fifteen," he said.

"Thanks!" A bright smile and sparkling eyes made her face beam. She zipped away on her roller blades.

A light breeze swept over the lake and made wavelets that shimmered in the sun. Mothers pushed infants in strollers around the asphalt path that rimmed the lake. Geese and ducks waddled on shore, while those in the water gave way to canoers that dotted the lake. Phil's thoughts went back to childhood days in South Milwaukee, and before long the sights and sounds and memories from his youth erased all trace of office and work. He would enjoy this day, live this day.

By the time he returned to his car, he was sweating and ready for more physical activity. He drove to the Wayzata Country Club, changed into tennis clothes he kept in his locker and found an opponent, a boy about sixteen. Mostly by luck and the inspiration of the day, Phil beat the boy six-four in the first set. Then came a quick one-six set. The kid was fairly good and played effortlessly. By the second set, Phil found the match grueling. No way could he keep up with his young adversary. But it was just what he needed while it lasted.

A shower and a sauna, another quick shower. He changed back into his suit, sans tie, and poked the numeral one on his cell phone. It was nearly six o'clock.

"I'll be late."

"Really stacked up?" Ellen said.

"I'll get a bite out. Then I'm going to the Ordway."

She had never cared for the symphony and seldom went with

him. Even so, the lack of explanation wasn't fair, but how could he begin to explain this day over the phone? The receiver clicked in his ear.

He resisted the impulse to dine at the Capital Grill. That was for special occasions with Ellen. Instead he drove to Murray's, which still had the best steaks in Minneapolis. He had no trouble getting a table because it was early. After enjoying his first martini in months, he ordered a filet mignon and a glass of Cabernet. No chicken or fish or seafood tonight. Only a thick filet would do, cost not withstanding. Deciding against a Frangelico after dinner, he paid the waiter and left.

In St. Paul the Chamber Orchestra filled the night with Dvorak and Tchaikovsky. Afterwards, Phil stepped out of the Ordway into the mellow evening. The glow of globe lights surrounded by huge shadowy buildings made Rice Park, with its pool and fountain and plum trees, romantic and quaint. The scent of lilacs mingled with exhaust fumes from the line of taxis. People laughed and said their good nights while engines roared to life around the square. He crossed the brick sidewalk and cut through the park to the St. Paul Hotel for a cold Schmidt beer in the oak-paneled bar before going home.

Ellen was awake when he slid into bed beside her.

"El?" he said after a few moments.

"What."

"I pretended I was footloose and twenty-one today. I took a twelve-hour sabbatical and spent money I shouldn't have."

The old pendulum clock, so ancient that Ellen had once had to find a clock smith almost as old to carve a wooden replacement part for it, tick-tocked in the hall as it had for years.

"And?"

"It didn't work. I had fun, but it wasn't the same without you."

Without attempting to explain anything, he told her in detail about his day.

"You give me the impression you're buried at the office, you go have a play day, then charge off to the symphony without so much as asking me along. Sound fair to you?"

"You wouldn't have gone anyway."

"That's immaterial."

"How material is your hanging up on me?"

When she didn't answer, he settled back and found her hand under the covers. She yanked it away and rolled onto her side.

Phil took a deep breath against a barb of disappointment, but within moments he felt content with the comfort of the room and bed, the clean scent of the sheets, the weight of Ellen next to him, the sounds coming off the lake. As if on cue, the staccato shriek of a loon lanced the night.

He was tired but wide awake and glad to be home. He had deceived Ellen and excluded her from his evening. She was probably more hurt than angry and had a right to be. He deserved the icy reception. There was something wrong, or at least highly suspect, in playing hooky on impulse, but he had done it and enjoyed it. His contrition for misleading Ellen and hurting her feelings was mild relative to the pleasure the day had provided, a fact that provided its own measure of guilt.

The clock ticked away, faster now, it seemed, than before. It raced, as if to get to the next hour before that hour moved beyond reach of the long black hands that crept along in the dark. Another sound in the clock's mechanism sounded forced, as if to hold the pendulum back, to restrain the relentless ticking from consuming the finite energy in its wound-up innards. Contradictory sounds, to be sure. But then, could an old clock with worn parts and variable rhythms be expected to remain forever constant?

Chapter Thirteen

Wagner's putt rolled through the dew. Throwing off a pinwheel of water and leaving a dark trail in the glistening gray surface, it lipped the cup and came to rest eighteen inches past the hole.

"You see that?" Wagner said. "Should've dropped!"

"Wasn't even close."

"Wasn't even close! Seen an eye doctor lately?"

David laughed in spite of the edge in Wagner's voice. A moment earlier, David had missed his own putt by three inches and gone four feet beyond the cup.

"Man, this is extreme. Don't you hate to see summer end?" Wagner said. He would leave in a few days for Mankato State.

David had missed the deadlines for the U and the dinky school in Iowa. As a result, his dad was all bent out of shape. All that reading. What was the point? Besides hating to read, he wanted to be a carpenter, a builder, so he could see what he had done; show it to people, know it would stand a long time, even after he was dead. Kind of instead of kids. No, not kind of. Instead of, period. Because he wasn't going to have kids. No way. That just wasn't going to be part of the deal.

The part-time job loading trucks at UPS was going great. The hard work kept his arms and shoulders in shape, and the pay was good. The longest he'd ever held a job was six months stocking shelves part-time at the Red Owl Supermarket. That's when he'd saved every cent to buy the Camaro. Except for Red Owl, he'd never worked anywhere for more than two weeks before he screwed up royally or ticked his boss off or got bored out of his skull. Something always happened to end the deal. Now he'd show his dad he could handle a real job and stay on it.

He hadn't touched a beer since that day with Greta Pederson. And his dad hadn't been on his case much, even on the college deal.

"You're up, Tag. Going to take all day?"

Wagner was getting on his nerves. David teed up but had no confidence when he addressed the ball. Maybe it was the oversized driver. *Whatever.* He duck-hooked the ball into the high wet grass between the tee box and fairway. He waited for Wagner's laugh and needling remark. Neither came. It wasn't the same with Wagner anymore. Probably his own fault. He was somehow managing to screw up his only real friendship. Was it something in his genes? Probably. Hell, his own birth mother didn't even keep him around. Why should anyone else?

"I'm sick of golf. I'm going in."

"Come on, Tag. Just because you mess up a shot?"

"You want to get some breakfast?"

"Yeah, why not."

David tried to smooth things over at McDonald's. "Wanna shoot some trap this afternoon?"

"Naw. I've got some shopping to do. You know, school stuff and clothes. Some other time."

"What's up, Wag? I was a dick back on the course, but something's hassling you. Has been all morning."

Wagner swallowed the last of his Sausage McMuffin. "It's heavy stuff, man. Like, one minute I can't get away from home fast enough, and the next I think I should stay."

David waited for him to continue. When Wagner didn't, David punched him on the shoulder. "Spill it, dude."

Wagner gazed out the window and took a deep breath. "I think my old man's got a girlfriend on the side. I don't think it, I know it."

"Aw, jeez, Wag. There's got to be a mistake. I mean, your dad's a great guy. Man, the times he's taken us fishing and— "

"She's from our church. I saw him with her. They weren't praying."

"Man, what're you going to do?"

Wagner sat motionless for a long moment. "I'm going to Mankato, and I'm going to party. Can't do any good here."

"Your mom know?"

"I don't think so."

"Jeez, Wag, I wish I could, I mean, I'm sorry. If there's anything—"

"Hey, no one can do anything. I'd kick the old man in the balls if I could. But what good would it do?" He glanced at his watch. "I gotta go. Need to pick up some things for school." He slid from the booth, leaned over and punched David on the shoulder. "See you around, man."

David watched Wagner get into his car and pull away. Then he ran to his Camaro and headed for Highway 12. It was too early. He had an appointment at eleven, but he couldn't wait until then. Greta Pederson had called last night and said she'd found his birth mother. All along he'd wondered how he would feel when the time came. Now he couldn't quite figure out how he felt. What a tough deal for Wagner. How could his old man do that? How was Wagner supposed to take on college with something like that on his mind? What would it do to Mrs. Wagner if she found out? It was all so crazy. Someone should kick Mr. Wagner's butt around the block, the jerk. David felt a powerful urge to get onto I-494 and wind out the Camaro. Peg it. Man, that'd feel good. He'd done it all summer and luckily never gotten a ticket.

He drove instead to the Children's Refuge Association. A woman in gray slacks told him Greta Pederson was in a meeting. He locked his eyes to the bridge of the woman's nose and said in a near-whisper, "It's an emergency."

The woman frowned but went down a hallway and returned a minute later with Greta. David's throat tightened. "I know I'm early. If you'd like, I can wait till you're ready."

"It's okay."

They went to the conference room they had used before.

"Driest meeting of the century," she said. "You rescued me."

"She doesn't want to see me, right?"

"My call was a shock. She'll work her way through it."

"She didn't want me around then, so why would she now?"

"Give me a break. Give *her* a break."

"Break, my butt."

"She's as confused as you are right now."

"Whose side are you on?"

"Don't try to make this a contest, David. There are no sides."

"Then quit making excuses for her."

Her face got red and her chest heaved. Her voice was controlled, though, when she spoke. "One, you drive here in your own car; two, wearing designer jeans with a silver spoon in the pocket; and three, you seem to think the world owes you something. Would you care to explain that to me?"

Her suppressed anger took the fight out of him. "Took you almost three months. You owe me a drink."

"So I missed by a few weeks. Big deal. Four o'clock, Smooch's?"

Their regular haunt. For weeks he had made up excuses to see her. He knew she liked him by the way she talked and laughed and kidded around. Nothing like all the other social workers and psycho-creeps he had seen, except for Father Banning, who was okay, but not as cool as Greta. Not by a long shot. Didn't look as good, either.

Chapter Fourteen

Her car was already in the parking lot when he got there five minutes early and ran to the entrance.

"Hi! I knocked off early," she said inside.

She had been wearing a maroon blazer earlier. Now she wore a white blouse he could see through and beneath it a filmy bra that left little to the imagination. Her hair was no longer in a bun but falling loose about her shoulders.

"You really look nice," he said, his voice thick.

"Thank you."

"Where're your glasses?"

"Can't a girl wear contacts when she's off duty?"

The waitress came. Not one of the regulars, she was skinny and had braces on her teeth.

"A Pepsi and a light beer," David said.

Greta put a large sealed envelope on the table.

"Your birth mother gave me this batch of non-identifying information. Mostly medical stuff, I'd guess."

His mind whirling, David peered at the envelope. His mom was probably home making dinner. Another woman, old enough to be his mother, with breasts that aroused him to the brink of pain, had just handed him an envelope from a woman who'd given birth to him in the first place.

"How's your daughter doing?"

"Fine. No, that's not true. She's getting rebellious. But we're not here to talk about her."

"Tell me. I want to know."

Their drinks arrived. The waitress left a ticket and walked away without a word.

"I'm afraid she's experimenting with alcohol. God, she's only fourteen."

"That's when I started."

Greta's head cocked up.

David spoke quickly, before she had a chance to start asking questions. "I abused alcohol and other stuff for three years."

She closed her eyes and shook her head slowly.

David covered her hand with his. "It's okay."

"It's *not* okay! I sat here and drank with you. Had you been dry before that?"

"Yeah, but it doesn't matter."

"Are you crazy? One, you're underage. Two, you have a problem with alcohol. Three, I allowed you to drink."

"It was my fault. I haven't had a drop since. I'm okay."

"Are you dependent? Do you attend Alanon?"

"It's kind of a split decision. I usually don't crave the stuff physically, but if I drink I get really smashed. I have to live like I'm hooked. I don't go to meetings. I'm going to show my dad I can gut it out."

"That makes no sense."

"He doesn't think it's a disease."

"So much for enlightenment. Is there anything else I should know?"

He shook his head. She leaned back against the booth and glared at him, her breasts rising and falling beneath the white blouse. "All right, David, let's have it. The whole story. You've never spilled your insides to me. You're going to now."

"That's it. I had some trouble and started using drugs and stuff."

"Tell me about yourself when you were little."

He squirmed, sipped his soda, and glanced around. No one was close enough to hear him. "It's hard to talk about, y'know? Embarrassing."

"Talk to me."

He took a deep breath. "I couldn't wait to go to school. I used to cry when the other kids went, and I was too young. Then I got there and hated it."

"Why?"

"I didn't know for a long time. I just knew I hated reading. Besides, I thought school was going to be play time. And from first grade on I knew I was as smart as the rest of the kids, but I didn't learn much. I wasn't interested. They all giggled and made fun of me. I was the dummy of the class. Pretty soon teachers started telling me not to be so stupid. After a while I shut everything out and just stared out the windows."

"Where were your parents when all this was going on?"

"They tried to figure it out right away, especially my mom. She was in school almost as much as me. She worked with the teachers and special ed people like crazy. Took me to a whole bunch of eye doctors, who said nothing was wrong, I just had an attitude. Funny though, I kind of liked to read history. It was hard but not impossible. I could figure it out and do it, but not my other courses. So maybe I did have an attitude. And I was stubborn." He cleared his throat and rubbed his eyes.

"Sounds like it went on for a long time."

"Till I was fourteen. Things were nuts at school, and at home we fought all the time. My dad finally had our whole family analyzed by a special team of doctors and psychologists at the university. Know what they found? Not much. I was a little dyslexic—they said moderately dyslexic—but no big deal. My folks got a tutor for me that took care of that, but nothing changed at school. I just didn't give a crap. My dad got really honked and on my case. It went like totally ballistic the next three years."

"Dyslexia is much more prevalent in adopted kids than in the general population. Lots of studies and theories, but no one really knows why. Probably has to do with a lack of prenatal care and the lifestyles of the biological parents. Things like smoking and lousy eating habits, to say nothing of drugs and liquor."

David fiddled with the parmesan cheese shaker. "I was mad at the world. Got into booze and drugs, began running with dirtballs and disappearing from home. My parents must have taken me to fifteen different counselors and psychologists. Then I got picked up for drinking and before I knew it, I was in juvenile detention—ha! we called it juvy ten—and detox centers and halfway houses more than I was home. It just about killed my parents. Didn't do my sister any good, either. Tension at home all the time, and I think she was embarrassed at school being my sister."

"You must have reached a turning point."

"Yeah. I stole my parents blind for a long time before they caught me. Then one day they found out I'd taken my mom's engagement ring. To get drugs, y'know? She never wore it, just kept it in her dresser drawer because she was afraid she'd knock the diamond off and lose it. When I confessed, Mom didn't say a word, just went to her bedroom. My dad came to my room a few minutes later. I thought he was going to kill me. He gave me holy hell, but all of a sudden he broke down and cried. The only time I'd ever seen him cry, and I wanted to die. I was sick of everything, but my dad's crying was the thing that kicked me in the butt."

"You've put them through a lot."

"No kidding. And Jessica, too. She got anti-social and began to exercise all the time like she was in training for a decathlon, and ate like a bird. The doctors said she had symptoms of anorexia, and probably was anorexic. She kind of withdrew. We're all still really worried about her."

"Don't start blaming yourself for everything. Were you ever suicidal?"

"Oh, man! I came close only twice, but it was always there. Sometimes I feel so guilty and worthless I wish I was dead."

"Well, wouldn't that be a wonderful solution? Number one, you'd be giving up. Number two, you'd be shifting the guilt to your family. Neat trick, mister. And a dirty one. Ever think how they'd feel if you off'd yourself?"

He stared at her. *Jesus!*

"Did being adopted play a role in all this?"

"I don't think so. Not much, anyway. I always felt a little different and wondered who they were, what they looked like. Funny, whenever I'm naked I wonder if my body looks like my birth father's. Does he have a dimple like mine in his cheek? Is he tall or short? Does he have tiny ear lobes like mine? A mole next to his belly button? Goofy things like that. That's partly why I work out with weights. I think of him as big and strong like Mr. America. Is that dumb or what?"

"Just healthy curiosity. There's more, though, right?"

He looked away and up at the ceiling. He rubbed his temples with his thumb and index finger, dropped his hand to the table. "I want to ask them why they gave me up. I mean, I can't complain. Look how I lucked out. But I still need to know. Once I know I think I'll be okay with it, but it just eats at me, and it will until they tell me straight up. I'll know bull from truth when I hear it."

"There had to be a starting point to it."

"The curiosity was always there, kind of like a little seed. Then one day I was watching Oprah when she had on a bunch of birth parents and kids who'd found one another. Man, some were happy, and others were kind of freaked out. I mean you could see they weren't exactly crazy about the whole deal. It was something else. I walked around for a week in a kind of fog, wondering what it would be like. That's when I decided to find mine."

"Thanks for confiding in me, David. Let's have one more. I want to tell you about a case I read about in Michigan. Kind of like your situation. Then I have to run."

He covered her hand with his. "Thanks for listening. I've never told anyone all this."

Greta laid her free hand over his and squeezed.

Chapter Fifteen

The Camaro's headlights reached into the darkness and reflected off a line of parked cars on both sides of Colorado Avenue in St. Louis Park.

It was the ninth or tenth time David had driven the length of the street since leaving a party earlier. He slowed to a crawl when he passed her house. He had seen the house many times in daylight, but it seemed strange seeing it at night. A faint light glowed through the curtains in the picture window facing the street.

Midnight.

He parked the Camaro near the end of the block and walked back past the tiny houses. Tricycles and Big Wheels and other kid things littered the lawns in the moonlight. The wind rustled through the trees. His breath fogged the crisp air, and goose bumps covered his arms. Autumn ripeness filled the night, as it had when he was a kid out trick-or-treating. His heart pounding, he knocked on the door and waited for what seemed forever.

"Who is it?"

"David Tag."

Silence. Then a chain lock scraped in its channel. The door opened. David's throat was so dry he nearly choked. She wore a fuzzy yellow robe and her hair was kind of messed up.

"What brings you here, David?"

"I'm … I'm, y'know, sorry about in the restaurant the other day. You shouldn't have to listen to my problems."

"Part of my job. Come in," Greta said, motioning. There was no foyer. The door opened directly into the living room. "Keep your voice down. The girls are asleep. Didn't you wear a jacket?

You'll catch cold."

He sat on the edge of the worn couch. Greta dropped onto a stuffed chair opposite, knees under her chin, arms locked around her legs. She pushed her glasses up on her nose. "Like a soda?"

"No, thanks."

He glanced at the TV. Jennifer O'Neil stood on the beach in *Summer of '42,* an old movie he had seen before. "There wasn't much information. She had hypoglycemia."

"Nothing," Greta said.

"Yeah, I looked it up."

The boy in the movie was talking to Jennifer O'Neil.

"I'm sorry about your daughter. What's her name?"

"Stacy."

She crossed one leg over the other. The robe parted. She flipped it back over her thigh.

"What's your middle name?"

"Louise. Why?"

"I wondered what the L stood for. You know, in the phone book? The number matched the one you gave me in case I ever wanted to talk."

Her head tilted back slightly, her lips parted. He could hardly stand it, the way she looked at him. What if she saw the sweat on his forehead?

"So what's up, David?"

"I don't know. Nothing. I mean, I was wondering what was happening."

"She still hasn't agreed to see you."

"What's her problem?"

"Give her some time, David."

At a loss for words, he looked at his feet and twisted them in semi-circles. Greta straightened her legs in a forward rocking motion, planted her hands on the arms of the chair, and bounced to her feet.

"Young man, it's late, and you have a long drive home."

"I'll take that soda."

"Nope. Some other time."

She took him by the hand, led him to the door and opened it. David gripped her arms.

"Tell her I need to see her. Only once. I need to know where she's from, where my birth father is, why she gave me up. I don't want to be part of her life, but I need to know! And I want to see what she looks like. Will you tell her?"

Greta nodded.

"You okay? You're shaking," he said.

"The air's cold. You'd better leave."

"I'm sorry I bothered you. You're the nicest woman I've ever known."

"Bet you say that to all the girls."

He tightened his grip on her arms and shook his head. She kissed him on the cheek.

"Good night, David. Drive carefully."

She closed the door. He stepped back into the cold night. September in Minnesota. No wonder she was shivering.

Chapter Sixteen

In the parking lot of Southgate Mall, the sun-heated tailgate warmed Ellen's hand as Jessica meticulously positioned the box in the station wagon.

"Mother, I can't wait to wear it. I'm trying it on again the minute we get home!"

"Let's celebrate at the Blue Point."

How could it be even remotely possible that Jessica was only a year away from finishing high school? She could still street fight with David and go into a snit in the blink of an eye. But she also enjoyed window-shopping, and had recently begun to prefer fashion mags to touch football. How nice having a young woman in the house!

They walked the short distance from Frank Murphy's to the Blue Point Restaurant. Inside, the zealous air conditioning made Ellen glad she'd worn jeans. Once seated in a window booth, she glanced at the menu and leaned conspiratorially toward Jessica.

"Let's have a dessert."

"Oh, Mother, you try this every time."

Ellen ordered Spumoni and carrot cake. Jessica had tea and Melba toast. The pale blue linen tablecloth felt starchy. The restaurant was simple, almost Spartan but spotless, and wonderful aromas came from its kitchen. Lake Minnetonka glistened in the distance.

"You eat anything and stay so slender. Have you gained a pound since you married Daddy?"

"Six, as a matter of fact."

"In twenty-nine years. I've gained that much in the last three months."

Ellen smiled wanly. Her daughter had gained six pounds in the last year, but not in three months. She was still far too thin.

Jessica ate one of the crackers. The second one remained in the cellophane wrapper. The signs had begun at the peak of David's problems two years ago: the running, the constant exercising, the fussiness, as if her life depended on everything being perfect. But for the past six months she had been more like her old self, though far more mature.

As to the extravagance of the gown, well, Jessica would have it not only for Wahoo, the Wayzata Country Club's annual fall dance, but also for the prom next spring. Phil never said much, but she knew the business was going through especially tough times. Why else would they be dipping into their meager savings at every turn? As to the gown, Ellen would alter it sufficiently for the prom, perhaps even dye it, if the fabric would take dye, so that Jessica wouldn't feel self-conscious. Jack Barker, last year's high school diving team captain, had invited her to Wahoo, the first for both of them.

"What does Jack like other than swimming?"

*"Div*ing, Mother." Jessica waited for the distinction to register. "He led the debate team and was sports editor of the school paper. He wants to major in communications."

"He sounds neat, honey. I look forward to meeting him." She held a spoonful of spumoni over her plate. "By the way, has David said anything about his search?"

A slight frown creased Jessica's face. "Why to you believe he would tell me?"

Ellen's heart raced. Heat rose to her ears. Was she coloring?

"Honey, you know I'd never want you to betray David's confidence."

They finished eating.

"Are you curious about your birth parents?"

"Sure, sometimes. Nothing like David, though. Maybe someday it'll be more important," Jessica said with a shrug. She fiddled with the cellophane wrapper. "Why is Daddy working so much? Is everything okay?"

"What do you mean? Why do you ask?"

"I don't know. I mean, he's always on the go, and edgy."

"He and Mr. Goldman are going to move the office. And they have to buy a whole new computer system. He has a lot on his mind."

"Is he okay? I mean, happy and everything?"

Did the shard of alarm show? Did Jessica sense the half-beat skip in her breathing?

"I hope he's not still upset with David. I think he is, though," Jessica said.

"Not upset. Concerned."

"Jeez, isn't it natural for David to want to find out where he came from? And kind of who he is?"

"Of course, but—"

"It's *his* life, Mother. You know his favorite subject. The only subject he ever liked."

"Of course. History."

"Don't you see? His need to know the past? What happened? Why it happened? That's why he aced every history course, and barely got through all the others. I think he's struggling with so many things."

Ellen, her chest a commotion, nodded her agreement. Only yesterday a girl of seventeen herself, now a woman of forty-nine, nearly three years older than her husband, a man under tremendous self-imposed pressure, a disciplined man deeply hurt by and worried about his unmotivated, baggage-carrying son. Was he unhappy or dissatisfied with her, too? For months she had attributed his moods and distances to work, to David, to middle age, to every convenient reason under the sun. Was she part of his discontent? Impossible. Their marriage had always been solid. *Don't start imagining things, El.*

"Mother, are you all right?"

"What? Yes. Yes, of course. I'm just thinking. Why are you looking at me like that? Why these questions? Of course everything is all right with Dad—with me—us!"

"I wasn't even talking about you and Daddy."

Hurt showed in Jessica's eyes. The corner of Ellen's mouth quivered. She tried to stop it by pursing her lips. When that didn't work, she forced a smile. Reaching across the table, she grasped her daughter's hand.

"I know, honey. I'm just so tired. Are you done with your crackers? I have to see Father Banning about the Spring Bazaar after I drop you off."

Before they left, Jessica stacked their cups. She brushed cracker crumbs and the cellophane wrapper into her palm, and dropped them into a wastebasket next to the cash register on the way out.

It had rained hard earlier. The rain began again as they reached the parking lot. Ellen wondered what Phil was doing, wished he were here, wished they could spend the afternoon together.

Chapter Seventeen

David rolled off the family room sofa and stretched. Yawning and scratching, his neck stiff from lying in a crooked position for too long, he shuffled to a window to peer out at the lake. The droning hiss of a steady, straight-down rain enveloped the house, and the smell of freshly cut spring grass, which he had mowed between bouts of rain, came through the open windows into the family room.

Should he put on his rain gear and go fishing? It was warm enough, and on a day like this there wouldn't be five zillion boats on Lake Minnetonka. He was kind of watching a tennis match between Federer and Nadal, though. Besides, he didn't like to use his binoculars in the rain, and it wasn't much fun going without them. He couldn't remember the last time he hadn't taken them on the lake. With binoculars, everything on the lake and on the shore could be brought up close and clear: boats and wildlife and people.

His mom and Jessica had gone shopping and weren't back yet. She said she had to study for one of her courses at the U later on. A mystery, why she'd decided to get a degree in nursing when she already was a nurse. But she was determined to do it, and once she made up her mind, that was it. End of discussion. Indecision wasn't in her vocabulary. Dad had gone to a Twins game with Mr. Boyd and Mr. Boyd Junior, who was a minus two on a scale of ten, a nerd right down to his goofy colored socks.

Neat that Dad had taken a Saturday off work to go fishing with him, but the rain had knocked that out. Then Mr. Boyd called with box seat tickets, and David agreed to go, even tried to show enthusiasm. But he backed out at the last minute by saying he didn't feel good, which wasn't really a lie because the thought of sitting next to the Boyds for a whole game did make him kind of sick. And baseball didn't thrill him much either, with or without the Boyds. Every game he'd ever seen had amounted to three minutes of action packed into three hours. Nor was he exactly crazy about the Metrodome. Kind of like watching a game in a tent. Even Dad wished they played outside on real grass.

Actually, baseball wasn't really on his mind. Neither was tennis. Inga Lindrud was. Popular, academic all-star, beauty queen Inga. Untouchable Inga. Pregnant Inga.

They said the kid's father was a junior at the U. No one even knew the guy. According to Sue Carlson, Inga was going to keep the baby, but not marry the U guy. David had dated Inga three or four times back before the beginning of that big golden black hole in his life, when he went totally bonkers, and liked her a lot.

Why'd she let it happen? And with a guy so old. Jeez, didn't the U have enough girls to go around? Weird thing, sex. Why would God make something so great and so bitchy? Banks had a penalty for early withdrawal, sex had one if you were late. So you always had to watch the fine print, no matter what.

Or did people make it bad? They sure got on a girl's case and made her do things like abortion or give up the kid. Everything was cool unless somebody got pregnant. When that happened, they reached for the nightmare switch.

Neat that she wanted to keep the kid; took a lot of guts. Be nice to help her in some way. The kid would always be with her, the way it should be. Maybe the U guy wouldn't marry her? What a jerk.

A car door slammed. Jessica came into the house calling, "Hello, anyone home?" until she saw David sprawled on the sofa.

"Home alone? What're you doing? Who's playing?"

"Yes. Nothing. Two tennis players."

"Go jump in a sewer, butthead!"

"Then quit banging on my ears." He couldn't help laughing.

"Oh, come off it, David. You've really been a dork lately."

What a seventeen-year-old piece of work. Next, she'd try to

make peace by going to something totally unrelated. It didn't take long.

"Hear about Inga Lindrud?" she asked.

"Uh-huh."

"Boy, you'd think if she's going to do it, she'd use something."

"Look, she made a mistake, okay? So get off her case."

"Sit on it, geek!"

She went silent. Translation: her feelings were hurt. David couldn't look at her then, so he turned away and closed his eyes. She was an okay kid sister, better than okay. Not someone you wanted to hurt. Except when she was on one of her ultra-competitive streaks. When that happened, her witchiness made you want to lock her in the basement for a week. For the last six months, though, she'd pretty much mellowed out. Still ran thirty miles a week and exercised like a freaked-out Olympian, but seemed to have her head on right. Didn't look like a skeleton anymore, either, and even had boobs and a butt. His friends were asking about her, and some guys were starting to suck up to him. It wasn't hard to figure out. She was tall—what, five-eight, five-nine?—had nice sandy hair, blue eyes and was usually outgoing. Kind of like he used to be, the outgoing part.

He could kill himself for saying Inga made a mistake. That kind of made the baby a mistake, too, which wasn't true. It would be the same as any other kid, except it might never know its father.

"Something's going on, David. Did that social worker find your birth parents? Is that it?"

It'd be easy to throw her off the scent by calling her Icka, as in the last two syllables of Jessica. But she'd pay him back for the next year and a half by calling him Davie in that nagging voice she reserved just for getting under his skin.

"Don't feel like talking about it, Jess. Okay?"

"You should talk to Mom and Dad about it. They'd understand."

"Not Dad. Anyway, it's my deal, y'know?"

"Well, set it up with my secretary any time you want it on the agenda," she said s she fluffed a pillow on the couch. She stood back and surveyed it before another fluffing and repositioning. Then she did it all again. Just when he was about to tell her to stop it, she did stop.

"How're you doing, Jess? I hope you don't let my deal get to you. You've got to take care of yourself."

"I'm okay. Dad gets to you more than he does to me."

"He thinks it's his mission in life to fix everything. He doesn't mean to be a royal pain. Know what I mean?"

"Yeah. I'm going to crash. Couldn't sleep last night."

When Jessica was gone, Federer held a huge trophy in the air for the fans and TV cameras. Everyone except Nadal looked happy. David turned off the TV, dropped the remote to the floor and stretched out on the white leather sofa. It was so quiet. Middle-of-the-night quiet. The shelves of books on both sides of the fireplace reminded him of a creepy library. Who would ever want to study in a library? A morgue would offer more fun. Muffled thunder rumbled in the distance. He gazed out the window at the maple trees twitching in the rain. It was dark enough outside to make the family room gloomy, in spite of all the windows. Tears welled up. He wished Jessica hadn't left. Why'd he been so rotten to her? He rolled to his side, drew his knees up into a fetal position, and closed his eyes.

"All right, Ellen, you win. Two bands: one polka and one rock. You line them up. Anything else on your list?"

Ellen made a check mark on her pad. "Nope. That should do it for now, Father."

"How's David coming along?"

"We hold our breath a lot. He seems to be holding his own. Thanks for asking."

Father Banning arose and opened a cabinet door. "Would you care for a glass of wine?"

"No, thanks, Father. Well, why not? Just half. Thank you."

He poured red wine, handed one glass to her, and sat next to her on the small sofa in his office. He raised his glass. "To the bazaar…and to its lovely coordinator."

"Thank you." Ellen couldn't help smiling in spite of a sliver of uneasiness.

"Life takes so many detours. If we had any idea when we were young, we'd either not believe it or would be afraid to begin."

"When did you decide to become a priest, Father?"

"Would you be comfortable calling me Gerard? Adults calling me Father day in and day out gets so tiresome at times. As if they're all kids and I'm the only grownup."

"I could try, but it's so automatic."

"Whichever," he said with a laugh. "I don't want you to feel awkward. You're too special to me." He took a big drink of wine. "I wanted to be a priest in grade school and never seriously considered other options. No vocation is perfect."

Ellen waited for him to continue.

"The lack of female companionship creates a real void. I don't want to leave the priesthood, but the older I get, the more I realize how empty it can be at times."

"Married life has its own share of problems."

"Celibacy isn't one of them."

Ellen sipped her wine. She was glad not to be drinking a full glass, though the priest had filled hers well past half. "Not that marriage is exactly saturated with sex after the first few years," she heard herself say, meaning it as a joke but not hearing it that way.

He placed his hand on her back just below her neck. "Are you unfulfilled?"

Feeling the warmth spread through her, Ellen set her wine on the end table next to the sofa and stood up. "I appreciate your concern, Father, but I really must be off."

Father Banning arose. On the way to the door, he embraced her. "I respect you far too much to ever violate your trust, Ellen. I hope to see you soon."

Her heart pounding, the walk to her car seemed to take forever. She still felt his hand on her back, and the feeling was not unpleasant.

Chapter Eighteen

David squinted and cupped his hand over his forehead to shade his eyes from the sun. Compared to inside the house, the driveway was like standing next to a fireplace. The weatherman had predicted seventy degrees, a real bonus for October.

He had his paycheck from UPS in his pocket and a date with Pam Linder, who was home from Iowa City for the weekend. Everyone would tailgate before and after the game, then move on to Susan Lund's house in Eden Prairie for a party. Booze would flow like water, but that was okay. Just something he had to contend with, no big deal. Besides, he didn't have the overpowering physical craving for the stuff he'd read about others having. That's why he didn't believe he was an alchy. He sure did like the buzz and the escape it offered, though, and once he started he didn't know when to stop, so maybe he was hooked. Whatever.

He joined his dad, who was waxing the Cadillac in the driveway.

"Need some help?" he said.

"Sure. Wax or buff? Your choice."

"Buff."

The wax dried quickly in the warm dry air, and the gray paint gleamed when he rubbed off the chalky residue. Maybe he'd go to school at the semester, give it a try. Couldn't hurt. For the time being he'd hang in there and hope his birth mother would change her mind and see him. He hated her for refusing. Problem was, the more he hated her, the more he thought about her, so his curiosity was running wild. But that could wait. Last night Pam Linder had practically asked him to take her to the game today. All he could think of was that day last summer when she had grabbed him in the swimming pool.

"You'll reach bare metal if you buff that spot much more."

David frowned. Then he saw his dad was only joking. "Yeah, they sure don't paint 'em like they used to. My Camaro has better paint on it," he said, which made his dad laugh.

Except for a few times with his dad along, David had not driven the Cadillac. His dad offered it to him occasionally, but it was no fun driving a lunker like that. He'd rather drive the Camaro. His baby. He was responsible for it and not about to run around in some chromed-up Cadillac that happened to be ten years newer. Hard to figure, why people bought new cars all the time, or why Detroit and Japan changed designs so often. His dad bought a new car just about every year until his business started going downhill. His mom drove an old station wagon. It still looked good and she wanted to keep it.

Nearly finished with the roof, he reached to the center and gave it a few last strokes.

"Ah, careful with your buckle, son."

David looked and, *damn,* beneath the chrome strip at the window, his Coors belt buckle had scratched the paint.

"It'll rub out with compound, son. Don't worry about it."

But David had caught the slight note of irritation in his dad's voice. Jeez, if somebody did that to the Camaro....

His dad threw an arm across his shoulders, gave him a jab to the ribs. "If you think you're going to get out of this job over a tiny scratch, forget it, *amigo.*"

Not that phony Spanish stuff like Mr. Goldman.

"Don't feel like it anymore, Dad."

"Okay, you wax. I'll buff."

David folded the buffing cloth and laid it on the fender. "I mean, I've got to get ready, and I have to cash my check."

"I'm not upset, David. It's nothing. I wasn't getting on your case."

"Thanks, Dad. I was going to quit anyway."

He walked into the garage and was nearly out of earshot when his father muttered, "Shit!" Lightheadedness hit David as if the blood in his brain had drained away all at once. It took a few moments for him to realize where he was and where he was going.

Well, at least he knew what the Old Man thought of him.

Phil continued waxing the car, rubbing on the paste wax and buffing with hard strokes. When he finished he applied a special rubbing compound to the scratch before waxing over it again. The scratch all but disappeared.

David left the house and climbed into his Camaro. As he backed into the street and roared off, Ellen appeared.

"What happened with David?"

Phil told her, adding, "I shouldn't have said that."

Her silence confirmed her agreement. "Did you use the new wax?" she said, turning the conversation. "The car looks nice."

He nodded and put his arm around her waist. "Let's go out tonight, just us. We'll give Jessica pizza money."

"Where?"

"How about a movie? It's been a long time."

"They're all violence and sex."

"We'll find a good one. Let's give it a shot."

The phone rang inside.

"I'd rather not. I have a test to study for. Let me get that call."

Iowa trounced Minnesota. David enjoyed the tailgating and the party in spite of a few college guys who thought they were God's gift to the world. He didn't drink a drop, though at times it took everything he had to keep from popping a beer and downing it when the college guys got on his nerves. But it was best to tough it out and stay away from the stuff. Who wanted to turn into a full-time wino?

At midnight Pam snuggled up to him and whispered, "Shall we leave?" Her lips brushed his ear and her warm breath caressed his neck, while her breast pressed against his arm. She must have applied fresh cologne or perfume because the scent of it, mingled with a hint of perspiration, radiated from her and went straight from his nose to his crotch. They slipped out and walked hand in hand to the Camaro.

"Some house, huh?" Pam said as they backed out of the driveway.

The Lunds had moved from Wayzata to Eden Prairie last summer because Mr. Lund liked the Olympic Hills golf course. Their house sat on a fairway with a lake on the other side.

David turned onto Pioneer Trail.

"God, it's so good to get away from the crowd. So nice and quiet. Shall we go talk awhile?" Pam said.

He knew where to go. There was a short spur of street that sloped down and ended abruptly about three hundred yards from the main road. He left the radio on when he turned off the engine. The sound of Celine's voice filled the car.

"It was a fun day," Pam said.

"It's really nice to see you again."

"I was afraid last night you wouldn't ask me to the game."

She had dropped broad hints, then Nikki Alt had asked him if he'd like to take Pam to the game. Only after all that had he approached her.

"Gosh, you looked nice today. I was really proud."

"What a nice thing to say," she said, and moved closer, onto the console between the bucket seats, and lay her head on his shoulder. "You're always nice."

He didn't care if she heard his heart thumping. He shifted his weight and looped his arm around her and ran his cheek against her hair. When she tilted her face, her forehead grazed his lips. He kissed her on the nose and on the mouth. Her lips parted, she put her right hand behind his head, and drew his face to hers. The tip of her tongue met his, retreated, returned, vanished. A second later it deftly swept the inside of his upper lip and darted against his tongue again. The kiss continued for a long time without interruption while she caressed his chest and arms.

She broke away, lay her face on his chest, her forearm across his lap. "Mmmmmm. I need to stop and get home, but it's so hard, isn't it?"

"Just a little longer?"

"I guess so."

He held his breath and put his hand high on her chest where he could feel her collarbone through the thin sweater. Angling her face next to his throat, her lips upturned to meet his, she engulfed him when he kissed her. The softness of her breast beneath the sweater gave him the courage to press gently. She took her lips from his and placed them on his ear, said “No,” and immediately exhaled. While he fought for breath, her tongue massaged his ear, then slipped straight into the center in a tight augering motion.

She stopped. “What’s that big building over there?”

“A church.” His chest heaved. “Pax Christi.”

“Oh.”

She laid her hand over his inner thigh and wedged her fingers between his thigh and the seat. “Gives me the creeps doing this so close to a church.”

He stared at her in the darkness.

“It’s so warm in here,” she said. “God, I’m hot!”

She rolled her sweater up under her breasts, leaving her midriff bare.

“There. That’s better.” She leaned over to him again.

He kissed her and slid his hand under the rolled up sweater. She jutted her shoulder forward so that her bra strap dropped down over her arm. Her breast came free into his hand, her lips crushed his while her hand stroked his thigh.

Her hand left his thigh. She tugged his shirt free and slipped her hand under his belt against his belly and down. She squeezed and stroked, then released him and ran her hand across his ribs and around to his shoulder blade, rolled over the console, straddled him and ground against him.

His hands came up under her skirt and grasped her cheeks. Hooking his thumbs under the elastic, he tugged at her panties. She brought her legs together so the panties could slide down. He reached between her thighs. She inhaled sharply and mashed against him. He unzipped, and she lowered herself to him.

She abruptly rolled away. “We have to stop.”

David’s head fell back to the headrest. He gulped air and swallowed.

“I’m sorry, I guess I’m terrible,” she said. “Kiss me?”

They melted together, his hand between her legs, her hand inside his jockey shorts. She pulled away. "Let's stop now."

"Why?"

"Because I'm—I—we have to, that's all. I mean, right here next to a church and—Is it a Catholic church?"

"Yeah."

"You're Catholic, aren't you?"

"Sure, but—"

"Do you have … you know. Anything?"

He raised off the seat, straight-legged, shoved his hand into his pants pocket, and extracted a packet of three Trojans.

"But you're not supposed to … I mean, being a Catholic.…"

"Come on, Pam. What's going on?"

"I don't want you to do anything wrong. I need to get home. Please?"

"Yeah, and if I didn't have the damn things, that would be your excuse."

He started the engine.

"I'm sorry, David. Here, put your hand here again. Just for a minute." She took his hand and began to guide it to her. He yanked it away.

"What is it? What's wrong?"

"What's wrong? Oh, nothing. Nothing at all."

He did a U-turn in reverse and headed for Pioneer Trail.

"Look, David, I think you're awfully nice, and—"

"Cut it, Pam! Just cut it the hell out!"

Chapter Nineteen

After dropping Pam off, David had an unrelenting urge to roll the windows down and lay the speedometer needle on the peg for about fifty miles with the wind howling and the engine screaming as he zephyred through the night. The interstate sign loomed up in his lights, but at the last second, instead of entering the ramp, he swerved and headed for the Excelsior Boulevard exit. A few minutes later he parked at the end of the car-lined street and walked back to the little house. A muffled voice came from inside when he knocked. He identified himself. The door opened. Greta, puzzled, beckoned him in.

"I hope I didn't wake the girls."

"They're at my sister's."

She motioned him to a chair. She went to the couch.

She had on the same yellow robe she'd worn the last time. She tucked it under her when she stretched her legs along the length of the couch.

"So, Mr. Tag, what brings you here at this hour?"

"Well, I—I was on a date and didn't feel like going home."

"Everything go okay?"

"Yeah. No, not really."

"Want to talk about it?"

No way. But before he knew it he said, "Why do girls talk in code? Why do they always say and do the opposite?"

Her head arched back. She closed her eyes.

"I mean, how does a guy know? When I was on stuff, I hit on girls in a second. Not any more. I don't know where they're coming from."

"Don't be so hard on yourself. Men are still confused by

women at fifty. And vice versa."

She swung her feet to the floor. Her hair was all done up. So was her face, and she might have had her contacts in, but probably not. Her eyes had a certain look, as if she weren't focusing too well.

"You really look nice," he said, and when she smiled he rose from his chair. "Can I sit with you for a minute?" She didn't answer but kind of shrugged in a little way that said yes.

"What'd you do tonight?" he said.

"Ha! Almost went to dinner and a play."

"Almost?"

"He didn't show."

"Oh, no. Jeez, I'm sorry."

"I think he's married. He says not, but now I'd bet on it."

"What a jerk!"

"A heck of a fun guy, great to be with. Maybe a jerk underneath, who knows? See what I mean? Women don't understand much, either, at times. Some do. Yesterday a real bitch in our department got promoted. She's practically incompetent, but she's sleeping with a big boss downtown."

She closed her eyes again. She looked like a religious painting in the pale light. The faint smell of alcohol made him wonder how much she'd had to drink.

"You're so nice," he said, "and so beautiful."

He put his arm around her. Her head fell back and she parted her lips to meet his. Her lips were moist, her tongue warm and soft and delicious with the taste and scent of alcohol mingled with perfume and powder. A low moan came from her throat. Her leg, free of the robe, curled around his thigh. His hand easily slipped inside the loose robe to cup her breast. She moved wetly over his face and throat, kissed his eyes and cheeks, bit him. He nearly cried out when she probed his ear, and again when she opened his shirt and nuzzled his nipples. He pulled her robe open and thrust his hand between her thighs. She clamped her legs together.

"Time to get up, baby." She sprang to her feet, grabbed both his wrists, pulled him up, and led him to the door.

"You have to go."

She pushed him through the door and closed it behind him. The cold air slapped him. He could hardly see, hardly breathe.

The door opened. “Come, baby.” She bumped the door shut behind him and let the robe slide off her shoulders to the floor.

He was alone when he awoke in the morning. He found her in the living room and tried to coax her back into bed. When she refused, he took a shower. Afterwards, she gave him two slices of toast and a glass of orange juice, which he devoured. An Egg McMuffin on the way home would take care of his hunger.

“Have you heard from my birth mom?”

“She called late Friday and said she’d meet you. With conditions.”

David held his breath.

“One, she won’t divulge her name or any other identifying information. Two, you’ll meet where and when she designates. Three, you won’t reveal your last name or address. If you do, she won’t see you again. She knows your first name.”

“But—”

“She cut no slack on the conditions. Today is the only time she can see you in the next two weeks. I’m to call her by noon to confirm a time and place.”

“Why didn’t you call me?”

“I tried three times yesterday. I didn’t think you’d want me to leave a message. Last night sure didn’t seem like the right time. I was going to call you after I picked up the girls this morning.” She raised her juice glass, which had been a jelly jar, to her lips.

He put his arms around her. She pushed him away.

“Please take a walk while I call her.”

He went outside until she called him back in. She handed him a slip of paper.

First lookout on Highway 13
South of Mendota Bridge
9:00a.m.

It gave him only thirty minutes.

Chapter Twenty

He sped through the light Sunday traffic and pulled into the deserted lookout parking area at eight-fifty. He hurried to the concrete rail that jutted out some twenty feet above the valley floor. Pacing around the lookout, he started to read the historical marker but lost interest before reading a line. He returned to the railing. Marshes and backwater of the Mississippi stretched out for miles. Jets screamed into the air from the Minneapolis-St. Paul Airport directly across the valley.

His dad and Mr. Goldman had gotten their flying licenses at the same time and for several years had flown off to places like Watertown, Sioux City and Wausau for fly-in breakfasts, barbecues and air shows. His dad always wanted one of the family to join him, someone to talk with and help watch for checkpoints. Jessica went along once in a while. David went once and got bored out of his skull in thirty minutes. His mom wouldn't go. Not till the kids were grown, she said. His dad didn't fly much these days.

"David?"

He whirled around. Her hair wasn't quite blond or red or sandy, but a soft, coppery combination that caught the morning light.

"I—I didn't hear you coming."

"You were so lost in thought, I hated to break in."

A nice tan made her complexion even nicer. She had to be five-eight or nine, like a model.

"I didn't, ah, sleep much last night. Went to a football game and a party," he said, feeling pretty stupid and not knowing what else to say. A jet roared over and made conversation impossible. Her blue eyes followed the plane into the sky. How could anyone be so beautiful?

"There are some things you should know," she said. "You weren't an accident or mistake. I intentionally became pregnant because I wanted you very much. Your father was three years older than I and couldn't wait to get into the Marines. He enlisted a month after high school. I was afraid I'd never see him again. You were conceived when he came home on leave in September. Then, two months later a letter arrived. He had fallen in love with a girl from San Diego and was going to marry her."

She looked out over the swampy basin where haze muted the autumn colors on the distant bluffs. Another jet lifting off a runway whined across the valley and thundered overhead a few seconds later.

"I'd planned to raise you myself if anything happened to him. I was fully prepared to do that, expected to have to do it because I had a foreboding about his going into the service. He wanted to get into Special Forces. A daredevil, and so impulsive.

"I ignored my parents' anger and resolved to finish school. You must understand, I was not one bit ashamed. I wanted you. I never told him I was pregnant. Never had the chance, really. When his letter arrived, I wasn't yet certain of it.

"I'd had this romantic thought that if he died you would be my link to him for the rest of my life. My family was dirt poor, but I would have found a way to provide for you. What I could not accept was his betrayal. I had to sever my connection to him. That's why I put you up for adoption."

"Where is he now?"

"He drowned ten years ago SCUBA diving in Hawaii. A friend from high school sent me a clipping from the Duluth newspaper."

A siren wailed in the distance. A gust of wind sent a flurry of yellow leaves streaming to the ground from nearby trees.

"I must go, David. I think of you frequently, have always wanted the best for you. It was necessary, however, to close that chapter of my life. Do you understand?"

"I think so." David wasn't ready to let her go. "Was he

smart? Was he an athlete?"

She smiled. "Yes and yes. Very smart. He played football and ran the mile in track."

"Did you ever get married?"

"Never did."

"Will I see you again?"

"Once more. In the meantime, I want you to have this." She handed him a white envelope. "It's your father's senior yearbook picture. I found it a few days ago while going through some old things. Until next time." She stepped down to a walkway at the north edge of the lookout and disappeared into the trees and foliage.

David opened the envelope with shaking hands. He became lightheaded as he gazed at the handsome face in the black and white photo. Except for the longer hair, it could have been his own senior picture. David stood transfixed, wanting to run after her but unable to move. "Wait!" he called out.

When he finally bolted toward the trees, she was gone. A red car pulled away. He couldn't make out the model through the trees.

Chapter Twenty-One

Phil rolled onto his elbow and squinted at the digital alarm radio. Four forty-five, Sunday. Classical music would come on in fifteen minutes, followed by the alarm chimes five minutes later. He decided to begin setting it for four-thirty, the same as on weekdays. He was usually awake by then anyway.

He jabbed the alarm button to disable it and swung his feet to the floor. The sound of the wind through the trees and against the house told him the weather had changed, that a raw, wet day lurked outside. He tucked the blankets around Ellen's neck and touched her shoulder. A little extra sleep would do her good.

Because he had gotten up three times during the night to check, he knew David wasn't home. It was the first time in over a year he had not come home by a reasonable hour, or at least called to let them know where he was. Maybe it was nothing, what with homecoming parties and all. He probably had stayed with a friend, but….

Phil dressed and parted the sheers to look outside. A rotten day, an extension of what had happened last night, when he and Ellen had walked the bluffs above the river near the seminary in St. Paul before going to dinner. Leaves had made ticking and rustling sounds as they fell in the calm Indian Summer evening, and the faint scent of wood smoke drifted in the air. Students and elderly people ambled the path that wound beneath the trees high above the Mississippi.

"It's so beautiful here in the fall. Maybe it's Nature's way of making winter bearable," Phil said. Ellen didn't answer, and a few moments later they made room on the path for a young woman pushing a baby stroller.

"I think David found his birth parents," Ellen said.

"Has he said anything?"

She shook her head. "But something is wrong. I can sense it."

A dart of alarm, but no one needed an I-told-you-so. Besides, he wanted nothing to ruin the evening. "All we can do is stay out of the way."

"I know that, and I hate it! He's going to be hurt. We all are. If I could, I'd put a stop to it right now!" Her hand went to her face. She allowed him to hold her for only a moment before she pulled away. "I'm okay. I didn't mean to cry. You're right. We have to stay out of it."

Was it unacceptable to allow him to comfort her? Had their intimacy gone AWOL? Was crying inappropriate, too, and something to apologize for? When had that begun? Beyond all of that, it was clear that beneath her tough-love posturing, Ellen felt threatened by David's search, and her intuition seldom failed her. The episode stayed on his mind throughout the evening. At one point during dinner she asked him what was wrong, and he said something about being tired, and so the evening went.

In the kitchen Phil forced himself to stop thinking about last night. While coffee brewed he built a fire in the den fireplace. The left-over logs from last winter burned readily, and the fire soon chased the dampness. Ellen joined him at seven-thirty.

Jessica came downstairs at nine. "David didn't come home last night."

Ellen looked at Phil. He nodded. As if by agreement, no one said anything further. They went to mass at ten and returned home to an empty house.

"What time did he leave yesterday, Mom?"

"About nine or ten in the morning."

"He's been—I don't know, different for the last month. Like, kind of distant," Jessica said.

Phil caught Ellen's arched eyebrow and sidelong glance. Her way of saying: I was right. He's found them and something's gone wrong.

The rain continued for the rest of the morning. No wind or thunder or lightning, just a dreary soaking rain that deadened the world.

"Daddy, shouldn't we look for him?" Jessica said. "How can we sit around and do nothing? What's wrong with us?"

"We will, honey. Everything will be all right."

"You say that, but what if he's hurt? What if he's been drinking? Aren't you worried about him?"

"Of course I am, honey, but David's an adult. We have to give him some room."

"That doesn't make any sense." Jessica whirled around and ran for the stairs.

Damned if you do, damned if you don't.

Phil told himself for the tenth time there was scant reason for alarm. A nineteen-year-old had gone to a football game, partied and stayed out overnight, probably at the home of a friend. He'd call or show up soon. There was a chance he had stayed with that little fox he had taken to the game. What was her name? Pam something. Linder. Pam Linder. Good-looking thing. Just the sight of her would kick-start a guy's engine. Still, because of the risks and other factors, a small parental part of him hoped David hadn't spent the night with her. But for the moment there was no reason to believe his son was lying in a ditch, or that he had been drinking or doing anything else he shouldn't have.

Logic didn't quite hack it. Phil went to the garage and lifted his heavy yellow poncho from its hook and put it in the car. David most likely would go to one of three places if he were deeply upset or depressed: Mankato, to see Wagner; the abbey at St. John's, home of Brother Lawrence, whom David had met on a retreat and admired so much; or the family cabin on Vermillion Lake. Had Ellen narrowed the possibilities down in similar fashion? If she had, she hadn't shared it with him.

Decision time.

After coming up dry on two phone calls, he told Ellen where he was going, exchanged his slippers for a pair of old sneakers, put on a jacket and curled his way into the DTS. Twenty minutes later the northern suburbs of Minneapolis thinned into splotchy patches of frame homes huddled on marsh-bound prairie.

* * *

Propped up by pillows on the family room sofa, with steam curling up from a cup of tea on the end table, Ellen spoke into the phone.

"We'll have to charge fifty dollars a booth, minimum, Jo. Twenty-five won't do it. Any idea where you'll have the signs and posters printed?"

"For God's sake, El, the Bazaar is over eight months away. I mean, come on!"

"We can't leave everything to the last minute. We need to start now."

"Listen, Tag, you go insane if you want. I'll take a rain check." After a long silence, she said, "Are you all right?"

"Sorry, Jo. I must sound like a slaver. Wound a little tight right now."

"David?"

"Uh-huh. He didn't come home last night. Phil is on his way to the lake to see if he's there."

"Maybe he got lucky last night. Sorry. I take that back."

"That's okay. I know you're kidding. I'm worried and I'm not. Something tells me he's in no danger. And I think Phil is right in going to the lake. David mentioned the cabin a week or so ago. Some remark about how peaceful it was up there. Can you imagine longing for peace at nineteen? I sure never did."

After she hung up, Ellen finished her tea and stretched out on the sofa. Father Banning always had the last mass on Sunday, followed by lunch. His motives were questionable; still, he was empathetic, attentive and always willing to listen. She didn't want to see him, but a conversation would be nice. Her hand shook when she reached for the phone.

Small stones pinged and thunked against the undercarriage when Phil turned off the asphalt road and headed down the narrow roadbed of rain-soaked red granite. He had been on the road for four hours, a long drive on a hunch. If David weren't here, Phil would spend the time winterizing the cabin. But something told him David was here.

The gravel road reminded him of the time his father bought a used Ford with three thousand dollars of borrowed money, which he paid back in sixteen months out of an annual gross of less than twenty grand. And what a sixteen months it had been: an endless succession of school lunches consisting of thick slices of homemade bread with little to separate them. But it had helped his father pay off the debt.

The DTS splattered through a big puddle and nosed around a cluster of highland birch. The trees stood sentinel at the end of the long driveway to the cabin that Ellen had long ago christened Rag Tag Point. The Camaro was parked beside the storage shed next to the driveway. No lights showed in the cabin windows.

Phil got out and stretched to relieve the kinks and aches. When he placed his hand flat on the Camaro's hood, the metal was cool, but that didn't mean the car had been there a long time. The rain was cold, and the wind had increased to at least fifteen knots.

The empty cabin smelled musty and damp. Phil stepped into the three-season porch. Aspens and firs swayed outside, and the lake kicked up whitecaps that lashed against the pier. Five o'clock and getting dark.

Phil lunged for the door and ran to the pier. The Nordic bass boat rested safely on the beach. The Starcraft johnboat was gone.

Christ, not out there in a flimsy fourteen-foot johnboat!

He rushed to the car for his poncho, then wrestled the white and blue Nordic into the water and started the Merc 60 outboard. The motor belched a puff of white smoke, settled into an even, guttural burping and veered away from the pier into the foaming water. It would be no picnic on that lake in the Nordic, but at least it was heavier, had a more powerful motor and wasn't flat-bottomed like the dinky johnboat.

He left the bay and headed into open water. It was a mile to a narrow rock-filled channel that stretched a quarter of a mile and emptied into another body of open water a mile across. The lake was black. The rain and failing light made the waves even more difficult to read. The Nordic was a good boat in rough water, stable and maneuverable. If conditions didn't deteriorate further, it would be relatively safe. Even so, going into open water in this kind of wind wasn't smart.

He made it to the channel, which was protected from the wind, and a strong current made the water less choppy. He avoided the massive submerged rocks that lined the channel by going with the current in the middle. Reaching open water, the Nordic nearly capsized as the wind pounced on it again. Was that thunder exploding over the sound of the Mercury outboard? His eyes sweeping the lake, Phil hoped he wouldn't see the johnboat. In all likelihood, it would be upside down.

Finally, the open water behind him, Phil eased the boat into a small cove protected from the wind. He saw the johnboat and beached the Nordic next to it.

The terrain sloped up steeply. Rock outcroppings and stunted balsam firs covered the ridge. He slipped and hit his knee hard on a rock. The pain subsided after a few minutes.

After clawing and slipping the hundred yards to the crest, he paused to catch his breath. About a hundred feet away among the scrub stood the small stone enclosure he and David had built six summers ago around the flat slab of rock that formed a perfect bench. It had taken them all day to stack the rocks, crudely tuck-point them with Sakrete, and cover them with a sheet of galvanized steel that they secured with additional rocks. All but invisible from the water, unless you looked for it with binoculars, the structure commanded an unobstructed view of the lake. They had fashioned a concrete cornerstone with *WPA 1937* scratched into it to discourage vandalism.

Phil stopped thirty feet from the structure. "David?"

There were only the sounds of the rain and his own pumping heart.

"David?"

David stepped out into the open. "Dad?" He was wet and shivering. They both ducked into the small stone shelter. An unopened six-pack of Schmidt beer lay on the stone slab.

"Been here long, son?"

David shrugged and sat on the slab. Phil sat next to him. The rain pelted the roof inches above their heads.

"The tough weather begins. We should winterize the cabin while we're here," Phil said. The cold wind moaned and whistled. "Son, I'm not very good at this kind of thing, but let me try. You're grown now. You need to be your own man and make your own decisions. It's your life; it's my job to get out of the way. I've hounded you about so many things. I need to stop that. If I crowd you, tell me to back off. I'll respect you for it. You mean more to me than I can tell you. You need to know that. I need you to know it."

Rain and mist obscured the lake. Scrub pine bent and twisted in the mounting wind.

"Maybe we can talk more at the cabin, Dad? I mean, the lake's getting pretty bad, and I don't feel so good."

Phil wasn't ready to leave, but David was right. Maybe they could talk at the cabin where it would be warm and dry. He threw his arm around David.

"I love you, son. Let's go." Phil reached into his jacket pocket under the poncho and brought out a Fuji apple. "Here. I thought you might like one."

David took the apple. "Is it your last one?"

"I ate two on the way up."

He put the apple into his pocket. "Thanks, Dad. I'll eat it later."

Phil stripped off the heavy poncho. "Put this on. It'll keep you drier."

Pine needles, moss, and rain-slicked rocks made climbing down the ridge difficult. At water's edge the lake appeared much worse than it had from the shelter. Three-foot waves turned the cold water to ragged froth beyond the cove. Phil pulled the johnboat farther onto the bank for retrieval some other day, and got into the Nordic.

Phil tossed David one of the Nordic's blaze orange life vests and strapped one on himself, not that they would do much good in the ice-cold lake. The temperature had dropped. It was getting darker. Good judgment gave way. He and his son would prevail over the elements, a true bonding adventure, one they would never forget.

"Do we have enough gas, Dad?"

Phil twisted the cap off the tank and caught the gleam of fuel. Plenty of gas for calm water, but blasting through those waves? "We're okay, son."

The Nordic edged its way to open water. When it cleared the mouth of the cove, the boat pitched violently as the wind and water caught it broadside. Phil angled the bow into the waves. Ahead lay a mile of treacherous water straight into the wind and stinging rain.

"Hang on to the backrest and crouch behind me, son. The wind won't be so bad," Phil yelled.

The bass boat was too light to bore through the waves. It rode them, bobbing like an empty jug. As each wave crashed against the hull, the bow pitched up and then nosed down with a *smack!* into the trough behind the wave.

Two inches of water sloshed in the bottom of the boat before they had gone a quarter of a mile. Each time the bow nosed down, the prop rose up out of the water, screaming and consuming fuel. Halfway to the channel Phil angled right to take advantage of the high shoreline that blocked the wind for several hundred yards.

Even with the wind blunted, the cold went to their bones. Rain and spray whipped across their faces. Where the shoreline cut deeply inward, it would take too long to follow it. Better to cut across open water.

A wave hit them from the right. The wheel whipped from Phil's hands. The boat plowed ninety degrees left and lurched hard left again to reverse its original heading. Then it dropped lengthways into a trough, teetered and nearly rolled over. It would have capsized if another wave hadn't raised it to its crest where it twisted left once more, hovered as if on a fulcrum, and came crashing down bow first into the breaking waves.

Phil opened the throttle slightly and shouted for David to hold on. He tasted the same vile secretion he had that time in the Cessna when he got caught trying to outflank a thunderstorm. His survival then had been blind luck.

Yard by plodding yard they approached the channel. He angled right. He couldn't see the shore, but it had to be there somewhere in the crud. The rocky cliffs, topped with evergreens, would lessen the force of the wind, and the shoreline would bring them to the channel. Once through the channel they could navigate the last mile with the wind to their backs.

Visibility had diminished to a hundred yards. Where was the damn channel? He eased the throttle open a hair and nudged the boat to the right. That put their heading on a bias to the waves, a more dangerous tactic. But if he could find the shoreline and keep it in sight, it would reduce the likelihood of missing the channel.

"Dad! Rocks!"

Rocks bigger than the boat materialized in the boiling water, then disappeared. Phil turned into a large rolling swell and rode it away from the cluster of boulders. He had to stay in open water.

"Tell me if you see shore, son! Keep watching for rocks!"

Phil kept the Nordic headed where he thought the channel would appear, but when the shoreline's jagged jumble of rocks took shape through the rain and fog, the channel wasn't there.

Should they beach the boat and spend a miserable but safe night huddled together on a bed of pine needles? It wasn't an option. The shoreline here, rocky with sheer walls, took that away. The channel was their only hope.

They bored ahead, parallel with the shore. The channel gathered form in stages, first as a hole in the blurry shore line and then as a gaping wound in the dark strip of boulders and tree trunks. Phil coaxed the Nordic into the channel. He nearly became immobilized with fear when the boat veered sharply right. The passage had become a wind tunnel over a driving current. The momentary panic passed. He added power and aimed for mid-channel.

No matter what he did, the boat drifted right. The foaming water swirled and smashed against rocks the size of a bus. Spray exploded twenty feet into the air.

Son of a bitching weather unforgiving fucking lake dear God don't let him drown I'm heartily sorry for having offended—

"Dad! Look out!"

Massive black boulders jutted through the surface a few yards ahead.

"Hold on!"

He swung the bow left and goosed the throttle. The stern wallowed, the prop dug in. The boat lugged forward. A floating sensation followed as the Nordic fell into the trough nose-down.

Water rolled in up to their ankles.

Christ, it's going over!

It held.

"Get a tight grip, David! Lean to the high side!"

Into the wind, they had to make a U-turn to put the wind behind them. Should he turn at the crest or in between waves? How long should he ride it? When could he make the complete turn?

He decided to turn nose low, ride the wave to its crest, go over it and then turn into the face of the next wave. He had no sooner angled into the trough than the water lifted him up and spun him sideways. The Nordic came down hard, bobbing and rolling, out of control. The boat could have been a hollow plastic toy, the way the seething lake tossed it around.

Phil gripped the wheel with all his strength and tried to look over his shoulder at David. The bow pitched high in the air. The stern lurched at the base of the wave. The Nordic bottomed down in a blast of spray. More water poured into the boat.

They somehow ended up in the right direction with the wind at their backs. Phil said a quick Hail Mary. This kind of luck couldn't hold. Glancing back he couldn't even see the channel or the shore, neither of which could be more than a hundred yards away. He envisioned David in the water. The image passed, but not before burning into his brain: if they capsized, his son would die, and he would live on with the knowledge of his own stupid recklessness. Life jackets? They wouldn't be worth a damn out here.

He couldn't stop shaking from the wet and cold. Little feeling remained in his hands. A swampy odor filled the air. The storm must have churned up every dead thing in the lake. The thunder, which before had rolled and grumbled in the distance, began to bang away in counterpoint to the lightning. Ozone pungency pierced the smell of rot.

Little by little the boat made progress.

"We gonna to make it, Dad?"

"Tough part's behind us. Hang in there, son."

If they did make it across, Phil had no idea where they would land, given his now marginalized sense of direction. Which meant that if they passed wide of the point and failed to stay within the bay, they would drift into a large body of the lake—more than five miles from the nearest landfall, maybe ten.

With the wind driving it forward, the Nordic progressed in spite of the pounding. But it wasn't long before Phil suspected they had swung wide of the point. There was no hint of land, only a solid wall of rain and mist merging with the white-flecked black of the lake. Every few seconds lightning illuminated everything when it flared. But he could not see land of any kind, let alone the point. They could do nothing but hang on and stay afloat as long as possible.

The motor coughed, ran smoothly, coughed again, quit. The Nordic wallowed, then tiltawhirled forward.

Phil heard a gasp and caught a glimpse of David's face. He looked sick.

"Can you hold on?"

"I think so."

What if he can't? Jesus Christ, what if he can't?

Phil decided to jettison the motor. Maybe without the weight, the bass boat would make better time.

He thought he saw a dark ridge of shoreline in the crud, then nothing. There! No more than a hundred yards straight ahead.

"Climb into this seat and hold on!" He eased out of the swivel chair and guided David into it.

"Grip that wheel as hard as you can and don't let go!"

David's head went up and down in slow motion.

Where was the shore? The damn thing was dead ahead just a moment ago.

There! Low in the water the point aimed at them like a giant fish hook curving away on the far side. If they drifted a few feet to the left, the wind would sweep them into the vastness of the lake beyond. They had to reach the point.

The Nordic was taking on too much water. David was sagging.

Phil crawled to the motor. The clamps were tight. One finally came loose. The other wouldn't budge. He disconnected the fuel line and battery cables. Then he clawed his way to the bow, grabbed the anchor, and dragged it back to the stern.

The boat heaved up. Phil lost his balance and tumbled head-first. His head hit the motor housing. A flashing white sensation, and he nearly passed out. He clung to the edge of the boat for a few seconds.

As soon as his head cleared, he swung the anchor and struck the clamp repeatedly. The clamp began to give. When he tried to turn it by hand, it wouldn't move. He lifted the anchor and hit the clamp hard. Part of it broke off.

He beat at the broken clamp with an upward motion again and again. The clamp inched up the metal receiving plate and slipped over the edge. The two hundred-pound motor vanished into the lake. The Nordic dipped and spun in the water with new buoyancy.

The black, watersmooth rocks of the point lay only forty yards away. The boat shot up, tipped, swung sideways. It slipped into a trough. Phil slammed against a gunwale. He tried to shout. No sound came out. He twisted around.

David was gone.

The boat pitched up again, rolled to its side, and held for a split-second. It went over when another slashing wave hit its underside. Phil landed in the water on his back. He sucked in the foul lake water and came up gasping and hacking alongside the overturned Nordic.

A flash of orange and yellow. David floated ten feet away, ten feet farther into the lake.

Phil pushed off the hull and tried to swim to him. He made no progress. David saw him and began to flail at the water. A wall of water sent David crashing down next to him. Phil reached out. David clutched at him and climbed over him. They went under. The rank water seared Phil's throat.

David's knee drove into Phil's chest. Phil grabbed the knee and heaved upward. David lost his grip on Phil's head and fell away.

Lungs burning, Phil surfaced, choking and gasping. A wave broke over him. David grappled him. Phil slapped David hard, then hit him with a fisted backhand. It stunned David long enough for Phil to loop his left arm around his son's neck. Holding David face up, he tried to swim for shore.

The current drove them forward but not fast enough. The cold water siphoned Phil's strength and numbed him. With every awkward stroke he gulped more water and lost more of his grip on David.

The unmistakable tug of an undertow swept against Phil's thigh. The point was still thirty or forty feet away. Little feeling remained in Phil's arm. David started to slide from his grasp.

The onrushing water split into two currents as it reached the point—one to the bay side, the other to the open lake.

"Son, don't fight me, I have to change arms!"

He curled his right arm under David's chin. When he tried to disengage his left, he could barely move it.

David must have sensed Phil's alarm. He began to struggle. Phil, both arms around David's neck, lay back in an attempt to avoid his son's clawing hands.

Panic gave David strength. Before Phil could react, David gripped him under the left eye and squeezed. A fingernail dug into his face and ripped out a chunk of flesh. Phil yanked his arm tight across David's throat and dashed his head into the water. David fought with newfound strength. Elbows, fingers, knees. They both went under.

Phil snapped his shoulder into a renewed stranglehold on David, momentarily not caring if he broke his son's neck. David went limp. They surfaced. The black slimy rocks of the point slid by.

So close, so far.

The current carried them toward the open lake.

Phil thrashed at the water. He gained a few feet on the surly pile of rocks. The pull of the outbound current got stronger. His strength gone, he could no longer hold David.

His will left him. He gave up. He had failed to save his son. His despairing scream drowned the sounds of the wind and the storm and the water. He sank into the black lake.

Please God let him make it.

He heard David's voice as if from a great distance. The water turned and twisted him. The current got stronger. It pulled and tugged him. He bumped into rocks. A dull pain enveloped his body. Blackness. Was that David's voice? He scraped over the underwater rocks. All sensation ceased.

Chapter Twenty-Two

Rain.

Something hard and unforgiving dug into Phil's back beneath his right shoulder blade. He opened his eyes. Lightning splintered a churning sky. Rain splattered on his face.

"Dad?"

He turned to the voice. A hand touched his face. He covered the hand with his, and drew David's face to his chest. Thunder cracked through the wind. The frothing lake blasted into the rocks a few feet from them. They held each other, and Phil heard himself saying repeatedly, "My son! My son! Thank God, you're safe!"

After several moments, Phil pulled away. "What happened?"

"I felt you slipping away, Dad. I shucked the poncho and preserver, then I grabbed hold of your jacket and started swimming for shore. Don't know where I got the strength, but the water got shallow enough to stand, and I was able to drag you up onto the rocks."

"You saved my life."

"You saved mine first."

Phil touched a stinging sensation beneath his left eye. The missing flesh left a hole the size of a pencil eraser. He recalled how David's fingernail had dug into him. Tender though it was, it felt like the most beautiful scar imaginable. Phil tousled David's wet hair. "We'll catch pneumonia if we don't get out of here. We need dry clothes and a restaurant. I'm so hungry, I could eat a steer."

"Me, too, Dad. Hey, I still have the apple you gave me."

"You eat it." Then, with a punch to David's shoulder: "But

it's the last time I give you my last one."

David laughed and took a big bite of the apple.

Phil didn't tell Ellen how narrow an escape he and David had experienced, but he knew that she dragged enough information from David to have a pretty good idea. Two days after returning home, Phil decided to put Rag Tag Point on the market. In addition to the mortgage, the place had a lien on it from their business loan, so he'd have to clear any sale with the bank and fork over his equity, but that was okay.

He told himself he was doing it because he could never again enjoy the cabin as he once had, that it now represented danger to his family, that it was too far away to be of practical use. All of which was true enough. On a deeper level, though, the close call enabled him to make a long-delayed decision to sell the cabin because he could no longer afford to keep it, a rationalization that enabled him to save face with himself.

Chapter Twenty-Three

Jeez, why'd she insist on meeting here in Rice Park? St. Paul is like the other side of the world if you live in Wayzata. Does she live over here?

David looked at his watch. She wasn't late yet, but almost. His eyes swept the square. He shifted his weight and hunched forward, leaned back, shoved his hands into his pockets and glanced at his watch again. Where was she? He was going fishing on Lake Waconia with a buddy from UPS, probably the last time until spring, so he didn't have much time.

Tough one to figure out, his birth mother. First, she wouldn't see him, then she did see him and was nice and told him all that stuff about when he was born. When they met the second time, last week, she hadn't said much at first, seemed impatient, short, a little bitchy. She volunteered some things. Like, she got lucky and went to school on a scholarship and loans, studied computers, moved to the Cities and lived in a filthy apartment by the river until she paid off her loans, that kind of stuff. But when he started asking her questions about his birth father, she opened up and answered them all and even told him stuff he didn't care about. And to top it off, when she was about to leave, out of the blue she said they should meet again.

He was glad and he wasn't. She had her life, he had his. She owned a computer company that seemed to be the number one thing in her life. He had the feeling she'd kill anybody who messed with it. Not because of anything she'd actually said, just a feeling he had, along with a feeling that they wouldn't get along very well if they were together much. Anyway, talking to her, getting to know her, wasn't as big a deal as before.

Everything seemed to change after that day on the lake with Dad. Things were ten times better at home. Everybody was happy and glad to be together, and it was great. Nice to know his birth mom was a neat person and doing okay, but she wasn't part of his life. She'd be his secret, one he'd keep in a special place because she was so beautiful and because he wouldn't be alive without her. That was the part that wouldn't let go of him. He wouldn't *be* without her, wouldn't *exist.* Awesome. They had separate lives, but they also shared something that was theirs alone in the whole world.

People were coming out of the St. Paul Hotel to his right. Opposite the hotel, the glassy Ordway Music Theatre gleamed in the morning sun.

"Hello, David."

He started at the sound of her voice.

"Been waiting long?"

"No, not very."

He didn't feel much like talking, really didn't. She must not have either because they sat on the bench and didn't say a word for a while. Boy, did she run hot and cold or what? Attitude, no attitude.

A fat girl walked past. When the girl was beyond earshot, his birth mother said, "She's so unfortunate. The other kids probably make her life miserable. I have a cousin named Ellen who wasn't at all fat as a little girl. Not even plump. Yet we all taunted her with, 'Ellen Fenellen, the big fat watermelon!' until she cried. We were so cruel."

"My mom's name is Ellen. She wouldn't think that's funny, either. She gets really mad at things that poke fun at people, like ethnic jokes. Comes unglued over racial ones."

Neither of them said anything right away. Her hair glistened in the sun, and her smooth face seemed to glow around the dimple in her left cheek.

"Isn't that a lovely old building?" she said, pointing at Landmark Center.

"It's on Christmas cards from that disabled people's place."

"The Courage Workshop."

"Yeah. My dad sends them out every year. Has the same

painting in his office. He's a lawyer but he's in the insurance business."

"It's popular with artists. I've painted it myself."

"I thought you were into computers."

She laughed her nice laugh and threw her head back. "To the world I'm into computers. In my other life, my real life, I paint. What a combination, hey? Perhaps one day I'll come out of the paint closet."

Snared by the way she spoke, by her looks, by her cool sense of humor that broke through every once in a while...he forgave her.

"So you live over here?"

"Oh, no. I live on Lake Minnetonka," she said.

"Really? So do I."

"But we won't tell each other where. It's for the best."

He nodded and sneaked a look at his watch.

"Another appointment?" she said.

"No. Well, yeah. I mean, I have to meet a guy from work. Maybe the last good day for it, so we're going fishing."

"Oh."

"I mean, there's no rush or anything." He stretched his legs out in front of him and slid his hands into his pockets. "I didn't mean—I'm going to school next quarter at the U."

"Wonderful! I hope you like it. There's always so much going on."

"I'm pretty excited. And scared."

"You're only young once, David. Be confident and make the most of it."

The look on her face was kind of strange.

"Thanks for seeing me. I understand things better now, and feel a lot better. Could I ask you a personal question?"

"Of course."

"Were either of you—I mean, was my father a heavy drinker?"

"What an odd question. Why do you ask?"

"Well, you gave me a lot of medical information, but I read somewhere that I should know stuff like this, too. I suppose it's important with some medical conditions or something."

She gazed across the street for a moment before looking back at him.

"It's hard to say. Your father was so young when he went off to the Marines. He didn't drink constantly in high school. When he did, though, he drank heavily. Sometimes he even passed out. Then he might not drink again for a week. It may have developed into a problem in the service. Looking back, I guess I'd have to say the signs were there."

"Thanks for being honest with me. If I ever need to see you, I mean, real bad, like if there's an emergency or something, could I have Greta Pederson call you?"

"Not a good idea. We need to make a clean break. It's only fair. To you, me, your parents."

"Well, it was nice meeting you and talking with you these few times."

She hugged him and shook his hand firmly.

"Take care of yourself, David. I wish you all the best."

"You, too."

When they parted, his eyes blinked fast and his breath came in short little gulps. He'd probably never see her again. It was kind of like having a relative die, a sense of loss coming at you from all sides and making you sad but not really because you didn't know the person very well and all you want to do is escape, but that brings feelings of guilt and makes you wonder why there are things like betrayal and death and grief, and then you need to eat or drink or swim or go to a party, anything to blot out the bad things.

He walked away fast. Lake Waconia would ripple in the autumn breeze and catch the sunlight, the air would taste fresh and cold, the fish would battle against his taut line and bending rod tip.

Chapter Twenty-Four

All Souls' Day, the hallowed eve of All Saints' Day, trivialized by modern secularism into Halloween, a time for pranks and sweets and scary movies, hardly a time for remembering and praying for the dead, lay sullen under a cold, driving rain.

Phil considered early mass at St. Olaf's, but decided against it when he saw the full parking lot. No sense getting soaked between the far end of the lot and the church door. The rain wouldn't deter Ellen, who would swim through a flood to attend daily mass. How admirable. How maddening. Maybe by noon the rain would let up and he would walk to the church from his office.

Ruth buzzed him at ten.

"Will you take a call from Lars Borglund?"

"Sure. Put it through. Thanks."

When he picked up, a formal female voice asked him to hold. A moment later Borglund came on the line.

"Mr. Tag, can you make yourself available for lunch today?"

"I could at one."

"The Minnesota Club at one then."

Later, Phil found it difficult to concentrate on the mass, which he had wanted to attend for motives other than justifying a late lunch, a fiction he had invented so as not to appear too eager to Lars Borglund. You didn't jump on command for anyone, not even Lars Borglund, and expect to deal from any kind of strength afterwards.

The Minnesota Club and St. Olaf's stood on opposite sides

of Eighth Street at Second Avenue, the club building by far the more imposing structure. Phil peered up at the five stories of the prestigious, old money place with its distinctive chimneys reaching long and slender into the gray sky. In summer the ivy, thick at the bottom and thinning as it climbed the dark brick building, conjured up an image of tattered money spilling over the top of a huge vault to gather in deep piles at the base. Phil had vowed, since coming to Minnesota, that he'd become a member of the club and be on the inside looking out.

Borglund met him at the entrance. The man was older than Phil had envisioned him. However, his blue eyes behind gold-framed glasses were alert, and his pale face was smooth. They took a groaning, creaky elevator upstairs to a private dining room. A mural on the north and west walls depicted a pioneer farming scene in Minnesota, a team of oxen pulling a plow through the sod ahead of a golden-haired man in a red shirt with a long whip in his hand.

"Would you like a drink, Mr. Tag? I'm having a brandy myself."

Phil ordered a light Scotch and water.

"I know how busy you are. My call gave you scant lead time, for which I apologize. Perhaps we should order lunch and get right to it."

Their drinks arrived, they ordered, and Borglund took charge again.

"When I invited you to my home this past summer, it was to observe you firsthand. I had heard good things about your work. I found your articles stimulating, a superb blend of the practical and the scholarly. You are obviously a student of Anglo-American legal history. I would hazard a guess you have an affection for the law shared by all too few lawyers. As a fellow graduate of your alma mater, I have the law as my intellectual hobby. It's how I keep my hat in the legal ring, if you will.

"I did my due diligence. Lawyers, accountants and trust officers hold you in high regard. You sell large amounts of life insurance to wealthy and near-wealthy clients throughout the area. In addition, you own one of the best employee benefit administration firms in the state. Not large, but topnotch. You enjoy a solid reputation. As important as these facts are, they do not in and of themselves impress me."

Borglund sipped his brandy. He dabbed his thick white moustache with the linen napkin. Adjusting his glasses, he cleared his throat and leaned forward.

"It is important to me that you have established your reputation without chasing speaking engagements at every turn, or otherwise indulging in self-promotion. On the contrary, you have remained a loner. Behind the scenes you have worked hard for your law school, for the American College in Pennsylvania, and for the local financial planning association.

"Your writing is not voluminous, but first-rate journals have published your work. I believe that two of your articles could prove to be quite seminal in Minnesota tax circles."

"Thank you."

"I also investigated Phillip Tag, the man. Married twenty-nine years, two adopted children, loyal to the Roman church. You have been faithful to your wife, or extremely discreet. I choose to believe the former."

The food arrived.

"Ah! Shall we? I believe you will find the poached salmon to your liking. Our chef has a talent for it."

Borglund did not talk business while eating. Instead, the conversation turned to the Vikings and their chances of making the playoffs, the problem of terrorism, the obscenely high deficit.

"Thank God, neither Gore nor Kerry won. They were indecisive demagogues," Borglund said. "Mr. Bush, on the other hand, was an idiot on immigration, developed tunnel vision on foreign policy and had a tin ear for the economy. I lost patience with him. Now that we have Obama and a blank check Congress, all of that will pale by comparison. The country has reached a tipping point in terms of political and economic philosophy. We are about to go the way of Europe, which unfortunately will open the door to China and the Asian Rim to fill the vacuum for the next century or two. To avoid becoming a second-rate power within two generations, we need another Truman or Reagan, party affiliation be damned. Give me a plain-speaking President. One who sees clearly, understands leadership and follows a sound moral and capitalist vision."

He got back on track as soon as the waiter removed the dishes from the table.

"The evidence indicates that you are not only an outstanding tax and insurance advisor, but also a devoted husband and father. Other financial planners fit that description. Moreover," he said with a half-smile, "they have not had the audacity to decline an invitation to my home."

Perplexity must have shown in Phil's face. Borglund's smile broadened.

"You offered no reason, which initially mystified me. But in a flash, I realized your phone call confirmed my appraisals of you. Clearly, something had occurred in your family that needed your attention. And you valued that more, without explanation or alibi, than you did access to my business. In today's world that is indeed refreshing. And you did not come whining afterward."

With that he reached for his coffee and drank it.

"I have been married to Mrs. Borglund for forty-eight years. She has blessed me with five children, not all of whom please me. One I have disowned because of his lifestyle. Another is on the brink. There is nothing I value or respect more than two people keeping their vows and making a good marriage.

"Give or take, I'm worth nine hundred and forty million dollars. I have corporate lawyers and practicing attorneys on retainer. I have an executive vice-president in my holding company in charge of, among other things, human resources and employee benefits for all of my companies. None of them can do what I want you to do."

Phil resisted the urge to lean forward into the pause. Borglund's words hung in the air, verbal brass rings that gleamed no less than metal ones.

"Which is to streamline, coordinate and minimize the cost of all employee benefits in the companies I own or control. The same for all property and casualty insurance, which will be your partner's bailiwick should you and he agree to take on these tasks.

"I also want you personally to plan my estate in the best way possible for my family and foundation to retain control of my holdings. I have some idea as to the complexities of estate planning, but nowhere near your knowledge and range of solutions. I will expect you to be creative. There are certain charities I wish to provide for. There will be liquidity concerns. I want you to cut to an absolute minimum the amount of probate costs and death taxes payable to the state of Minnesota and the federal government. The IRS did its level best to keep me from accumulating what I have. I choose not to pay one dime more than necessary in death taxes. Not for a minute do I believe the current phase-out of the federal estate tax will be made permanent. The sunset provision will prevail, mark my words."

"That's a tall order for a team of experts, let alone two people."

Borglund pushed back from the table and cleared his throat. His eyes bored into Phil.

"I'm well aware of that. If you accept, I will place you on retainer at fifty thousand dollars per month for one year. Should Mr. Goldman agree to handle the casualty end, I will pay ninety thousand per month, to be divided as the two of you decide. The commissions you generate will be paid above and beyond the retainer. I will also pay you twenty percent of all premium reductions and documented administrative economies you create in that year and the next.

"It will take you at least six months to assemble the information you need, another six to analyze it and formulate your recommendations. And you may well have to seek out—and compensate—specialists for some aspects of the work. One year could be overly aggressive. Therefore, I would consider extending our agreement six months. Beyond that, we will work out an arrangement to keep you abreast of any changes in my personal and business affairs throughout the process."

Borglund reached down and opened a briefcase. He handed Phil a thin sheaf of legal-size bond paper stapled to a light blue cover.

"Please take this contract with you and read it carefully. Shall we meet again in one week? Would that give you adequate time?"

"For discussing and clarifying the contract, a week will be

fine. Beyond that, my partner and I will have to do some restructuring. We'll need time to work that out and implement the changes."

"Understood." Borglund contemplated his coffee spoon for several long seconds before returning his gaze to Phil. "I'm a hard taskmaster. If you don't measure up, I will terminate your services without hesitation. I hold my senior people to high ethical and performance standards. You will be no different. The conditions are all in the contract."

"There's one important issue I need to address. You previously told me you sent my articles to your executive vice president for review and handling." Phil paused long enough for Borglund to grow impatient.

"Yes, that's correct. What is your point?"

"I never heard from him. I have reason to believe that he'll have little interest in my coming aboard."

"You feel that Mr. Lankar won't cooperate. Is that it?"

"I don't know what he will or won't do. It's a concern I have."

Borglund leaned forward. "I'm sure your concern is unfounded. I will of course communicate to Mr. Lankar that you and I have executed a contract for services. In view of his many years of loyal service, it is inconceivable to me that he would be uncooperative in any way. I might add that I do not appreciate your implying otherwise."

"I believe it's important that you and I be candid with each other."

"Agreed."

Phil looked at his watch. "Thank you for lunch. I have an appointment I can't be late for." He shook Borglund's hand and rose to leave. "I look forward to working with you."

Outside, it was raining again. Phil leaned into the wind and hurried back to his office wondering about this grand new venture. Was it a Halloween trick or treat?

The contract was specific and carefully crafted. A few provisions needed tweaking for clarification, but whoever had drawn the document for Borglund was good and knew exactly what the man wanted. Had Borglund written it himself? He was, after all, a lawyer by training. Was the man pompous and full of himself? Without question. But he spoke without affectation when it came to compensation. Why was he willing to pay so much?

"It looks perfect, Marty. We can do him a lot of good and make a fortune."

"*Bueno.* What's the catch? This is your big chance to kill two birds with one stone and realize your obsession. Your enthusiasm underwhelms me."

"Guess it hasn't caught up with me yet. So many pieces."

"Two big pieces: the office move and the computer system," Marty said. "We need a smooth move, and now's the time to build the system right."

"Okay, let's go with both."

At home Phil related the Borglund meeting to Ellen.

"He's checked us out with a microscope, honey. You, me, Marty, Liz."

"Good thing he didn't find out about my boyfriend," Ellen said.

"He probably overlooked that harmless wimp."

She put her arms around him. "Oh yeah? No wimps for this gal."

They laughed and held each other.

"Are you happy?" she said.

"It's a heck of a challenge. We'll generate megabucks. No way can we get it done in a year."

Her eyes searched his face.

"This will be my swan song, El. You'll have your degree by then. I'll try to hook on at the U, or maybe St. Thomas. We'll have the time and money to do what we want. Work the school year and take summers off."

"Let's celebrate."

"You've got it. Your choice."

"Let's take the kids to a pizza joint and cut them loose."

Dear God, she gave so much and asked for so little. Maybe things were getting back in sync.

David and Jessica picked up on the festive mood and decided on a deluxe at Pizza Corner. Ellen tried to protest. She was hooted down until Phil reminded Jessica that the deluxe would have onions.

"No way!"

"I don't want olives," Ellen said.

"I just want one piece and a small salad, anyway," Jessica said. "I'm not very hungry."

In the end they deleted olives, onions and anchovies. Jessica became particularly expansive about everything under the sun while they ate, but as soon as they finished she began to pressure them to leave.

"He'll call back if no one answers," David said.

"Who?" Phil asked before he caught Ellen's glance.

"Yeah, who, Jessica?" David said.

"Get off my case, Davie!"

"Does his name rhyme with bait?"

"Grow up!" Jessica said and slid from the booth. "I'll wait in the car." She marched to the door.

"Big crush on Nate Landon," Ellen said.

"The all-conference running back?"

"And Big Man on Campus in general. She's walking on air and eggs. Very touchy."

The skirmish ended in a truce on the way home. David, at Ellen's prior insistence, apologized in his own fashion by poking Jessica on the shoulder and saying, "Next to me Nate's ugly. Next to anybody else he's semi-awesome."

Jessica ran upstairs when her bedroom phone rang within five minutes of their return from the restaurant.

"Could we talk for a minute, Dad?" David said.

"Sure. What's on your mind?"

"Well, I … I found my birth mother, and I'd like to tell you both about her."

"Have you spoken with her?" Ellen asked.

"Uh-huh. Three times."

The roomed seemed ready to implode from the silence.

"And?" Ellen said.

"Well, we talked. Like, it was weird, y'know? I mean, she was a total stranger, and yet she was my, uh, mother, I guess? That's kind of different."

Ellen sat as motionless as the Lladró figurines on the shelf to her left.

"She agreed to see me if we didn't tell each other our names. She's okay, but we have our own lives, and we don't want to change that."

"What's she like, honey?"

"Well, she doesn't look too much like me, except for this dimple right here. And her hair is like mine, only shinier. She told me why she gave me up, and I'm okay with that now. Mostly, I satisfied my curiosity. It's not as important as before.

"The first time, she was, like, all business, but nice, and didn't stay long. Told me about when I was born and stuff. The second time, she told me what she does and about when she was young, her family and all that. This last time I think she wanted to spend more time, but I was going fishing with Mike from UPS, so I had to leave. We aren't going to meet again. Would you believe it? She lives somewhere on Lake Minnetonka. She kind of let that slip."

Phil was about to ask about the birth father when Ellen broke in. "What does she do?"

"She's into computers. And art. Has her own company—I don't know exactly what she does. Just computers and stuff. Painting is her hobby."

Ellen smiled. "A modern woman. How nice. How old is she?"

David looked up at the ceiling and shrugged. "Gee, I don't know. She looks, well, she said she had me when she was sixteen. So I guess she's about thirty-five."

"Pretty?"

"Beautif— Not as pretty as you, Mom."

Ellen slid off the sofa and hugged him. "Flattery, flattery! I'm so proud of you, honey. You did it all on your own. I'll bet she's as proud of you as we are."

David blushed.

"Two lucky women have a very special son."

Later, when David was gone, Ellen was pensive. "Something tells me it won't be as simple as it sounds."

"David seems to have his arms around it."

"Just a strange feeling, but I feel it down deep and can't shake it."

Phil lay in bed listening to the sounds of the night. Ellen was still downstairs having tea. Would David's birth mother cause trouble? Would she want to see him again and maybe get involved with his life? The maternal instinct was unpredictable. David didn't need any more complications and could certainly do without torn loyalties.

And Ellen? She'd handled the news like a champ, but given her outburst that night during their walk on the bluffs, she obviously had misgivings—misgivings underscored by the fact that she said nothing of substance after David had gone out for the evening. She would analyze it from every conceivable perspective and probably say nothing to anyone, including Phil, until something further happened. Hold her counsel though she might, her intuitions and conclusions were seldom off the mark.

Phil slipped from bed and went to the window. The rain had stopped. Wayzata Bay glimmered in the moonlight, and the wind rustled through the trees. Ghosts roamed out there, ghosts with the power to confuse and hurt. If only they could be seen, they might be kept under control. His father had always said, "To win at poker, you've got to watch the players." Good advice then, good advice now.

Chapter Twenty-Five

"Mr. Barnhill," Phil said into the phone to the Star's computer columnist, "my name is Phil Tag. My partner and I are looking for a consultant to help us with a new computer system. We heard good things a while back about a local woman, but we misfiled her name. Thought you might be able to help us locate her."

"Any clues?"

"She has her own company, and she's an artist, a painter. Lives somewhere on Lake Minnetonka. That's about all I know."

"I'll give it a go and get back to you. What's your number?"

Phil gave him their number and added, "We'd be glad to pay a fee."

"How about a hundred bucks if I find her? I've got a deadline staring me in the face, so I can't spend much time on it."

"Fair enough."

Barnhill called back the next day.

"You're looking for Nora Helstrin. Runs Computer Spectrums out in Deephaven. Has a good reputation."

Phil went to Marty's office.

"Got a lead on a good computer person. I checked with Barnhill, who said good things about her. I know I'm on your turf, but it can't hurt to meet with her." He handed Marty a slip with the name and phone number.

"Okay. But she's the last one. I have appointments with two others this week. Then I make my decision."

* * *

"I need to see you," David said. "Could we go for a Pepsi?"

"I'm waiting for my sister to call," Greta said. "She has the kids."

David didn't know what to say.

"You can come here," she said.

"Twenty minutes."

When she opened the door, she wore brown slacks and a blue button-down shirt. She didn't have her glasses on. "Like a soda?"

"Sure."

He liked her so much, always would, was crazy about her and wanted her in bed again. But it was kind of crazy. She was the same age as his birth mother. What if she got pregnant? Wouldn't be exactly fair to the kids she was raising now, or to her or the baby. He sure couldn't help her with any money. Abortion? He shuddered.

"Here you go," she said, returning from the kitchen.

"Thanks."

The soda was a supermarket brand. Which was okay because she didn't have much money to spend on things like that, and jeez, what if she had another kid?

"So how've you been?" she said.

"Fine. Why won't you ever see me?"

"You know why. Ready for Christmas?"

"Almost." *Oh, no.* He'd forgotten to bring her gift. It was almost a month until Christmas, but he had wanted to give it to her early.

She sat on the couch and leaned back. He set his soda down and joined her. She gave him a hug when he put his arm around her. He tried to kiss her.

"None of that," she said. "We need to talk."

"What about?"

"About your blowing in here, mister, and expecting to get into my pants."

"Gosh, I'm sorry. I didn't mean it that way."

"It's okay. Not entirely your fault."

"The reason I called, I'm enrolling at the U and wanted to

share it with you. I—I thought you might be happy about it."

A tender expression came into her face. "That's great, David!" She leaned over and hugged him. His hand slid down her back. She grasped his wrist.

"We can't repeat that."

"I want you so bad!"

She placed a finger against his lips.

"One, it's wrong. Two, it's unprofessional. Three, it's non-negotiable."

He looked into her eyes and dropped his hands to his sides.

"I probably shouldn't come back?"

"I won't let you. The night we spent together was a one-time thing that shouldn't have happened, not in a million years, but I was so … it's not that I wasn't attracted to you. I was, even before that night. Then when you showed up, after the nightmare day I'd had, believe me, you looked so good and I was so down—anyway, that's over. You need to be with girls your own age. Don't be afraid to approach them. Girls will welcome your hitting on them, even if they're coy or play hard to get. Remember, you look as good to them as they do to you. But be careful. No babies, no STD."

He put his hands on her shoulders and kissed her on the cheek. "I know you're right about you and me." He took a deep breath. "Thanks."

"Merry Christmas. Be happy."

Phil watched Marty wend his way across the dining room to the table at a south window of Windows On Minnesota. Right on time, as always.

"How'd it go?"

"One sharp lady, that *señorita,*" Marty said. "She can help us. Her staff looks good. Nice office. I like her. Not one negative in three meetings."

"Where'd you leave it?"

"We're almost there. All three of us need to meet before we ink it. Then we'll have to give her and her people a lot of nitty-gritty input."

"Sign the contract if you feel good about it. You don't need me there."

"What's the deal, Phil?"

"I'm working on the move."

"You'll need me on that, I need you on this. Don't jack me around."

Phil ground his teeth and leaned back. "Okay."

"Good. I'll set it up."

They ordered lunch.

"When do you see your buddy, *amigo?"*

"Two-thirty this afternoon."

"Decided on your strategy?"

"Straight up. That was then, this is now."

"You're on his dance floor. Get him on your side, it's a waltz. Otherwise, you limbo. You've waited a long time for this dance."

A cool breeze with a subtle scent of lilac wafted through the warmth of a perfect June day. A door to the administration building groaned open behind Phil.

"Still in that sling, Tag?"

Squinting against the sun's glare, Phil didn't turn to the voice. They hadn't spoken since it happened.

"You did it on purpose."

"Aw, come on. Don't be a sore loser."

"It was bush league and you know it."

Lankar stepped in front of Phil and got in his face. "You are one mouthy son of a bitch. If you didn't have that sling, I'd kick your ass around the block."

"I'll never forget it, Lankar. Or that you embarrassed my dad. Corvette and all, you're a busher."

Lankar flushed. "You're a loser, Tag. You'll end up in a sweatshop just like your old man." He sauntered down the steps to his car, which was parked in a no parking zone.

"Someday you'll eat those words, Lankar. When I'm in the Bigs, you'll have to pay to watch me play."

Lankar flipped him the bird and climbed into his car. A mo-

ment later, the Corvette's squealing tires left two black ribbons of rubber on the pavement.

His left hand clenched into a fist, Phil hoped he would never see the jerk again. Lankar's mocking cough at his dad's car would never fade. Someday he would drive any car he wanted, and he'd buy his father any car he wanted, too. Life was a big game—the big game—and he was going to win it. He was going to win it, not in a one-run pitching duel, but with so many RBIs the opposition would run out of pitchers.

"So you're Mr. Tag," the secretary said. Her inflection, though pleasant and professional, spoke volumes.

She led him into a spacious office that reeked of tobacco. The man behind the desk had matured into a caricature of his youth: huge jaw, broad, toothy smile, thin hair that was once golden but now platinum. No amount of expensive tailoring could disguise the protruding belly of Wade Lankar, Executive Vice-President, Borglund Enterprises. Phil saw him in a Marquette baseball uniform; heard him mocking his father; saw the pitch and heard the dull crack and felt the sharp pain that ended his dream of pro ball. *How had such a jerk ever become Borglund's ace?*

"Hello, Tag. Have a chair. Care for coffee? Soft drink?"

"No, thanks."

"Thanks, Nancy," he said to his assistant. "Be sure to buzz me at three."

"You have another meeting in thirty minutes? We were supposed to meet for an hour."

"To review our retirement programs. Couldn't duck it. I've had a committee on it for three months. Got to make sure we're getting a good bang for our buck. These days if you don't—"

"I'll keep it short." Phil paused and leaned forward. "We'll be working together for some time, Wade. I'm glad we could meet today to get the process underway. What's your understanding of my role?"

A hint of color came into the man's face. He extracted a red pack of cigarettes from his shirt pocket and lit up. He had to be one of the few people left in the world who still smoked unfiltered Pall Malls.

"You've been retained by Lars to review our insurance. We've had consultants in before."

Phil leaned back in his chair. Limbo time.

"Actually," Phil said, "the analysis will encompass all your employee benefits, executive perks, and stock purchase agreements. My partner will review all property coverages, workers' comp plans and liability insurance. We'll need plan documents by company, plant and division. And I need to know all administration costs absorbed by the companies. Hard dollars initially, soft stuff later."

Lankar took notes. He finished scribbling and looked up, smiling. "That it?"

"For now."

"No problem! I'll form a committee and get them cracking."

"How soon can I have it?"

"Six months."

"I need it next week."

"No way! Impossible! You can't expect—we just can't do it that fast." Lankar snuffed out his cigarette in a large ashtray that contained numerous half-smoked Pall Malls.

"Look, I understand you've got the holidays and year-end stuff facing you. Let's agree on December tenth for the first batch of material. I'll let you know in writing exactly what we need. Then you and I will set up a schedule for deliverables."

"Consider it done." Lankar reached into his pocket, brought out a clipper, and began to trim his nails.

Phil stood to leave. "Wade, I appreciate your cooperation. Let me be clear. For years you've blocked me. So I went around you and I'm in the door. I've got a job to do and I'm going to get it done. Do we understand each other?"

"No speeches, please. Let me know what you need." He continued clipping his nails.

"Just don't try to jack me around. I'm not that freshman you hit with a pitch. This time, I'm holding the ball."

Lankar flushed. He didn't look up but merely continued his nail work, so Phil wheeled around and headed for the door. Just as Phil opened the door, Lankar grunted, "Fuck you, Polack!" Phil turned and smiled at him. Then he swung the door open wide and walked out without closing it.

When Phil left the building, a blast of frigid wind greeted him. Sand, salt and exhaust fumes had already begun to sully the new snow, and the temperature had plummeted. He'd have to psyche himself up. It was the coup of a lifetime, one that called for excitement and enthusiasm. And as an added bonus he had Lankar, at long last, right where he wanted him.

Phil pulled into the parking lot outside their apartment and turned off the ignition. A breeze flowed through the car's open windows and through the wet sweatshirt from Saturday practice.

He gazed through the windshield, but his true gaze was inward. After a minute or two, he took a deep breath, grabbed his glove and spikes from the passenger seat and swung from the car. He hated what he had to tell Ellen.

"Hi," she said when he entered the apartment. "How was practice?"

"Great."

"Doesn't show."

"I quit the team."

Ellen draped a dish towel over the towel rack. "Little soon for that, isn't it?"

He dropped his spikes and glove onto a chair. "I've been kidding myself for a month, El. The elbow doesn't work in the field, and it sure as heck doesn't work when I hit. That is, when I try to hit. Oh, it'll be okay for slow pitch softball. Not for baseball."

Ellen put her arms around him. "Maybe you need more rehab. More time to heal."

He held her loosely, then more tightly. "The quickness is gone from my swing. There's no snap, no bat speed. It's over, El. But, hey, we'll get the degree and be okay. More than one way to win. Making the pro's was always a long shot anyway."

She kissed him lightly. "You would have made it. I just know it. Maybe you can give it another try next year."

"Nope. It's over. Now I have to figure out what I'm going to do."

"You'll get your degree and do what you've always wanted to do when your playing days were over: teach and coach."

Phil stripped off the sweatshirt. "Yeah, you're probably right." He threw the shirt into the hamper inside the tiny closet. "Whatever we do, we're going to make things happen. Good things."

He slumped into the begrimed Cadillac, lay back against the headrest, and closed his eyes. A minute later he started the engine and backed slowly from the parking space.

Chapter Twenty-Six

Phil had placed the small digital clock on the bookshelf across the room from his desk in order to keep track of time without glancing at his watch when he had someone in his office. The red numbers glowed 1:59.

Marty appeared in the doorway.

"Nora, I'd like you to meet my partner, Phil Tag. Phil, Nora Helstrin."

They sat in the stuffed chairs around the oval oak coffee table with marble inlay. Ruth had brought in tea bags, hot water, coffee and two bottles of Perrier. Nora Helstrin took hot water but no tea bag.

"Café solo, Marty?"

"Please."

Phil poured cream into his own coffee and watched Nora Helstrin sip her hot water.

"We're about ready to move ahead, Phil. Nora needs to interview both of us separately in the next week or so."

"Marty will give you great input, Ms. Helstrin. I'm not sure I'll be of much help."

"Oh, but you will. I also need to spend time with your employees." An easy smile animated her expressive face and caused a dimple in her left cheek to appear and disappear. "My initial presentation should raise dozens of questions. My challenge will be to answer them and resolve any problems before we implement." Her unselfconscious smile revealed perfect teeth.

"How long will it take? We're fighting some damn tight deadlines." His tone was accusatory. The woman's expression hardened for a fleeting moment before she recovered with a smile.

"We'll be ready before or after your move. Your choice."

"Ms. Helstrin—or is it Mrs.?"

"Nora or Miss or Ms., whichever you prefer."

"Miss Helstrin, what can you do for us that a big company like IBM can't?"

"Why don't we run through it?"

"Yes, why don't we?"

She set her cup on the coffee table.

"You mean more to me than you would to IBM. You're a bigger fish in my lake than you'd ever be in IBM's. And I'm a more objective filter. You'll have an immediate, unlimited range of hardware and software. Finally, you benefit because I don't sell product. Only my expertise and creativity."

"But IBM has to stand behind its applications and its products. What guarantee do we have from you?"

She opened her maroon leather briefcase, brought out a three-ring binder and handed it to him. Phil flipped the cover and quickly leafed through several pages. It was filled with testimonial letters on familiar corporate letterheads representing an impressive clientele. Lars Borglund owned at least two of the companies in the binder.

"You'll find nothing in IBM's product warranties covering advice," she said, playing hardball very nicely, and with a smile. "My clients must be satisfied or I'm out of business. I have no product margins to fall back on."

Phil handed the binder back to her. "No further questions."

A few minutes later, Phil saw Marty and Nora to the door. She stopped to admire the picture hanging next to a bookshelf.

"What a lovely painting," she said. "Landmark Center. From Courage Workshop."

Phil nodded.

She extended her hand. "Until next time."

He shook her hand and watched her walk away. So what if she probably was David's birth mother? No reason to have acted like an ass and embarrassed Marty after he'd already checked her out.

"Ruth, I'll be gone the rest of the day," he said into the intercom.

Forty minutes later he parked next to the chain link fence at Classic Aviation. He phoned Flight Service for a weather briefing and went downstairs to prepare his flight plan.

Judy Cichon, a flight instructor, entered the room.

"Haven't seen you around," she said.

Phil smiled at her and said hi before turning to his sectional map. She was a former TV meteorologist who had gotten a divorce, given up television and become a flight instructor in the space of one year. Had someone laminated her jeans to her perfect thighs?

"Where're you headed?" she asked.

"Duluth. Wanted to go to Fargo, but there's a front coming in over Bismarck."

"Have a good flight." She touched his shoulder lightly.

He filed his flight plan, preflighted the Cessna, twisted into the plane, tuned in ATIS and called the tower. "Flying Cloud ground, Skylane niner seven five zero four at Classic with echo. Northbound."

"Two eight left, five zero four."

Nora Helstrin sat in the Le Café Nicollet with her best friend, Connie Denning, a buyer for Dayton's Department Store.

"Tell me you're making a sick joke," Connie said. Her eyebrows arched. "You are not joking."

Nora shook her head.

"But you're going on bits and pieces, Nora. I mean, so he's an insurance man who lives on Lake Minnetonka and has a picture of Landmark Center on his wall. This is the Twin-Cities. Pictures of Landmark Center are everywhere."

"I know it sounds crazy. Just a hunch, you understand. Question is, why? I'm not saying his partner knows anything, but Tag has to. It's all too coincidental otherwise. His partner told me Tag got him to contact me. In one of our conversations, Marty mentioned that Tag was a lawyer years ago. And he had no reason to get abrasive in his office. He's up to something."

"Why not ask him? Lay it on the table."

"Because it might scare him and cost me the contract. At the very least, it would make it more awkward for both of us if I'm right. And what if he let it slip at home? I don't want David to know. He and I have reached our understanding. I'm sure the wife wouldn't be thrilled. No, I'll let him play his little game, and I'll play right along. Stay tuned."

Duluth International's runways looked wide and interstate-long when Phil touched down. After refueling, he hurried up to the After Burner Café for a soft drink. The café gave him a perfect view of the 148th Fighter Wing of the Minnesota Air National Guard shooting take offs and landings in their F-16s. After watching them for a half hour, he returned to his Cessna and flew back to Flying Cloud.

She was professional and classy. She had a lucrative career and didn't strike him as a troublemaker. What motivation could she possibly have to make waves? David, who seemed to be okay with everything, was two decades in her past. But could you leave it to chance? Didn't you have to watch the players and have some kind of plan to fall back on if necessary?

Chapter Twenty-Seven

The fireplace in the Tag den popped and crackled in defiance of the wind and falling snow. Heat radiated up Phil's legs, the smell of the fire reminding him of their lake cabin. Midwinter in Minnesota. Decent weather still three months away. In the meantime, what better way to spend a Sunday afternoon?

"Ta-dah!" Ellen crowed. "Spring training can wait. It's time for fat food!"

The aroma of spiced tea and party mix entered the room with her. David and Jessica were gone for the day, so instead of hard rock banging away from two radios, the notes of a Mozart CD floated in the background. Phil was catching up on reading from the office while Ellen read the "Saint Anthony Messenger" magazine.

She set the magazine aside. "Mind if I turn on the TV?"

"It's kind of nice without it."

Ellen leaned over him. "Who makes the best party mix around?"

"Well, I once knew a gal from Nantucket.…"

"Who had a face like a bucket."

"Not how it goes."

"Did she serve white chocolate with party mix?"

Phil set aside his papers. "Okay, you win. Where is it?"

"Beg me."

"I'm begging! I'm begging!"

She handed him a tin of white chocolate, kissed him and sat beside him on the floor. She opened the TV Guide and said something about a National Geographic special. Moments later, the clattering of countless hooves and a sonorous voice-over began to distract Phil. The program dealt with wildebeests and their migration patterns. The endless migration of countless wildebeests soon gained his full attention: how they began, millions of them, on the Serengeti plain, galloping, always galloping, to the north for a thousand miles in search of grass; and how, once having reached the northernmost tip of their annual journey, they looped back and returned by a more easterly route to their starting point on the Serengeti. Then, after only two months of grazing on the lush plain, the dry season would set in again and the wildebeests would begin yet another northward trek.

"This reminds me of that old bumper sticker," Ellen said.

"Which?"

"'Life is a bitch and then we die.'"

"Ha! Maybe our migration is a daily thirty-minute commute."

Great numbers of them, though a small percentage, died through drowning and in the jaws of predatory cats, hyenas, wild dogs and crocodiles. Newborn calves were especially vulnerable, as were females giving birth. If a calf became separated from its mother, it had no chance of finding her in the massive herd, and was doomed.

The graphic photography made Ellen gasp and turn away. The narrator reminded viewers that the deaths of thousands of wildebeests meant life for many more thousands of other species—predators, vultures, storks and even moths that laid their eggs in the skeletal remains of those long dead. The cycle worked extremely well for the wildebeests, had for two million years.

When the program ended, Ellen appeared lost in thought as she gazed into the fire for several moments. "How are the computer consultants working out?"

Phil reached for the poker. "They'll help us."

"You haven't said much about them. You seem … I don't know … kind of hostile toward the whole thing. Is Lankar cooperating?"

He poked the embers and threw a log on the fire. "They don't come cheap. The new stuff should pay off in the long run, though. Lankar is a jerk; no change there. The first batch of documents came two weeks late all jumbled up in a box. Some weren't even identified by company. It hasn't gotten better."

"Have you gone to Borglund?"

"I went to Lankar. He's so slippery. All smiles and 'I'll get to the bottom of this.' As if he hadn't personally had a hand in it. He feels he's losing face—to me of all people. I have to work with him. Borglund wants and expects that. Lankar is his main guy. But if I can't get what I need when I need it, I'll have to pull an end run somehow."

"Strange that Lankar is the one you have to work with after all these years. Of course, you manipulated the whole scenario. "

"Not really. Gives me a rush, though, thinking about going *mano a mano* with him."

"I still worry about your holding a grudge that long. But there's no need to go over that again." Ellen left the sofa and sat on the hearth. "Jessica and I decided on a Chicago date. The only time we can do it is April first."

They would fly down on a Friday, sightsee and shop through Saturday, catch a nightclub act in the evening and round out the trip with mass and brunch on Sunday before flying back. A mother-daughter thing Ellen had seized on when the Borglund contract was signed.

"We'll be moving the office that weekend, so I won't be around much then anyway." Phil caught himself massaging the indentation under his eye where David had gouged him in the lake. "I'm thinking about having something done with this. A surgeon could smooth it out."

"Really want to?"

"It's pretty ugly."

"Wish you wouldn't. It means something."

The wind howled and the fire curled around the new log.

"You said something last week about Bob Danner getting an award in Des Moines," Ellen said.

"The Chamber of Commerce named him Man of the Year. It's a big deal. I'm looking forward to seeing him again. God, I can't believe we've been out of law school for nearly twenty-three years."

"Are you sure you don't mind my not going along?"

"No problem. I've covered it with Bob."

"What sounds good for dinner?"

"Let's have dessert first. You look delicious. I'll even tell you about the girl from Nantucket."

"Oh, brother."

She stretched out beside him on the deep pile carpet in the warmth of the fire with the snow falling and the wind moaning and whistling in the gray afternoon.

"Mmmmm," he said, "I still like White Linen. Remember the first time you wore it?" They had gone to dinner at La Tortue when it was still in business and made love when they returned home, the fresh scent of her new perfume forever commingled in his mind with marvelous food and sex. His hand went to the zipper of her slacks.

"Let's wait till tonight."

He persisted.

"I'll go lock the doors," she said.

"Why?"

She gave him a look. "I'll be right back."

After they made love, he tried to remember the last time they had done it any place other than in bed. He wished she hadn't locked the doors. Ellen went upstairs to freshen up, and Phil lay under an afghan and closed his eyes. How could he get Lankar to play ball? The computer overhaul would cost a bundle, probably a great deal more than even Marty anticipated. Helstrin was competent, but not likely inexpensive. Phil rolled closer to the feeble warmth of the fireplace embers as images of the driven wildebeest clattered through his imagination along with flashes of Nora Helstrin.

Chapter Twenty-Eight

"Phil, you've got to spend some time with her."

"I'm up to my earlobes, Marty. Whatever you agree to is okay with me."

Marty slammed his palm against the wall. "It doesn't work that way! She needs your input and you promised to give it! It's time to deliver!"

This from Marty the Imperturbable, a man as tough-minded and determined as you could find, but one who almost never showed his anger or frustration.

"I have an hour in the morning before I leave for Des Moines. See if she can be here."

"You've got a phone. Call her yourself," Marty said and stalked out.

Jesus, what was going on? Was it the pressure? There was always pressure. So Lankar was a jerk. Dealing with jerks was nothing new. Sick of winter? So was everybody else. Ill at ease around Nora Helstrin? Threatened? Curious? Who the hell brought her in, Tag? You did. So why not cooperate, get it over with, and paint her out of the picture?

He picked up the phone and dialed.

"Computer Spectrums," an eager young female voice said.

"Miss Helstrin, please."

"May I tell her who's calling?"

"Phil Tag."

The ever-so-slight hesitation before the girl said thank you suggested much. How many times had her boss called him an impossible so-and-so?

"Hello, Mr. Tag. This is Nora," she said in an upbeat voice

that nettled him.

"Miss Helstrin, could we get together tomorrow morning? I'd have an hour open."

"I need more than an hour, but that would be a start."

"My office at nine then."

"Won't work. I have an eight o'clock in Excelsior and a nine-fifteen back here. Can you come to my office? I'll reschedule my nine-fifteen."

His calendar showed a seven-thirty breakfast appointment in Apple Valley. He could conveniently go to her place but didn't want to. "Look, let's try for a day next week."

"I really need your input to move ahead."

Okay, Marty, okay. "I'll be there."

Under pressure of traffic both ways, Phil missed the driveway twice. On the third pass he slowed to a crawl, impatient commuters be damned, and realized why he had missed it. A thick stand of fir trees camouflaged her driveway at the tip of a sharp turn in the road.

He snaked up the long asphalt drive to the crest of a knoll that commanded a tree-obscured view of one of Lake Minnetonka's bays. Except for the partial view of the lake, evergreens surrounded the property and gave it remarkable privacy.

The home of Computer Spectrums and of Nora Helstrin was a neat, well-maintained white ranch with a two-car garage. Three cars were parked in a small asphalt parking area. A life-size naked man of white marble rose up from a decorative pool. The sculptor had chiseled in all the details: rippling muscles, flowing hair, pronounced genitals.

Nora opened the door when he rang.

"Good morning and welcome."

She wore navy slacks and a pleated caramel-color blouse that complemented her complexion and hair, which was at the moment burnished by the morning light. She took his coat.

"Coffee?"

"With cream. Thanks."

She disappeared through a doorway and returned a minute later with a steaming cup.

"Our work area," she said with a wave of her arm. She stepped down into a large room that resembled a mission control center. At least eight computers, several printers and various pieces of collateral equipment filled the room. Three people, a young man and two women, looked up. She introduced them.

"We call it the Braincane Room, as in hurricane," Nora said. "One step beyond brain*storm.*" She rolled her eyes. "We're a little driven here."

She led him into her private office. "We don't have much time, so we'd better begin. I have a list."

Her incisive questions led to other questions and considerations not on her list. She saw possibilities and pitfalls quickly and, though she knew next to nothing about his business, she spoke on a conceptual level that challenged him. Her thought process brought to Phil's mind an image of a tightly racked set of billiard balls expertly broken by a cue ball, the balls scattering across the table, caroming off the rails, clicking into one another, coming to a stop and then, like a film run in reverse, coming together in a tightly bunched pyramid once more.

"I have to go," Phil said at ten.

"But we—I—How can I do good work for you if you don't give a little? Why are you so elusive?"

"I'm very busy these days, Miss Helstrin."

"Balls! No one is that freaking busy!"

"My coat, please."

She yanked the door open and whipped through it. When she returned with his coat, her face was flushed. She held the coat at arm's length, standing sideways to him, her free hand in a fist on her hip.

"What time is your next appointment?"

"Don't have one. I'm flying to Des Moines."

Her head jerked back. She straightened. "Extraordinary circumstances require extraordinary measures. I'll get a ticket on the same flight. We'll talk in the air."

"Sorry, I'm flying my own plane."

"How long will you be gone?"

"Overnight."

"Perfect."

She became a blur of controlled movement. Briefcase, BlackBerry, purse. She went to the door. "Tracy, please cancel everything until tomorrow noon and reschedule. Thanks." She looked at Phil. "Give me ten minutes to throw some things together. I'm going with you to Des Moines."

Totally taken aback, he could think of only one good reason for her not taking her. If they bought the farm, he could see the Star-Tribune's story: "A local businessman and his female companion were killed when their small plane…." Nice legacy for Ellen and the kids. He picked up Nora's phone and jabbed the buttons.

"Marty? Phil. Guess who's going to Iowa with me."

He explained the situation. Marty laughed and said something like *Qué mujer!* Phil figured it was either ironic or lascivious.

Chapter Twenty-Nine

She interviewed him for the entire flight until he contacted approach control twenty miles from Des Moines. His law school classmate met them at Elliott Aviation.

"Nora Helstrin, Bob Danner. We need to drop Miss Helstrin off at her hotel."

Awkward chit-chat about weather, inquiries about families and old friends and other small talk took up the drive to the downtown Marriott, where Phil asked Nora to meet them at eight in the morning. They were pulling away from the hotel when Bob gave Phil an okay-come-clean-what's-this-all-about look.

Phil punched him on the shoulder. "You won't believe it. Damn, it's good to see you! We've got a lot of catching up to do."

"And so in recognition and appreciation of all you've accomplished, and of how much you've given of yourself, it is indeed an honor to present you with the Man of the Year award."

Bob Danner accepted the plaque and shook the presenter's hand while cameras flashed and people clapped in the ballroom of the Marriott. The audience rose in a standing ovation. Bob handed the plaque to his wife Betty and stepped to the microphone. He glanced down at Phil, front table center, and winked. Deservedly proud of the award, he also saw through the politics and hypocrisy surrounding it.

"So much bullshit, you know? What does it all mean, Phil?" he had said that afternoon at his club where they had gone to catch up with each other's life. "What does it all really mean?"

But now at the lectern he was playing by the rules and doing it superbly.

"Thank you, Jack, for those kind words. Coming from you, they mean a lot. Truth of the matter is, I don't deserve this any more than a dozen other people here tonight."

He spoke in a halting, low-key manner that conveyed humility and a common-man image. A big man who had put on weight, he always looked a little frumpy in a suit. His thick, graying eyebrows moved up and down above the rims of his reading glasses.

"When you come right down to it, we all need good luck and good people. I've had both in abundance. First of all, I'm lucky to have married the woman I did. I simply wouldn't be here tonight without her."

He motioned to Betty next to him at the head table. The crowd applauded her. She smiled wanly. Oddly, there was no detectable spark of pride in her eyes.

"My kids are good kids. My health is good. How much luckier can a guy get? A lot luckier." Danner proceeded to recognize five of his key people. By the time he finished, all credit for his success seemed to belong to his employees.

"These people are the best. My only problem now is, what do I do tomorrow when they all want raises?" He waited for the laughter to subside. Because he'd been hanging on the lectern, his sleeves had crept up his arms to expose three inches of shirt cuffs. He wrapped up his speech a minute later with a tribute to the Chamber of Commerce and all the people he'd had the opportunity to work with over the years.

It was past eleven by the time Betty, Bob and Phil drove to the Danner home, a huge tri-level stone affair in Clive. Bob suggested a nightcap.

"I'm going to bed," Betty said. "Excuse me, Phil."

In the den Bob lit the gas starter in the fireplace and in minutes had a leaping fire going. They each had a Scotch. Bob downed his quickly, poured another and sat in a stuffed chair at an angle to the fireplace.

"Mother, flag and apple pie, Phillip. Isn't it a grand life? Betty and I are divorcing."

The Scotch caught in Phil's throat. He coughed and set his drink down.

"I know. I find it hard to believe myself. There's no going back. It's over. Has been for three years. Maybe longer."

"Bob, I'm sorry. You know how I feel about you both."

Danner swirled his drink. The ice cubes rattled, the fire crackled.

"There's no other woman and, so far as I know, no other man. We're just different people than before. She's still a fine woman, but the fun isn't there.

"I say there's no other woman. That's not exactly true. I've messed around some in the last year, but that's after it was over. It's like—"

"Do the kids know?"

"They've got to suspect. We're waiting till school lets out to tell them."

Phil drained his Scotch and waved off Bob's offer of another. "Some speech you gave tonight."

"Thanks. Meant every word of it. And felt like a hypocrite at the same time. No, that's not accurate. I meant what I said, including the things about Betty. But it seemed pointless. Like, what's the purpose? So what if I can show you buildings I put up all over the city? No one gives a damn, and the world keeps turning."

"Did you feel this way when it was still right with Betty?"

Danner poked at the logs in the fireplace and sipped on his Scotch. His face sagged in a way Phil hadn't noticed earlier. He looked noticeably older than before.

"I guess back then there was a reason to do daily battle. I can't bring that back, don't want to. I'm going to make a right angle turn when this is all over, Phillip, my fellow Minnesota Golden Gopher."

He probably had needed a sounding board for a long time. Under the veil of alcohol, he could confide in an old friend with minimal loss of face if he didn't say too much.

"My old man had a dinky construction company that put up single-family homes. Once in a while a duplex. Today we build twenty-story buildings and other things that my dad wouldn't believe. Made a fortune, but I'd rather have been a zoologist. My undergrad major, remember? Thought I'd observe the wonders of Nature and quench my thirst with pure water and purer Scotch."

Phil went to pour another drink. He'd go to bed if Danner didn't regain his grip and dispense with the false jocularity.

"How about you, Phil? Happy? Still think about teaching someday?"

"Just took on a client worth nearly a billion."

"You don't seem overjoyed."

"It's a ton of work."

Danner eyed him closely. His expression changed. He threw down the last of his drink. "I've known you a long time, and I know it's stupid to give advice, but here it comes anyway. Don't wait it out because of what others might think. They don't give a damn. Do what you want, my friend. When the grim reaper taps you on the shoulder—"

"Damn it, don't play Digger O'Dell with me. This is Phil the Serious, remember? You had the gift of gab and all the one-liners. Besides, you blasted Hawkeye, I never could keep up with your drinking, so lighten up on the Scotch."

It worked. Danner laughed and got another drink. He talked about the breakup of his marriage until he'd emptied himself of it. They turned to politics and sports and old times. Phil quit drinking at one-thirty because of his nine-thirty a.m. flight time, but they talked until three.

Bob showed Phil to his room. "I let you turn the conversation back there. But what I said stands, Phil. Take care of yourself."

They ate breakfast at seven-thirty and left to pick up Nora at eight.

"Thanks for listening last night," Bob said on the way to the Marriott, where Nora was waiting at the curb. When they got to the airport, Phil gave Danner a thumbs up. "Great seeing you again. Let's keep in touch. You're on for that fishing trip in the fall, and I'll hold you to it."

Phil preflighted the Skylane and they took off. When they reached altitude, Nora said, “A number of things came to mind last night that I’d like to clear up, okay?”

“Not today, please. I’m not up to it.”

“But this is a perfect—”

“Look, the interview is over. No more questions. Or do you need to hear it in computerese? And please pull your skirt down!”

Chapter Thirty

Ellen said no by touching his hand where it touched her.

"Just hold me," she said. She rolled to her side and snuggled against him spoon fashion. Phil's hand cradled her breast. Not as firm as before, but still so smooth and warm and wondrously soft.

"I couldn't wait to get home today," he said.

He had gone to the office but had left early, bought a single red rose, a bottle of wine, a pound of veal and insisted on preparing dinner. He had grilled burgers for David and Jessica before they went out for the evening. Then he and Ellen ate in the dining room and went to bed early. He wanted to make love to her as soon as the kids were gone. But the way she said "just hold me" told him it was out of the question.

He lay back and took a deep, quiet breath. "How's Jessica?"

"In case you haven't noticed, she's turning into quite the young lady. She's eating well. Added a few pounds, in fact."

"You've become buddies."

"It's nice to have her nearly grown up. Sometimes we talk nonstop."

"Seems only yesterday she was a baby."

"You haven't said much about Iowa. How are Bob and Betty?"

It was no time for evasiveness. "They're getting a divorce."

Ellen tensed. "Why?"

"I'm not sure." He hoped she wouldn't press, but knew she would.

"Twenty-some years. Another woman?"

"I don't think so. Not directly, anyway."

"Don't be cute. Tell me."

"I think it's a little more general than that."

"Bob was sowing middle-age wild oats and got caught. Did you talk to Betty at all?"

"Not really. And I don't think there's another woman. The whole thing is clouded. In the end, who knows? I'm not sure Bob and Betty know when it all started, or how it got to this point."

"What did Bob say? He had to tell you about it."

"Please don't ask me to give you a second-hand version of something I don't understand myself. He didn't really tell me anything, except they weren't having fun anymore."

Ellen snuggled against him and said nothing for several moments, waiting, he knew, for him to open up. "All right, don't tell me," she said, finally.

He moved his arm and shifted his weight to draw her closer.

"Have you ever wanted to have an affair?" she said.

"Come on, El. The Danners are the Danners, and we're us."

"Do you find other women attractive?"

"Sure. That doesn't mean I want an affair. I don't."

"Are the ones you're attracted to younger?"

"They're old and fat with warts. How about the guys you look at?"

"I'm serious. Please don't joke."

"Look, I don't want another woman. I love you, and I don't want anyone else."

"Does my age matter to you?"

Phil rolled from his side to his back and draped his forearm over his eyes. "Come on, El. Give it a rest."

"Does it?"

"No. It never has and never will." He rolled back to his side and put his arms around her. "You know that, don't you?"

"Such a waste. Nobody wins. Not them, not the kids. I don't want it to happen to us. It won't, will it?"

"Never."

"They get through the tough years, only to grow old alone or with someone else. How sad." She rocked to a sitting position. "Makes me so angry I could spit! I know you're tired and don't want to talk." She swung her feet to the floor and grabbed her robe from the stuffed chair next to the bed. She left the room but returned a moment later. "Don't say anything about it to Jessica. It would be threatening to her. If it can happen to them, it could happen to us. I'm going to make a cup of herbal tea."

Too little sleep and too much Scotch last night were no guarantee of sleep tonight. The clock in the hallway tick-tocked like an hourglass for the blind.

Chapter Thirty-One

Phil pressed a button on the attachment connected to his phone, lifted the receiver, and dialed the number from the file on his desk. First the secretary, then her boss.

"How can I help you?" Lankar said after his secretary put the call through.

It was easy to envision the smirk on his face. This was the eighth call in the past two weeks.

"Wade, we've talked and talked. Why do I continually receive obsolete information?"

"You don't."

"Benefit schedules from 2006 are current?"

"Well, ah, no. Hell no! I'll get you more recent stuff."

"Not 'more recent.' Current. Everything you've sent me has been useless. How many times have we discussed this? And the information you send arrives in shambles."

"Tag, people do make mistakes."

"Not this many. Your people are either incompetent, or someone is trying to sabotage this project."

"Bullshit!"

One … two … three.

"Are you giving this your personal attention?"

"You're fucking right I am."

"Then you're incompetent."

A grunt came through the receiver.

"What are you hiding, Lankar?"

"Don't you dare question my integrity, you cocksucker!" His voice was high-pitched and forced. "I don't know why you're here, you blue collar Polack asshole. You're not needed, you're not wanted. Give it up, loser!"

Would he say more?

"The job isn't getting done, Wade."

"Let us know what you need. We'll deliver. Have a great day."

Phil placed the phone on the cradle. Five letters and eight phone calls. This was the capstone.

Marty walked in. "Nora Helstrin just called. She's close to wrapping it up. Needs to run some things past you."

"Okay."

"She said the trip to Iowa was an experience."

"I was rough on her."

Marty shrugged. "She didn't say anything negative. I assumed she meant the plane ride. Know what I like about her, other than the fact she's competent and professional? Her upbeat nature. Great personality. Heck of a woman."

After Marty left, Phil dialed her number. "Nora Helstrin, please," he said to the young woman who answered. "This is Phil Tag." Even Helstrin would be a welcome change from Lankar. Besides, he owed her an apology.

"Hi."

"Marty said you need to see me. Can you make lunch?"

They met at the Calhoun Yacht Club, an upscale place on Lake Calhoun. The March sun flooded through the high vaulted windows. The dining room always looked bright and airy, even on cloudy days.

"Oh, look at the organ," Nora said on their way to a table. An ancient, perfectly preserved organ stood in the southwest corner of the room. As soon as they had been seated near a window, Nora insisted that they examine the organ more closely. She inspected the instrument, which was painted in pastels and gilt. Her delight was infectious. "I'm so glad we came here," she said.

She ordered a seashell salad. He selected a grilled chicken breast in grape sauce. Snow-covered Lake Calhoun stretched out to the gray tree line on the far south shore. Dark blotches mottled the surface where the snow had turned to slush in the first stage of spring breakup.

People began to file in. The maitre d' greeted many of them by their names and offered his arm to lead them to their tables. Most were women whose average age had to be well over seventy. They reminded Phil of the elderly population of Miami Beach who daily migrate from their apartments and condos to the beach, walking like crabs, stiff and deliberate, across the sand for one more day in the sun—a sight so depressing that Phil had moved the family to the Gulf side on their first vacation trip to Florida years ago.

"Let's have a glass of wine," he said, leaning forward. "To spring."

"Be a crime not to."

He ordered the wine.

"Tell me about you," he said.

She contemplated him, her expression the closest thing to a Mona Lisa smile he had ever seen on a living woman's face.

"I'm a long-standing member of those two indigenous Minnesota majorities, Swedes and hardheads. I grew up near Duluth, went to the university there, ended up in computers."

The waiter placed the wine on the table. On the street, young lovers across Excelsior Boulevard walked along the lake, coats open, laughing and enjoying this fine day of false spring.

"So there I have it. The definitive biography of Nora Helstrin."

Color rose in her face. "Yes, there you have it!"

What a bitch. Okay, Marty, okay. "I didn't mean it that way. Tell me more. By the way, my apologies for the Iowa trip."

"Accepted."

"You're too resilient to be a hardhead."

She screwed up her eyes. "I'm a survivor. First and foremost, I'm a survivor." As if catching herself, she leaned back, smiled and raised her glass. "To spring."

"And to our project."

"Skoal." She drew the glass to her lips. "It's all in the wrist."

The fume blanc tasted pleasingly tart.

"What do you enjoy in your free time?" he said.

"Many things. Hiking, swimming, downhill skiing. Music, theatre, reading. Painting."

"Oils?"

"Water colors. My oils turn into grease jobs."

The waiter brought their food. His chicken was too sweet, but succulent.

"Ready for the big change?" she said.

Puzzled, he tilted his head.

"Your office move."

"Oh, sure," he said too quickly. Their eyes met for a moment as the waiter approached.

"Is everything all right here?" the waiter asked. When neither of them answered, he swished off in a snit.

The snow was turning gray-black at the edge of the street, but the sun brightened even the slush.

"The only constant is change," he said. "So trite but so true. In most ways, I've always resisted change. I'm a lawyer who gave up law to sell insurance. The move to the suburbs is the only other major change that comes to mind."

"Not true. You were single, you married. You … had children?"

"Two. But beyond those kinds of things, I've stuck to the familiar. I like to try things—new places, different foods and sports—things like that. But always with a lifeline to the familiar. I come back to the same things I've always liked. Computers. Ha! I delegate most of that. Without Ruth, I wouldn't turn one on, except when I'm running financial programs. Don't know what I'd do without her. If it were up to me, I'm afraid we'd still be doing everything on three-by-five cards."

"I know you exaggerate, but for a while there, I nearly recommended that you do exactly that."

"But once I get a heading, I hold it. I finish what I begin."

"Why did you leave the law for insurance?"

"Money. I specialized in estate planning. I'd draft a will and trust, and maybe some business agreements, and collect a few thousand dollars. It was frequently a life insurance agent who brought the client to me in the first place, and the agent would often make ten times more in commissions than I did in legal fees. Sometimes, a lot more than that. So I switched. Then I bought a third party administration business and hired a darn good manager for it."

"Do you love what you're doing?"

"It pays the bills."

They both contemplated their wine for a moment.

"When you began working with us and kept calling me Mr. Tag, I felt like a senior citizen."

"You certainly don't look like one."

"Thanks. You should see the wrinkles on the inside."

"Would love to. Oh! Look at the time. I'll be late for my appointment if I don't fly."

He sifted through the pile of paper on his desk, went to the window every few minutes and paced the floor. By three o'clock the sky had clouded over. Another dark day in the endless Minnesota winter. He had enjoyed lunch with Nora Helstrin.

The intercom buzzed.

"Borglund's secretary. He wants to see you at eight tomorrow. Your calendar's clear."

"Set it up, Ruth. Thanks."

Borglund had twice made it clear that he was unhappy with the lack of progress. Phil was ready for him. Ready, but not feeling good about it.

"Mr. Borglund, your concern is justified," Phil said the following morning in the Northstar Hotel coffee shop. "The project is not progressing. You're not getting your money's worth and you won't." He opened his briefcase and extracted a large brown envelope, which he placed on the table. "This envelope contains a tape of several phone conversations and copies of correspondence. I give them to you without comment. The tape is the only copy. Do with it what you wish. I'll await your call."

Neither of them said anything while they put on their coats. On the street Borglund held Phil with a cold stare for several seconds. Then he nodded once and turned away without shaking hands.

Chapter Thirty-Two

"Ellen called while you were gone," Ruth said when he returned to the office. "She has to come downtown and would like to have lunch. You're open."

Ah, this gentle, unspoken conspiracy of females that had become part of his life over the past decade.

"In a pig's ear! No more free lunches for that dame!"

"Ha! I hope she soaks you good."

Lunch with Ellen. The perfect antidote to Borglund and Lankar.

"You had an avalanche of calls," Ruth said. "I handled all but two. Jack Dessing wants you to call tomorrow, and Nora Helstrin needs a call back by ten. You have a ten-fifteen in New Hope and a three o'clock in Eagan."

He called Ellen and agreed to meet her at Leeann Chin's in International Centre at noon. He returned Nora's call.

"Hi," she said. "I have to run into town later. May I buy you lunch?"

He hesitated. Lunch dates were popping up all over the place. He pondered the word "date."

"Let me do some juggling. It would have to be later, say one-fifteen."

"MR's at one-fifteen."

He called Ellen to meet him earlier.

"Eleven-thirty will be tight," she said, "but I can make it. It'll cost you a glass of wine."

"You've got it. Sorry for the change, honey. See you in a bit."

He hung up and rushed through the mail before leaving for

his appointment in New Hope. By the time he finished, returned and parked, it was eleven-forty.

Ellen was at a table, waiting.

"Sorry I'm late, El." He kissed her.

"I just got here myself."

"Long enough to drink half your wine."

"Well, I did get here a little early."

He smiled and squeezed her hand. "How was your morning?"

"The Spring Bazaar is getting bizarre. No, Father Banning is. I work out a million details, and he second-guesses everything. Seems he needs to meet with me every ten minutes."

"Sounds like his pastoral humility isn't up to his financial anxiety."

"His paranoia overwhelms his ability to delegate."

"Maybe he likes you. In fact, I think he does."

"What's that supposed to mean?"

"Just kidding. But he does like you. My God, you're his work horse."

He ordered plum wine with the buffet. Ellen seemed inclined to linger over her meal. Meeting Nora on time would be difficult.

"Is something on your mind, Phil?"

"Nothing in particular. Why?"

"You seem preoccupied."

"My afternoon is packed."

"We need to decide on the Oregon trip."

"It's months away."

"There's no sense leaving it till the last minute. We have to let Humberto and Yolanda know one way or the other, and we need to cancel the reservation in Maine if we decide on Oregon."

"We haven't seen Humberto in ages."

"We've never gone to Maine."

"We practically promised them."

"Didn't I tell you? I made a deposit at that lodge in Maine. It's nonrefundable."

Phil closed his eyes for a second before glancing at his watch. "Okay, let's do Maine. I have to cut."

"We hardly see you anymore."

"It'll be worth it."

"How many times have I heard that?"

They kissed and Phil ran to his car. He parked on the street near MR's, rushed in and collided with Nora in the darkness. He lost his balance and held on to her to keep from falling.

"Goodness, I should stand in dark entryways more often!"

He followed her up a stairway lined with dozens of framed photographs. They emerged from relative darkness into a solarium with tables of wrought iron and glass, only one of which was set up.

The glass enclosure afforded an upward-angled panorama of the edge of downtown. A block away on the left a slender black steeple rose into the sky. Clockwise from the steeple were City Center and, cut off at the knees by Dayton's, the Radisson Hotel, followed by the IDS Tower, Foshay Tower, International Centre and the Piper-Jaffray building, which reflected scattered clouds moving across an azure sky.

"Are we the only customers?"

"This room is reserved for group functions only," she said. "Can't you see all the people filing in? Luckily, I know the owner. He held this one last table for us."

Phil laughed at her charade. How many similarly unusual restaurants existed in the Cities? Probably dozens. Years ago he and Ellen had loved finding cozy places that gave them a sense of intimacy and adventure. Later, as the kids grew into toddlers, they fell into the Perkins and Country Kitchen habit, followed by McDonald's and Pizza Hut as the kids got older. On their nights out alone they gravitated to conventional steak and seafood restaurants.

"I didn't know about MR's," he said. "My secretary looked it up for me. A popular spot?"

"The Comedy Porch packs them in. Up-and-coming comics do their routines here four nights a week."

A waitress appeared. Phil ordered only a small salad and a Pepsi.

"Are you in training?"

"Always. Tell me more about Nora Helstrin."

"Like what?"

"You decide."

Tires screeching on pavement pierced the solitude of the solarium. On the street below, at the end of two black ribbons on gray asphalt, a blue car had stopped inches from a small child in a yellow coat. A woman ran from the sidewalk to scoop the child up. The car proceeded. Nora's face was pale.

"You okay?"

She nodded.

She had long tapered fingers and beautifully manicured nails. What made her tick? Did her temper flare up often? Was she religious? What kind of music did she like? What kind of reading? Did she swear when she stubbed her toe? Did she have any other kids? Ever married? Who was the father? Still alive? Where? Did she have a lover? Lovers? Did she wear panties under her panty hose? What color? Did she look as perfect naked as she did clothed? When—

"Hello in there. Still with me?"

He raised his hands in apology. "Sorry. Just thinking."

"Life is brief enough without violence," she said, "even accidental violence. Especially when it's a child. Children are so—so— I believe we should execute anyone who abuses or molests a child!"

"Have you ever been married?"

"What does— No. Never."

Their food arrived. Phil sipped his soda. "What's your perfume?"

"Obsession."

They said little while they ate. At one point Phil noticed her studying him. She twice caught him doing the same. Her hair changed with the light and with the angle.

"You said you have two children?"

"Correct."

"Boys or girls?"

"One of each."

"Ages?"

"What is this, Q and A time?"

"It's important for me to know my clients."

"Nineteen and seventeen."

"Their names?"

"David and Jessica."

"David is the older?"

It was getting warm in the solarium. Across the way, high on the side of the black Twin City Federal building, two life-size neon trees glowed eternally green.

"You'll make your final recommendations Monday?"

She had already made two presentations, and she and Marty had spent untold hours on follow-up details.

"As planned. Implementation two weeks hence. Ninety percent of the equipment has arrived. The rest will come in this week."

They had scheduled the office move to Bloomington for a weekend two weeks after Nora's final presentation, a perfect timetable. The new computer system essentially would be in place for the start of business on Monday. Of course, the training would take time, and they would have to deal with glitches galore, but the coordinated transition of space and equipment appeared perfect.

"Your system will be state-of-the-art for years to come."

"What's the total cost?"

"Let's wait for the presentation."

"How much?"

"It won't exceed one million six."

He bent forward. "Damn, that's up a hundred thousand since your first presentation and double your original quote. We can't afford it."

"Can't not afford it. It'll pay for itself."

"So you say. Does that include all your fees?"

Smiling, she reached over and touched his hand. "Of course. Wait till Monday. You'll love the package. Marty has approved every dollar of it."

Her hand was warm, her smile warmer.

"I'll go over it with Marty."

"Your wife is a homemaker?"

"Correct."

"What does she like to do? Is she pretty? Of course she is, isn't she?"

"She's lovely."

"What's her name?"

"Ellen. Where's that waitress? I have an appointment in Eagan."

"What are David and Jessica like? Do they look like you?"

"Not at all. Our waitress must be on sabbatical."

Why was she looking at him like that? And why all the personal questions? She was as beautiful as they come, but she was too damned nosy. It seemed forever before the waitress showed up.

"Screaming certainty replaces whispering intuition," Nora said in the Embers restaurant on South Hennepin later that afternoon. "Connie, he's not a good liar. He gets nervous and hostile just being evasive."

"Will you continue working with him?"

"How could I possibly stop? He manipulated this whole situation. I need to find out why."

"And?"

"There is no and."

"Nora, how long have I known you?"

Nora ran the tip of her tongue around the small finger of her left hand. She brought her gaze back to her friend. "It does go beyond curiosity. I'm intrigued." She puckered her lips tightly on her finger. "He's good-enough-looking, a good dresser. More than a little successful. I could like him—do like him— now that he's not acting like an ass. Out of the question, of course."

"Sounds dangerous to me."

"So what's a little danger?"

"When I wrote in your yearbook that you'd lead an exciting life, I didn't realize my own prescience."

"You melodramatize."

"Do I?"

The gray day hovered outside the rectory windows.

"Father," Ellen said, "everything is under control. Please

don't worry."

"I never worry when you're handling a project. I simply wish to be supportive. The priest came around his desk. He curled his arm loosely around Ellen's waist. "How's David doing? Are you all right?"

"We're working through things one day at a time."

He pulled her slightly closer and smiled. "If you ever need me, you know I'm here for you."

Ellen did a quarter-circle turn and moved free of him. "Yes, I know, Father. Thanks. If you'll excuse me, I need to get over to the gym. Today is blood pressure check for seniors."

"You're doing a wonderful job with Parish Nurses. We all appreciate your leadership."

"Have to run." She hurried through the door keenly aware of his eyes following her. As inappropriate as he could be lately, she had to admit that the attention he gave her was nice, and he was so darn good-looking to boot. So long as she didn't encourage him, things would be fine wouldn't they? Trouble was, she was less inclined these days to discourage him. His advances piqued her and gave her that indefinable rush that comes from being desired.

Chapter Thirty-Three

David stood in the driveway next to his Camaro.

"The main thing is, I know I can do it, Dad. I was really scared when I signed up. Never thought of myself as a college guy, y'know?"

Phil threw his arm around David's neck.

"You can do anything you want to, son." He broke away and punched David lightly on the arm. "Except beat me in golf."

"I'll waste you this year."

"When I'm eighty. Maybe seventy-nine, if you really work at it."

"Sure, Dad, sure. Just remember to count all your strokes, old-timer!"

David climbed into the Camaro and roared off with a wave. Phil swallowed the lump in his throat. Maybe prayers did get answered.

Nora made an outstanding presentation. Everything seemed to fit their needs, and she had built in flexibility for current usage and future expansion. Marty went to great lengths to convince Phil that the cost was no problem in view of the Borglund retainer and the commissions it would soon generate. In the meantime, on the strength of the retainer, they took out another hefty swing loan from the bank.

The changes reflected the input of the employees at every step. As Nora had predicted, dozens of questions arose during her presentation and Q & A. She answered them on the spot. Afterwards, Phil excused himself so that Marty and Nora could discuss training schedules. Ruth held up a phone message. The orange slip meant it was urgent.

"Borglund," she said.

"I must see you in my office immediately," Borglund said when Phil called.

"I can't get away for an hour."

"Mr. Tag, I insist that you come to my office immediately."

"I'll get there as soon as I possibly can."

"See that you do."

Borglund's executive assistant always projected an inscrutable professional decorum: clothing between mature conservative and austere, a smile with the warmth of a twenty-five-watt bulb, a vocabulary that consisted of clausal suffixes to "Mr. Borglund." She was not a passive woman. Taciturn, but not passive. Today she seemed particularly reserved.

Her phone chimed. The retaliatory fifteen-minute spite-wait was over.

"Mr. Borglund will see you now."

Phil went in and closed the door behind him. Borglund sat behind his desk. On previous meetings, he had joined Phil at the conference table.

"I have terminated Mr. Lankar's services. At this moment security personnel are supervising his vacating. He has a noon deadline. You will work directly with me until the work is done. There will be no middleman. That is the importance I attach to this project.

"I do not believe you are a man to gloat, Mr. Tag. Nor do I believe you necessarily wanted Mr. Lankar relieved of his duties. I took this action only after great deliberation. I had overlooked other—shall we say, indiscretions?—on his part over the years. The man could be very abrasive and crude at times, but he worked for me a considerable length of time, and I valued his contribution. What he did was petty and stupid. An ego thing, the last straw. I'll never know what possessed him to behave as he did.

"That is behind us. I decide; I act. I do not hesitate to dispose of those who stand in the way of legitimate enterprise. Then I move on."

He paused to pour himself a cup of coffee from an insulated pot on his credenza. Phil waved off his offer of a cup.

"It is possible that you inspired intractability in Mr. Lankar. Not probable, but possible. Culpability hides in many corners, as does mendacity, though I do not believe you are a mendacious man. If I believed that, I assure you we would be having an entirely different conversation.

"Without comment as to legality, I find your taping of telephone conversations irrevocably odious. I gave Mr. Lankar no specific reason for my action. Certainly, I made no reference to taped phone calls. Rest assured, Mr. Tag, that our phone conversations will be short and of no substance from this day forward."

"I would never—"

"But you already have, sir!" Borglund's hand flew up and slammed down on the desk. "The principal is not inviolable to you. Circumstance dictates." He adjusted his glasses on his nose. "But enough. I wish to proceed. It was important to have this discussion. You still have my confidence and support. Do you have any questions?"

"None."

One of Marty's Spanish proverbs came to mind, something about carrying a bucket of gold in one hand and caping a bull with the other. Nailing Lankar was worth two buckets of gold.

Chapter Thirty-Four

On April first, a Friday, Ellen and Jessica flew to Chicago for their long-awaited shopping junket. That same afternoon the move from the IDS Tower to Bloomington began. The haulers loaded furniture and equipment on trucks and transported them during the night. The employees, having long ago become familiar with the new floor plan, had prepared well. All desks, chairs, file cabinets and other equipment had color-coded numbers that corresponded to numbers on the floor plan.

On Saturday morning, the employees readied their work stations for business on Monday. Nora's company would work in concert with the phone company to connect the phones, computers, data ports and all the other hardware paraphernalia Saturday night and Sunday. The entire effort would minimize downtime and be well worth the overtime pay.

At noon the Keys Cafe delivered fifty-five box lunches. Phil brought in six pizzas and five coolers loaded with soda on ice. By four most employees had equipped and appointed their workstations. By four-thirty only Marty and Phil remained.

"I propose *tres partidos,* three games, of racquetball for the price of dinner, amigo. With Ellen gone, it's my duty to see that you eat right," Marty said.

"You're on."

Marty beat him two straight in a tough workout.

"You played like you meant it, wetback."

"No fué nada. It was nothing. Winning is in the mind. And in the wrist, of course."

Marty's wrist remark brought to mind Nora and her comment during their toast at the Calhoun Yacht Club.

"You have the honor of buying my dinner at Tubbs," Marty said.

"Way downtown?"

"River Place will be nice. On a beautiful spring night we'll view the IDS Tower from across the Mighty Miss and wave farewell.

"You're in a real mood, *señor.*"

As it had been for two weeks, it was unseasonably warm for the first of April, a night to complement Marty's buoyancy. The scent of early spring wafted through the air as they walked from their cars to the restaurant. For as long as Phil could remember, the first warm days of spring had filled him with a quiet excitement and sense of escape from layers of clothing and shoulders hunched against the cold.

"Marty," he said as they finished dinner, "let's do the town. Like the old days. We've got the Borglund deal, the move is done. Let's celebrate."

"Wish I could, but it's bridge night. I'd better take off before Liz comes looking for me."

Phil ordered an Amoretto when Marty left. Although he enjoyed the drink, he felt the night go empty while he watched passersby strolling on the sidewalk. After finishing his drink and paying the check, he walked along the Mississippi. Traces of thin ice still clung to the shoreline, but in the channel of the darkly flowing river the lights of the Minneapolis skyline danced on the current. The wistful notes of "Lara's Theme" came from somewhere down the street and revived the magic of the night. When the song ended a few moments later, the night went empty again. Maybe David had stayed home. They could play cards or watch a movie on TV. Or he'd read a book. It had been forever since he'd had the house alone on a Saturday night with a good book. He headed for his car. Were the comedy routines at MR's any good? A couple of good comics might dispel the loneliness.

The bar at MR's was packed. The bartender, a skinny man with a lopsided moustache and big ears, told him the first show started in thirty minutes. Phil ordered a Scotch rocks, went to a pay phone and poked the numbers with an unsteady index finger. She answered on the fourth ring.

"Nora, this is Phil Tag. I'm at MR's. Can you join me for a drink?" He cleared his throat. "Hello?"

"You caught me going out the door. Sorry."

His hand shook when he hung up, but in spite of how lonely he had felt only minutes before, he now felt more relieved than disappointed. It wasn't a good idea to be alone on such an evening with a woman as beautiful as Nora Helstrin. He'd catch a show and go home. First, though, he took his cell phone from his pocket and pressed memory number one for Ellen's cell phone. Jessica answered.

"Oh, Daddy! We had such a great day! You won't believe the beautiful outfit I found. We're going to the Palmer House for a show. Wish you were here. Here's Mom."

Ellen came on. "Hello, dear. Your daughter walked my legs off. Johnny Mathis won't keep me awake, I'm afraid."

"You'll fall in love after three notes."

"Maybe just a little. He's not Jessica's cup of tea, but she can't win them all. How did the move go?"

"Better than expected."

"I tried to call earlier."

"Marty and I played racquetball and went to dinner."

"I don't know where you find the energy. Honey, we have to run. Love you. Give David a hug."

"Love you, too. Have a good time."

He returned to the bar for his drink. The bartender's off-center moustache and crooked smile amused him, so he tipped the guy five dollars. Looking forward to a good show, he went upstairs to the nearly filled Comedy Porch and took an empty seat at the rear. If the show bombed he'd slip out and go home.

The first performer had gotten well into his routine when Phil felt a tap on his shoulder.

"April Fool!" Nora Helstrin whispered. Her Obsession perfume accompanied her warm breath. She wore a dressy black pant outfit with spaghetti straps and a sheer wraparound shawl. Phil had forgotten it was April Fool's Day.

A funny, outrageously raunchy woman of about thirty came onstage. Her perky delivery, fetching looks and genuine laugh, combined with perfect timing, enabled her to spout smutty lines without a loss of femininity or humor, either of which would have turned Phil off. She flirted unabashedly with men in the front rows. Her humor ranged from home to brothel, school to city hall.

Nora laughed easily and often. At the most graphically sexual jokes, she glanced at Phil and grimaced playfully. He wasn't at all ill at ease, which surprised him, because he had never quite become comfortable with truly off-color stories in mixed company. Would he be uncomfortable with Ellen at his side? Yes—not that she would sit through this kind of performance in the first place. Right now, the amusement and titillation ruled out self-consciousness. The next comic finished at ten-thirty.

"Let's have a nightcap," he said.

"My treat, my spot?"

"You got it."

He followed her red Lexus out of the city and west to the little town of Spring Park on Lake Minnetonka, where she pulled into the parking lot of Lord Fletcher's without using the valet parking service. Phil stopped behind her and left his engine running.

"Let's find another place."

"But it's my choice."

"Then change your choice. I could know a dozen people in there."

"That's their problem."

"Mine, too. See you later."

"Wait. I know a place."

The Lexus wound through the darkness until it stopped across the street from a rundown little bar that appeared to be part of a bait shop and marina. A rusty sign featuring a bosomy, smiling redhead with a Salem cigarette in her hand stood sentinel at the entrance. The dark interior smelled of tobacco. Deciding to drink beer from the bottle, Phil ordered a Schmidt. Nora asked for a Miller Lite.

"Let's go outside. Nels," she said to the bartender, "we'll take our drinks lakeside. Too nice out, you know, to breathe this foul air."

"It's not summer yet, Nora. Everything is stacked up out there."

"What a fine upstanding Norwegian you are, good Nels. We absolve you of all liability."

"Suit yourself."

"And sell me the largest cigar you have. And matches." She looked over her shoulder at Phil. "Join me in a smoke?"

He shook his head.

They followed a narrow boardwalk to a small deck with a railing at the edge of the lake. The air had turned cold. Without removing the white and gold band, Nora lit the long, thick cigar with a flourish and tossed the still burning match into the darkness.

"Soon the lake will shimmer incredibly blue as far as you can see," she said. "Oh, the life on the lake then! A panoply of color and movement. I love to paint it—the marinas, the boats, the people. Winter serenity is one thing, but God, the life on the water in summer!

"Don't you just hate winter towards the end? The deadness of it? God help me, I love it and hate it. I'm destined to live my life in Minnesota while my soul yearns for the sunny Southwest."

"What keeps you here?"

"Nothing and everything. That female comic was funny, yes? God, I nearly died. Did you like her?"

"The raunch didn't destroy anything else."

"That's the trick. 'Woman's virtue is man's invention.'" She balanced herself on the railing, one knee cocked up, and drank deeply from her bottle of beer. Then she curled her lips outward, pushed the cigar in and out several times and puffed on it.

"You're a different woman when the sun goes down."

"No, I'm a different woman when the sun comes up." A car door slammed somewhere in the darkness. An engine started. "You're smirking."

"I can't believe you're smoking a cigar."

"My conventional insurance man. Every so often I must have a cigar. Everyone does it now. I smoked them long before they became fashionable. Started in college seventeen years ago. The first few puffs are delicious in spite of the smoke. So sensuous. And so Freudian, don't you think? Downright phallic. Correction. So upright phallic."

The mild crudity did nothing to deflect the titillation that brought immediate arousal.

"This is a cruddy place to end the evening. Your place isn't far."

"No, not far. Don't think we should go there, though."

"You're probably right. I—" He took a deep breath, reached out and touched her cheek. "Your face, your voice—they don't belong in this place. Is there somewhere we can say goodnight over a civilized drink?"

She touched his hand on her cheek.

"When you called tonight, I was on my way out to meet someone in town. Had no conscious intention of going to the Comedy Porch. Told myself all the way in I wouldn't. And here I am." She slid off the railing to the deck. "One drink at my place."

She poured two Bailey's in her den.

"Come. I'll show you the rest."

Her furnishings were a curious blend of modern and trendy with a good dash of traditional. Watercolor and oil originals shared the walls with prints and posters. Some frames were wood, others brushed aluminum, stainless steel or even vinyl. An occasional piece of stuffed furniture with floral print upholstery nestled alongside rattan-framed Papasans.

"You like windows," he said.

"You noticed."

"Hard not to."

"I spent forty thousand dollars getting adequate light in here. Let me show you my workroom. It's actually a sunroom, but it's where I love to paint."

The sunroom had a thirty-foot, curving wall of windows.

When Nora flicked a switch, lawn, bushes and trees leaped into stark prominence.

"The windows and skylights make this magnificent for painting."

Dozens of paintings covered the walls. Colors in them ran rampant. Brightness and energy gave life to those that bordered on the abstract.

"My babies. I didn't paint this one, but I love it so. 'The book stalls of Notre Dame,' by LaRue. Bought it in Las Vegas, of all places."

The painting captured the feeling of Paris he recalled from the trip to France with Ellen on their tenth wedding anniversary, an extravagance he had insisted upon over her protests.

"Where do you sleep?"

Her eyes held his for a moment before she led him down a short hallway and through a door. "Here."

He raised his glass until their eyes met over the rim. He held it to her lips, then to his own, before setting the glass on a television at his side. He cupped her face in his hands and kissed her. She didn't respond. Then her face tilted and her lips parted. She leaned into him. He inhaled her scent and tasted a vestige of the cigar on her probing tongue. She arched against him before drawing back.

"Are you sure?" she said.

"Positive."

She switched on a dim lamp and pressed the play button on a CD player next to it. With the unmistakable voice of Barry White pervading the room with sensuality, they lowered themselves onto her waterbed. At first, she repeatedly removed his hand from her breast, would not allow him to touch her too high on the legs. Otherwise, she was totally physical, lithely rolling over him, pressing him to the bed, spread-eagled, as if holding him in bondage, biting, poking, raking, caressing him with expertise in every move. When Phil finally pinned her back, his hands gripping her wrists, she rose against him.

"Wait," she said. "Only a minute."

He rolled away. She unzipped him, held him gently, kissed him wetly there and lingered. She swung her feet to the floor and disappeared into the bathroom.

He kicked off his shoes and lay back, all nerve ends, chest heaving, not wanting to think, hoping he wouldn't think, afraid to think. The full moon poured in through two walls of glass. Every object inside and outside stood out, as if the floodlights were on, exposing him to the world, to the heavens. Just as Barry White reached a staccato crescendo, the clinking of glass against enamel came from the bathroom like an alarm. He had to get out. He clenched his fists, rolled off the bed, pulled on his shoes and hurried from the room.

The front door squeaked when he opened it. He paused before slipping out, not wanting to leave. He left. Moments later, the engine exploded to life and the Cadillac roared down the long driveway. Numb but alert, he drove through the night, taunted by an ancient ejaculation screaming in his ear: *April Fool! April Fool!*

Chapter Thirty-Five

David wasn't home. Phil laid the mail on the kitchen counter and went to bed. Were the sounds of the night always so clear? He tried to identify each one, wanted to hear the cry of a loon. Hundreds of times over the years they had lain in bed and listened to the haunting, shrill calls of the loons. Not tonight.

The most vivid images of Nora bombarded him. Her clear eyes and silky golden hair. Her soft skin and perfect teeth. Her movements beneath and over him. Her lingering scent, her taste, the sound of her voice. Attempts to think of baseball, of fishing, of business, didn't work. Nora swept everything aside. He'd had the strength to leave, the right thing to do, but what about her feelings? Leaving her like that at the brink of intimacy had to be cruel and humiliating. But it would have been more wrong to stay, wouldn't it? *Of course it would, idiot! But....*

Logic failed. So did praying. If only sleep would come. A hiatus of sleep followed by full daylight would change everything. Things were always different in daylight, always easier.

The burning in his stomach wouldn't stop. He went downstairs for an apple, but there were none so he poured a glass of milk and took one of the two chocolate chip cookies in the cookie jar. Ellen probably had baked four dozen yesterday, but the way David attacked them they never stayed around long. The only things the kid ate more of were apples. How many times over the years had Ellen threatened to buy an orchard? She had made the cookie jar, a fat brown squirrel on its haunches with a nut in its paws, in ceramics class. It was during the time they waited to hear from the adoption agency twenty years ago. "You can't have kids without a cookie jar!" she said the night she brought it home.

The cookie and milk and memories didn't help. He dragged himself upstairs and climbed into bed. A short time later, David came home, used the bathroom and went to bed.

Exhaustion and enervation would surely lead to sleep. Phil reached over and deactivated the alarm. He would sleep as late as he could in the morning, go to mass, busy himself around the house, maybe even take David fishing until it was time to pick up Ellen and Jessica at the airport. And then he would never look back.

He retreated from the edge of sleep at five. After a quick shower and shave, he looked into David's room. David had talked him into putting the Caravelle Interceptor into the water much earlier than usual because of the warm weather. Except for coves and north-facing shorelines, the lake was free of ice.

The red and white Interceptor's 350 Magnum V8 thundered in the early morning solitude. The boat knifed through the smooth water at low speed in the darkness. He knew exactly where to go because he had envisioned it fifty times during his night of fitful near-sleep. Twenty-five minutes later he knocked on Nora's door. He did it again and again, eight or nine times in all.

"What do you want?" she said finally.

"I need to see you."

"Go to hell!"

"Let me explain last night."

"Just leave."

"Not before we talk."

He stood at the door for five minutes before going to the end of the driveway. From there he walked for a quarter-mile on the asphalt road before coming back and knocking hard on her door.

Silence.

He searched along her drive until he found a rock the size of a golf ball. Using his handkerchief as a pad so as not to damage the wood, he maintained a steady beat on her door. When he had done this for several minutes, something—it sounded like a pot or pan—banged on the other side of the door frame.

"I'll call the police!"

"Open the door."

"Stick it!"

"If you were half the woman you think you are, you'd open the door. What's the matter, can't handle a little rejection? I thought you were tough. Maybe you're just another blonde!"

The latch clicked. The door swung open.

"Who do you think you're talking to?" she said.

"Who do you think?"

"Fuck you!" She turned away.

He lunged in and kicked the door shut behind him. She strode to the kitchen, where she stood at the sink with her back to him. He approached her, put his arms around her and held her when she tried to twist away. She kicked him on the shin with her heel. Pain shot up his leg.

"Let go of me, you bastard!"

"I need you!" He buried his face in her hair.

"Too bad!"

"I'm sorry about last night."

"After you called, I went through hell trying to decide what to do, you son of a bitch. Because you're married, because I had a date, because of many things. I was only going to drive past MR's. But I parked and went in, hoping you'd left and hoping you hadn't. By the time we got here, I was so ready for you I thought I'd scream. And you ran away with your dick standing at attention. Well you can run again!"

He released her. She wheeled around and slapped him hard. His face contorted. He blinked back the stinging in his eyes. She touched his face.

He embraced her. "I thought of you all night. Every minute, every second!" He held her hand and took a step toward the hall to her bedroom. She jerked free.

"Don't you dare presume!" She pushed past him. "I'll lead."

When she entered the bedroom, she flipped a switch next to the light switch. A moment later, "Fanfare for the Common Man" filled the room. Next to her bed, she unbuttoned his shirt, peeled it from him, unbuckled his belt, tugged his pants down over his hips and let them drop to the floor. She pulled his briefs down to his ankles. While Phil removed his shoes, she untied the belt on her robe and let it fall to the floor. A moment later the satin sheets intensified his arousal. Her scent intoxicated him even more than it had last night. The minty taste of her tongue told him she had used mouthwash only minutes earlier. Her veneer of control evaporated.

"Touch me there, there! Keep doing that!"

Her desire and energy were greater than before.

"Do me! Do me!"

Lost in her own ecstasy, she seemed to derive pleasure in a way that had nothing, necessarily, to do with him, but it didn't matter. Soon, too soon, he crested like a flash flood in a sun-parched arroyo, and thirty years of fidelity vanished.

The sound of running water was muffled, as if coming from a long distance, but the thrilling notes of the "William Tell Overture" were far from muted. Nora nudged him.

"Come shower with me."

Wondering about her choice of music, but excited by it, he rolled off the bed and followed her to the shower with images of the Swiss Alps and the Lone Ranger racing through his brain.

They lathered each other and moved in and out of the force of the spray. Nora rubbed her breasts across his chest, and slowly caressed him from his thighs to his temples.

"Lock your arms behind my neck," he said. He lifted her to him and cradled her buttocks in his hands. She wrapped her legs around him in a scissors hold, grasped his arms and leaned back against the shower wall so that he could enter her. Impaled on him, she tightened her grip on his arms and moved on him and against him in a way he had never known. He did everything he could to hold off but didn't last long, just long enough. When she came a moment later, she bit him hard between his neck and shoulder.

"Lie with me," she said after they had toweled each other. They lay on her bed as the sun rose in the morning sky and flooded the room, along with the insistent sensuality of Ravel's "Bolero." Even in his fog of sexual satiation, Phil sensed he was more the seduced than the seducer.

"What are you thinking?" she asked.

"I'm not." How could he possibly articulate the jangle of half-thoughts and fears and recriminations assailing him, the silent scream that wouldn't stop?

She kissed him on the throat and snuggled against him. After a while, they got up and stood at one of the large windows. Lake Minnetonka glistened blue and silver in the distance through the trees.

"Are you sure no one can see us?"

"Not to worry, it's special glass." She slipped into a billowy dress of yellow muslin. "Join me in the kitchen."

Earlier, the groundwater of reality had begun to seep into the drywell of spent passion. Now it poured. If only Ellen were frigid or shrewish, a witch, a bitch—anything that would fractionally sanction what had happened. Could he contain this infidelity in its own small compartment, without repetition and without meaning? What effect could one day have on three decades? And what about David? *Christ, what about David? If he ever found out... And Jessica? Dear God!*

"Coffee's on," Nora called through the doorway. "Or you can have herbal tea. I'll be right back."

He dressed and had read part of the Sunday paper by the time Nora returned with fresh croissants. These were joined minutes later by piping hot strips of pastrami, cream cheese, honey, raspberry preserves, wedges of cantaloupe and cold whole milk.

"Any good news in the paper?"

"I don't remember a thing I read. You have enough food for a battalion."

"I try different combinations every Sunday. Have some."

"How do you stay so slender?"

"Exercise. And, uh, you know." She arched an eyebrow.

He kissed her and cupped her breast. She fondled him. He broke away and waited for his breathing to slow.

"You drank hot water that first day in my office. Any significance in that?"

"Absolutely none. I'm not much of a coffee or tea drinker, but hot water soothes my throat and relaxes me."

After they had eaten, she showed him her studio by daylight. They stepped outside and began walking toward the bushes and a stand of trees that surrounded her lawn.

"Painting and computers. Which do you enjoy more?"

"Hope to make my living by painting one day. Not as an escape from computers, but to escape other peoples' schedules and rules. I can paint anytime, anywhere, and the finished product will endure. Nothing lasts in the computer world. Hardware is virtually obsolete as soon as you install it. Have you ever noticed the deterioration rate of computer paper? Worse than newsprint. There has to be something in life more lasting than that."

"Your beauty will last."

"Ha! That will disappear faster than today's technology." She took his hand. "Don't get sentimental."

He turned to face her. "I can't imagine your beauty not existing."

She tugged his hand. "Time to walk." They walked in silence until Nora squeezed his hand and leaned up to kiss him on the cheek. "Let me explain something important. I grew up dirt-poor. My parents hated each other and shouldn't have stayed together. Why they did, I'll never know. I think marriage made them the way they were. I was lucky. One of my high school teachers worked her buns off to get me an academic scholarship, my ticket out. As much as I love my painting, I would trash it to survive financially. I'd do it without hesitation. I'll never be poor again, will never get locked into a limiting situation."

They followed a path through the woods and over a small rise. They looped back, crossed a road and reached a marsh. Nora knew the names of the trees and birds and even the ground animals that had left markings on the ground. Her delight in seeing and knowing them was evident.

"Nature. Another counterweight to commerce and convention," she said.

Back inside, she served hot spiced cider.

"My own version. A cross between applejack and a Swedish spiced wine we had when I was a kid. Like it?"

"It's delicious."

"One product disclaimer: There's a touch of demon rum in this grog. For character. And stimulation."

"Unnecessary. I know you're naked under that dress."

They made love for the last time on a thick sheepskin spread before a low fire in the den. Afterwards, he sat up and looked at her. She moved her legs so that he could see her better, and cupped her breasts with her hands.

"I love your body. Your beauty will never fade. It would be too great a loss."

Nora put a finger to his lips and shook her head. A clock on an end table glowed red. David might be up by now.

"What's wrong? You tensed," she said.

"I need to go."

"Mmmmmm. Wish you didn't."

"I want to sleep and see you as soon as I open my eyes."

"Me too."

He kissed her eyes, her hair, her lips, her breasts. Only the thought of David kept him from staying.

He dressed and returned to the Interceptor. The water was smooth except in a few spots where the breeze ruffled it. While he crossed the lake at low throttle, an old refrain came to him again and again. It was from childhood when someone tried an April Fool's joke a day late: *April Fool is past, and you're the biggest fool at last!*

Chapter Thirty-Six

Winter succumbed, after several blustery protests, to the gentle insistence of spring. The move to Bloomington succeeded beyond expectations. Two employees quit before the move, and two or three more would probably leave in the months ahead due to their longer commute. Most employees, however, liked the new location because they lived on the south side of the city and neighboring suburbs, which meant a shorter drive to work, to say nothing of free parking.

Marty's side of the business had picked up handsomely. Borglund's retainer made the debt on the new computer system manageable and also provided a nice cash flow. They paid off the swing loan. The new system proved efficient and cost effective.

Accurate information flowed in from Borglund Enterprises. Phil and Marty met often with Borglund, who was pleased with the energy devoted to the project. Ellen continued taking a full load of courses for her degree, and devoted most of her scant free time to church activities.

Impatient to graduate, Jessica hoped to be accepted by Northwestern University. More immediately, she lived on a cloud because one Barry Groves had asked her to the prom. David was holding his own at the U, and every time the phone rang it seemed another girl was calling him.

Maybe it was time to approach Bob Aagard, dean of the law school, about a teaching position a year or two down the road. They had talked about it casually in the past. Aagard had not shown much enthusiasm, but they had talked. Of course, the Borglund project made all other options possible, so it had to stay at the head of the line. Once that was wrapped up, Phil could sell out to Marty in installments. He and Ellen would have summers free, a quarter of each year to re-create. If they began to set some money aside, they'd be able to make it with ease financially. Money, professional position, and time to enjoy it: what winning was all about.

Where did Nora fit into these plans? He had no answer. The affair couldn't go on like this indefinitely. What if Ellen found out? What if Borglund did? Or Marty? He did not have answers, did not even want to pose the questions, let alone dwell on the consequences. They were always there, though; hovering, lurking, ready to strike without notice, which they did with regularity, no matter how hard he tried to keep them at bay by ignoring them.

He left for the office by five every morning, including Saturday. He had to in order to get the work done. And to free up time for Nora. His feelings for her were in an uncharted region of emotional schizophrenia. On the one hand, he couldn't wait to see her and couldn't get enough of her. On the other, the guilt fed an equally consuming anxiety. He thought of her as soon as he awoke each morning, thought of her dozens of times during the day, and she filled his thoughts in bed at night until sleep came. Yet, he daily vowed to break off the affair. Only the sheer volume and intensity of Borglund's work enabled him to maintain any semblance of equilibrium. By turn she energized and enervated. Was it like this on drugs? He wanted to die every time he looked at Ellen or the kids. A moment later, he would find himself luxuriating in sensual thoughts of Nora.

They met often for lunch at out-of-the-way cafes in the Cities and in nearby towns like Shakopee, Stillwater, Anoka and Lakeville. Nora knew an endless number of delightful rendezvous that served good food and were unlikely to be frequented by his friends and clients. They had met today on short notice at Figlio's in Calhoun Square. Hardly a chic place, or discreet, but convenient, and they could pass for business associates, which, in fact, they were. From their window table, they had a perfect view of the noon crowd at the intersection of Lake and Hennepin.

"You've got to stop sending me so many cards," Phil said. "I love them, they make my day, but you send too many."

The cards—humorous, teasing, erotic—arrived in brown envelopes with typed *personal and confidential* mailing labels. Once in a while she sent a love poem. On one occasion she enclosed the smallest imaginable pair of bikini panties, another time a condom.

"I like sending them. I see them and I think of you."

"Two came yesterday. Ruth is getting suspicious."

"I'll send only two a week."

"One."

"Once in a while two?"

The teasing, expectant look on her face, aided and abetted by the sheer white blouse she wore, brought a wave of arousal. He covered her hand with his.

"What a work of art you are. Save the second one and give it to me when we meet. Now tell me everything you've done since I saw you."

Nora shook her head. "Time out. You know my life story. What about yours? Born in South Milwaukee. Then what? You're so guarded about yourself and your family."

"Actually, I was born in Gary, Indiana. My father worked in a steel mill there. Didn't want me to grow up and work in the mill, so he moved to South Milwaukee for a job with Bucyrus Erie. Work just as tough as the mill for less pay. Must be a Polish joke in there somewhere."

"Polish?"

"It wasn't always Tag. That's only short for Taglowski. My father was more American than apple pie and Chevrolet, but he wasn't born here. Came over when he was five. Loved music and played a trombone in a band to raise extra cash. He'd planned to name me after James C. Petrillo, a long-time president of the American Federation of Musicians. But in the hospital when I was born he bumped into Phil Cavaretta, a first baseman for the Cubs back in the forties. So just like that I became Phillip James Tag. Not too emotional, my dad."

"He sounds delightfully impetuous. Does he still live in South Milwaukee?"

"Both my parents are gone."

"I'm sorry. So, Phillip James Tag, what came after that leadoff home run?"

If she knew I raised her child, how would she react? Wouldn't it violate something between her and David? Between her and me? David and me?

"Hello? Anyone home? You have a habit of leaving me."

"Sorry. My life is pretty dry stuff."

"Got a skeleton or two in your closet, that it? Cross my heart, I won't tell."

"My older brother died in a car accident. I ended up getting a last-minute partial baseball scholarship to Marquette."

"Your naming was an omen. I'll bet you hit home runs."

"Ha! My baseball career was a strikeout. Broke my elbow before our first game, and it never healed right. End of baseball. Ellen held a nursing job at a nearby hospital, so I finished my degree with a double major in four years."

"When did she possibly have time to become a nurse?"

"She went into training right out of high school. She's three years older than I am. We came here in a U-Haul truck."

"Your children are Minnesotans."

"Native as loons."

"Are they handsome like their father, or beautiful like their mother? I'm sure Ellen's beautiful. Do you have a picture? I'm insanely curious."

"No," he lied, and quickly continued. "I practiced law for a few years before getting into the insurance business, and here we are."

Nora picked at her salad. "Do you enjoy what you do? Want to do it the rest of your life?"

"The years ahead should be comfortable."

"But unsatisfying."

"Does it show?"

She lowered her chin a degree or two and waited for him to answer his own question.

"I might teach. Law fascinates me. Not so much the nuts-and-bolts daily routine, but its history and theory, its evolution. I like research and writing, seeing it all come together, which it ultimately does. I like an academic environment—the energy and vitality. It's what Ellen wants, too. It'd be tough to walk away from what Marty and I have built. But I've wanted to teach law since I was in law school."

"How are you getting along with the Impressionists?" she said, referring to a coffee table book she had given him that he kept in his office.

"They fascinate me. I always wanted photographic detail in art; thought the Impressionists were sloppy. Now they've opened up a whole new world. I'm getting hooked on them. Your timing was perfect."

"You needed a fresh look, a new beginning."

"It's hard to believe those people in the paintings were once so alive, only to grow old and die after their brief time in the sun."

The warm spring day had brought people out in droves. Glancing across the street, he saw Wade Lankar fumbling with a parking meter. Lankar cuffed the meter with the heel of his hand, gave it one last look and checked his pocket for something before he strolled down Lake Street toward Hennepin, a long camera lens jutting up from his belly like a dildo.

"Is something wrong?" Nora said.

"I just saw a man who used to work for Lars Borglund. Name of Lankar."

"Mmmm. I met him. Never had to deal with him directly but saw him in action several times. Know what he did in a meeting once? Ate a bag of popcorn. Tacky enough, but when he finished it, he tilted the bag up and tapped the bottom to get all the crumbs, then spit the kernels back into the bag. What a pig."

"Doesn't surprise me in the least."

"But he's a very smooth and sophisticated charmer, too. When he was around Borglund, he was completely proper and professional. I suspect he handles himself that way whenever circumstances dictate. He's a cutthroat."

"But you said you never dealt with him directly."

"I once met with some of his direct reports to gather information I needed. Lankar wasn't there. Anyway, one of his guys—it was a young woman, actually—came up with a truly ingenious idea—it really broke new ground in several ways—and I complimented her at the time and, later, in writing. Months later, I became aware that, beyond any doubt, Lankar had taken credit for the whole concept insofar as Borglund was concerned."

"Hard to imagine how he could keep good people."

"He may have treated the woman fine. Who knows? He might have given her a hefty raise. But in Borglund's eyes, Lankar was the creative star. He somehow finessed it. As I say, he can be smooth. Did I mention I've worked with three of Borglund's companies? Still work with one."

Lankar disappeared into the crowd.

"Lankar is part of the reason I'm in Minnesota," Phil said. "I turned down better offers and came to the U for a number of reasons. I liked Minneapolis and it wasn't too far from my parents, but in my heart of hearts I'd have to admit that I came because Lankar was here. It's an old grudge from college."

"Must be some grudge to last this long."

"Like it happened yesterday. He humiliated my father and hit me with a pitch on purpose. That's how my elbow got broken. It ended my chance for a full scholarship and my dream of playing pro ball."

"Can't blame you for hating him. Can you get away at all this weekend?"

"Not a chance."

"Then I'll paint furiously Saturday and go to church on Sunday."

"Church?"

"You're surprised."

He shrugged. "Which one?"

"A different one almost every week." She laughed at his incomprehension. "The different rituals fascinate me. So do the varieties of architecture. Of course, I have favorites for special times like Christmas and Easter."

"But don't you feel—don't you miss a sense of belonging? Of community?"

"Not in the least. Each Sunday starts with adventure. I don't need the social involvement of religion. I want the liturgy, the pageantry. I suppose one day I'll settle into a church and join the Ladies Auxiliary, but not yet."

"So you have religious feelings."

"Of course. God's in the world. There's proof everywhere."

Phil winced and finished his iced tea. He twirled the ice cubes in the glass.

"Are you grimacing or just thinking hard?"

"I didn't go to mass that Sunday after returning to your place. First time I've missed in years. The next Sunday I received communion and almost choked on it."

"Had you gone to confession?"

He shook his head.

"So in your church's eyes you committed a sacrilege."

"And every Sunday since."

She shoved a spoon across the table. It banged into a salt shaker and caromed off the table to the floor. "The transgression is against your wife, not the church."

Phil snaked a finger between his neck and collar where the fabric chafed his skin. "Liturgy satisfies one hunger. And sex another?"

She looked incredulous, then furious. "A real *non sequitur* and a cheap, cheap shot. Are you as hypocritical as your church? They all are, but yours is the worst. The cardinal sins—what a joke. You can be as lazy as a tomcat, eat yourself into a stupor, drink until you're blind—no problem, so long as you're sexually pure everything is hunky dory."

"It's not that simple."

"How can you belong to a church like that? Of course sex is important, and it's none of the church's business. I have no problem doing it all night and going to church in the morning. Where's the conflict? It's a gift from God. We'd be ungrateful not to use it. It's so natural you'd think, with all their chatter about natural law, they'd be all for it. My God, all of human history has been a struggle to dominate and enjoy Nature."

"Please keep your voice down."

"Just as reason is a gift. Don't you think God wants us to use the very faculty that separates us from all other life forms? Our leaps of faith should land squarely in the garden of reason."

Phil glanced around. No one was paying any attention to them.

"The Christian church from day one has tried to suppress our natural instincts, especially sex. We're genetically promiscuous, but the church and society demand social monogamy."

"There's something to be said for rising above certain inclinations. Isn't that what civilization is all about?"

Nora laughed. "Here we are, debating doctrine. As if we could solve the ancient mysteries over lunch. You're the first married man I've ever had an affair with. Oh, there've been a few one-night stands, but no affairs. I willingly gave myself to a boy when I was fifteen. He was going to the Marines, couldn't wait to enlist, and I wanted his child. He married someone else. There's no logic in it, none whatsoever, but I vowed never to have anything to do with a married man. Marriage itself never appealed to me. Maybe because I grew up in a bad one. And married men held no attraction for me. If I disliked politics, would I find a politician attractive?"

"Please stop."

"Am I prattling?"

"Nothing you do disappoints me."

"That's what you say."

"You had his child."

"Twenty years ago next month. Gave it up for adoption."

Don't go there! "Tough decision."

"Not really."

"I have a business dinner Tuesday evening. May I see you?"

"Why are you changing the subject?"

"I guess it's making me…uncomfortable."

"Why?"

"It just is. Will you be free?"

"Available, yes. Free, never." She smiled. "If a woman you loved deeply were devout in a different faith, would you convert if she wanted you to?"

"I would."

"Some open windows then, in your storm-shuttered house of orthodoxy."

"Never thought of it that way."

"Would you be comfortable with it, or forever feel guilty?"

"If I loved her I'd be okay with it."

"So it gets back to your relationship with the person, not the church. I rest my case."

"You gloss over complexities like a sports car blazing past road signs."

Nora glanced away and then locked her eyes on his. "Life travels the interstate. Only theologians and the befuddled rove the back roads of doctrinal nuance. They argue and debate scripture until their last breath. You could lay them all end to end, and they still wouldn't reach a consensus, let alone truth. It's all interpretation and speculation. Our choice is to be believing agnostics or unbelieving agnostics. So why should the monks of the world have any credibility?"

"Details can find truth."

Nora leaned forward. "What's our truth? What effect would details have?"

"Maybe a great deal."

"Oh? How so?"

"I'm not sure."

"You're evading again. For someone who believes there's truth in details, you never get into any. You are one close-to-the-vest guy, Mr. Tag."

The look on her face was the same as it had been at the Calhoun Yacht Club. He couldn't read it and he was tired of fencing. He took thirty dollars from his wallet, dropped it onto the table and said, "I'm late."

She scooped up the money and slapped it into his hand. "It's my turn."

"Get it next time. I've got to go."

"I'll get it *this* time."

"What's the difference?"

"You'd never figure it out." She threw thirty of her own to the table. "I'm out of here."

She slid from the booth and swept out of the restaurant without a backward glance.

Chapter Thirty-Seven

Nora cut the throttle. The small aluminum boat from Gray's Marina plowed ahead for a few yards. When its forward motion stopped, it bobbed and rocked in the light chop on the lee side of a gentle bluff that rose up from the water.

She raised an old rod and reel and cast a lure toward shore. After leaning the rod against the gunwale, she uncased a pair of binoculars and draped the strap around her neck. Dressed in old slacks and shirt, a floppy straw hat and a pair of large, pink-framed sunglasses, she could have been anyone, young or old.

On the bluff, immaculate lawns sloped away from large, well-maintained homes. There was little movement on shore because it was only eight in the morning. A man appeared in boxer shorts on a lakeside patio. He retreated through a doorway when he saw the boat. He came out a few minutes later, wearing a robe, to read his Sunday paper and drink coffee.

She knew exactly which house to watch. She had driven past the large brick two-story at least ten times in recent weeks. A woman in white shorts and a yellow blouse stepped through a door to the patio. She had a golden tan, long slender legs and a high, full bust. Nora raised the binoculars slightly. The woman was lovely. After examining the abundance of flowers on the patio, she reentered the house.

No one appeared for some time. A power mower started up in the neighborhood and howled away. To the left a man washed his car. Robins sang. An angry-sounding blue jay nearby overrode the robins' singing. A young girl came around the corner of the brick house. She too was a beauty. A moment later she retraced her steps and disappeared.

Nora must have been looking away, or lost in thought, for when she looked again he stood in full view. She knew the set of his shoulders, even from this distance without binoculars, knew the small buttocks and slender thighs that pleasured her to see and touch and cradle between her own.

She looked through the binoculars and felt her throat constrict when the broad shoulders and the shock of curly dark hair came illusively close. She trained her focus on the boy next to him. It took only a moment to confirm all earlier suspicions.

Phil, his arm around David, pointed to something overhead on the house. Suddenly, the two of them began to butt each other shoulder to shoulder, as if they were on the line of scrimmage in a football game. They stopped and entered the house laughing.

The water lapped against the side of the boat in bumpy little wavelets born of a rising breeze. Nora lifted the rod and dropped it into the lake. She started the motor, turned the boat around and headed across the bay to open water.

"God, Nora, what if he'd seen you?" Connie said over the Appleby's menu.

"He'd've never recognized me. I had to go. I knew what I'd see before I went, but even so, it was a jolt seeing them together. Hard to describe; there I was, watching my kid with a man I desire as much as I did the kid's father. It makes me want him more. Crazy or what?"

"His wife has your son and your lover."

Nora slid her hands up and down the glass of iced tea on the table. Her fingers came away wet with condensation. "That, too. It doesn't matter so much up here." She tapped her temple. "Know what I mean?"

"She has them both."

Nora sipped her tea. "You oversimplify."

"Sure about that?"

Nora didn't answer.

With a polka band at one end, a rock band at the other and

food and drink everywhere in between, a cacophony of music, laughter and the conversation of hundreds of people filled the parking lot. Rides and games attracted small children and teenagers, and a flea market flourished inside a huge tent. The St. Bernadette Spring Bazaar had attracted what appeared be its biggest turnout ever.

Phil strolled through the crowd alone, enjoying a rare Saturday off. He knew Ellen was handling an endless stream of minor emergencies that kept threatening the perfect result of her months of planning.

"There you are, Tag. Man, you've been a real stranger," Don Boyd said.

"Hi, Don. How've you been?"

"Just great. Looks like Ellen's done a fantastic job."

"Thanks. Where's Carlene?"

"Believe she's in the tent buying some junk. Last I saw, she was talking to Ellen."

A young couple sauntered past, the boy's hand on the girl's backside.

"By the way, you rascal, who was that fox I saw you with a while back over in Stillwater?" Don said.

"What?"

"About two weeks ago, at noon. I yelled, but you were going around a corner and didn't hear me. I was with some people, so I couldn't run you down. But your friend was something else." He elbowed Phil in the ribs. "You getting that?"

"Must have been a client."

"Sure looked like you were enjoying your work."

Phil waved Boyd off and drifted toward the polka band. He would have to be more careful. If Don Boyd had seen him and Nora together, how many others had? Lost in thought, he looked up just in time to avoid bumping into Father Banning and Ellen.

"Hi, Father. Looks like a money-making turnout."

"Ah, yes. Ellen has done a magnificent job." He glanced from left to right and didn't seem to know what to do with his hands. Why was he so ill at ease? No, he wasn't ill at ease; he was nervous and downright uncomfortable.

Smiling, Phil watched the priest closely. "She's sure put in some long hours planning it. I'm glad it's paying off."

"Yes, yes. I am, too. If you'll excuse me, both of you, I have to check on a few things." The priest hurried off towards the throbbing rock band at the other end of the parking lot.

"I didn't mean to scare him off, El. He looked like he'd seen a ghost."

"I think the Bazaar has made him paranoid. I'd better scoot inside and take care of things. See you at home."

For some reason he couldn't put his finger on, Phil couldn't dispel a tangible sense of apprehension. Why would he make their pastor so nervous?

Chapter Thirty-Eight

Bells rang nearby. Jubilant, jangling, Easter Sunday bells. A naked man walked with two clothed women along a stream in the sunshine. The man remarked on the bells, that they sounded different. When he said that, one of the women began talking dramatically but inaudibly. She turned away, still mouthing words, while the other woman acted as if she had heard nothing and kept walking. The women, the creek, the sunny day faded. The bells continued ringing.

Phil reached to the nightstand and turned off the chime alarm. Ellen stirred.

"What time is it?" she asked.

"Four-fifteen. Stay in bed, El."

"I'll make coffee. I can nap later."

It would be futile to protest. She insisted on getting up with him during the week. Borglund's business forced him to get up earlier than ever. It was about the only thing he and Marty worked on any more. He went downstairs and poured a glass of orange juice.

"Would you like toast?" Ellen said when she joined him.

She wore more makeup these days. Not much, just eye shadow and liner and a touch of blush to highlight her cheeks, that was all, but it went on first thing before she came downstairs.

"No, thanks. Marty and I'll get a bite later."

"Is everything okay at the office?"

"The two new people are a good fit."

"We don't know you anymore. The kids have been great about it, but it can't go on forever, Phil."

"Gosh, El, the kids are so busy doing their own things, I can't imagine my hours meaning much to them."

"You really believe that?"

"It was true when I was that age. My dad worked, I went to school or work and was always with my buddies in between."

"Is there something else, Phil? Other than work?"

"Hell no!"

"Honey, you don't have to bite my head off. I only asked you a question."

"It's five in the damn morning."

"Something has changed," she said. "I don't know what, but it has. Even when you're here, which isn't often, you're off in a world of your own. And you're short with me so often. It's not like you. What's happening to us?"

"I think you're imagining things."

"Am I?"

"I'd better get going." From the corner of his eye, he caught a movement in the doorway. "Hi, Jess. You're up early." He crossed the room and hugged her. "See you tonight."

"Why are you and Mom fighting again?"

He hugged her tighter and closed his eyes. "We're not fighting, honey. It's just morning grumpiness."

"I think there's grumpiness all the time in our house."

He glanced at Ellen, who turned away. Phil released Jessica and strode to the garage. He backed the car out vowing once again to quit seeing Nora. Ellen was right. Something had changed. As much as he loved Ellen, his thoughts focused on Nora. She was the object of his desire. All of his desire? Pretty much. He loved Ellen. Did he love Nora? Yes. Can you love two women at the same time? Probably not for long. It had to stop. The lunches, the movie matinees, hurried art exhibits, visits to her home—all of it had to stop, especially the trips across the lake. It was so easy, under the guise of going boating or fishing, to jump into the Interceptor and race across the lake to her. If they hadn't planned it beforehand, he'd stop at Gray's Marina to call ahead, rather than use his cell phone. She never told him not to come. If she didn't answer, he was devastated. Yet, it was all so wrong, so terribly wrong. Wrong and unfair and selfish. It had to stop.

By the time he pulled into his reserved parking space, he wanted to see Nora so badly he could hardly stand it.

Ellen put her arm around Jessica, who was crying. “It’s okay, honey, don’t worry. Things will be fine.”

“No they won’t. Everything is all mixed up, all messed up. Why can’t we be a happy family?

Ellen hugged her harder.

At eleven-thirty Marty suggested lunch. They drove to Vescio’s in St Louis Park.

“Sarah’s using drugs,” Marty said as soon as they had ordered. “She admitted it last night.”

“Jesus, Marty, not Sarah!”

Sarah, that lovely, full-of-life girl who had developed into a remarkable young lady, an outstanding student, a budding singer. Marty and Liz had always worried about their devil-may-care son Steve, who was now eighteen and doing fine. But Sarah….

“We called Renaissance and made an appointment for three this afternoon. What should I expect?”

Marty had to be dying under his calm demeanor. Always, the more worried he was, the calmer he appeared. Sarah, the sparkling jewel of his life! How radiant she had been at her Bat Mitzvah. No one could ask for a sweeter disposition in a human being.

“They’ll explain the program and get some forms completed,” Phil said. “You’ll meet with a counselor. After that, a family lecture once a week, family therapy weekly and two all-day Saturday sessions.”

“She goes every day?”

Phil nodded. “School in the morning, dependency counseling in the afternoon.”

“How’s David doing?”

“Still turning the corner. He’s held onto the UPS job. Grades are passing. Big milestones.”

"By the way, *amigo,* your new-found interest in computers hasn't gone unnoticed. Ruth tells me you're becoming a whiz."

It was Marty's way of turning the conversation away from his problems, so Phil turned with him. "Hardly. Just trying to keep up with technology."

While they talked, the three years with David came back, a sledge hammer to the gut. How a good kid had slid to the edge of a precipice and dropped off. Was he an alcoholic? It wasn't a certainty. David always denied having a physical craving, but it was undeniable that when he drank, he drank to excess. Drank to excess? Hell, he couldn't stop and got bombed out of his skull. The only safe course for him was to abstain one day at a time for the rest of his life. Dear God, how unending that road must look to someone so young.

Phil climbed into the Lund bass boat, one of the two power boats he kept for their use on Lake Minnetonka. He pushed clear of the pier while David steered and throttled up. June had come and nearly gone, and this was their first time fishing together.

"I'm glad you wanted to go, Dad. They bit like crazy off the point at Lafayette Bay yesterday. Let's try it there first."

"Let her rip, son."

The fish didn't bite. David changed spots every fifteen or twenty minutes, and they both changed lures repeatedly, but the fish weren't interested. Nor would David rise to Phil's attempts at conversation. He got irritable instead. Finally, he took his binoculars from their case, slouched down in the swivel chair, propped his feet on the rail and scanned the water, while ignoring Phil. "There's a pair of loons," he said after a bit.

"Any young ones?"

"Nope."

David had loved to use binoculars since adolescence, especially on the water. Smiling, Phil recalled the time he caught David at thirteen watching a woman lying topless on the bow of a large cabin cruiser.

"Hey!" David said.

His rod slid across the gunwale at an angle, its tip jerking and bending to the water. In quick, coordinated movements he set the binoculars aside, grabbed the rod and crouched into position.

"Get the net, Dad! It's a beaut!"

The fish dove under the hull, shot out on the other side and broke the surface with a swirl. It went deep, then exploded into the air again and ran off ten yards of line before David skillfully retrieved it to the side of the boat and into the waiting net. He'd caught a trophy largemouth.

David slipped the bass onto the hook of his tackle box scale.

"Wow! Almost six pounds!"

Handling the fish carefully, David put it on the metal stringer and lowered it gently into the water.

"We'll bring it home and take pictures, Dad. Then we'll release it. Wow!" He checked his lure and began casting from a standing position.

"It's kind of like golf, Dad. You can have four or five rotten holes in a row, and you want to quit the game forever, then all of a sudden you shoot a birdie and think you can beat Tiger!"

Phil laughed.

"I've really felt great lately, Dad. Not all the time, but most of the time. I know I can handle college, and know I can stay off the stuff. Never had so much confidence, know what I mean?"

Phil nodded and swallowed a large lump in his throat.

"I'm not sure yet, I mean I have to give it a lot of thought, but I think I'd like to go into counseling. I could help kids with problems. Kind of, just like that fish, most kids are keepers, don't you think?"

"I do, son. I sure do."

He wanted to throw his arms around his son and hold him for dear life. David's wide mood swings aside, Phil wanted to believe he would make it, would find the strength to create, to live and love. The fish had catalyzed this flood of hope. It, too, deserved to go free and live as Nature meant it to live. Phil looked over the gunwale. The fish lay on its side, its gills laboring.

"Give me a hand, son."

They took the bass off the stringer and moved it slowly

through the water so its gills could extract oxygen without too much effort. David was good at it, but in spite of his efforts, in the end the fish rolled belly up. It lasted another few minutes before it died. Phil put his arm across David's shoulders.

"The fight was too much for it, son. It broke him."

Tears streamed down David's face.

"You could have it mounted."

"No. I won't clean it, either, or leave it here for the turtles. I'll take it home and bury it."

Phil tightened his arm around David before releasing him.

"I don't want to fish anymore," David said. He started the motor and waited for Phil to sit down. Then he jammed the throttle forward and hurtled across the water.

Phil faced aft. The cool twilight air flowed over him. The wake trailed out white and churning before it died in the calm dark water.

Chapter Thirty-Nine

Waiters scurried from table to table amid the talk and laughter of customers. Tableware clinked and clattered. The aroma of fresh baked goods filled the air at Keys Cafe.

"I'll have the last three bids by Thursday," Marty said. "The biggest ones."

"Still looking good?"

"Better than good. Even better than I thought. If I can't save him five hundred thou, I'll run for Pope. It's hard to believe anybody was minding the store. Only a handful of agencies placed most of the business, one or two in particular. It's not like it was so scattered nobody could keep track of it."

"Same on the benefits side." Phil said. "Know what I'm thinking?"

"Same thing I am?"

Phil nodded. "We can't say a word to Borglund. Not even a hint. Let him reach his own conclusions. No wonder he was willing to pay so much. "

"We have a week to get ready."

A stout waitress, about sixty and wearing ornately framed glasses, brought their breakfasts.

"How's Sarah doing?" Phil asked when the waitress left.

"Hard to tell. She's beginning to settle down. I try not to let myself think about it during the day." He sipped his coffee. "How do the numbers look on your side?"

He would talk about Sarah when he was ready.

"I'll save a quarter-mil a year on benefits for openers. It gets really wild on the estate planning end. He'll save tens of millions in death taxes and settlement costs. And with what I've learned about the man, I could write a book."

"Skip the book and stick with the numbers. I haven't been this excited in years! I've got to add another benefits clerk and get her up to speed quick. We're going to make a bundle on this. It's our annuity."

"We'd better. If we lose it, we're in trouble. It's all we work on anymore. If we lose another account like Dalbarm, well, not good."

Marty reached over and cuffed him on the arm. "We won't lose it. It's a sweet deal you carried through the door. I'm buying a Beech Bonanza to celebrate. Found a beauty with low hours. Flies like a hawk."

"Expensive maintenance, the Beech."

"It's only money."

When Phil went to his car later in the warm sun of a flawless July morning, he nearly broke into a trot. He'd have to make time to buy a new car, maybe that red Corvette he'd always wanted.

In one of Lars Borglund's conference rooms, Phil advanced the PowerPoint slide and paused. Then, touching the screen with his pointer, he said in a measured voice, "Total annual savings for all insurance coverages and employee benefits will amount to nearly eight hundred thousand dollars. As we become more familiar with the various operating units, we should realize further economies. Your companies will also do less administration. We conservatively expect annual hard-dollar savings from that in the one-hundred-thousand-dollar range. We'll provide you with full documentation within sixty days."

Lars Borglund glared at the PowerPoint visual. Borglund's new insurance and employee benefits vice president, Tim Hollings, a likable man of thirty-five with JD, CPA and CPCU after his name, sat next to him.

"How did these costs run so amok?" Borglund asked in a quiet voice. "And for how long?" His eyes shone like cut diamonds behind the gold-rimmed glasses. "Was there collusion?"

"We have no way of knowing," Phil said.

"I know thievery when I see it. You have done excellent work. I will review your analysis and recommendations in detail with Mr. Hollings. Insurance and benefits will never get out of line again."

Tim Hollings shifted in his chair.

"Mr. Tag, are you still interested in considering a faculty position in the School of Law?" Dean Robert Aagard said on the phone.

"I'm committed to a project for at least eighteen months. I couldn't think of making a change before then."

"That should pose no problem. We are at least a year away from putting this together."

"Let's talk."

"I'll have a better grasp of the details in a few weeks. Perhaps we could get together in the next, ah, thirty days? I'll call you."

Like a huge muskie hitting your lure when you're reeling in to quit for the day, the law school opportunity had come from nowhere. Aagard had sounded civil, even friendly. A first for him.

Chapter Forty

Phil arrived home at seven.

"Where're the kids?"

"Jessica went downtown with Sue Larson. David's out fishing. He said he wouldn't be back till late."

"I thought I'd go fishing for a while."

"Again? I was hoping we could spend some time together for a change." She smiled. "You never catch any fish anyway."

"I'll only be gone a couple hours. Why don't you pick up a video? We'll watch it when I get back."

"No, because you'll come home and go to bed. All you do is work and sleep and read art books. Or go out on the lake. Have you become addicted to that lake?"

He didn't reply.

"Fine. Go." Ellen turned and marched from the room.

He threw his tackle into the Interceptor and started the motor.

Ellen watched Phil get into the boat and head toward the bay. When he got about a hundred yards from the dock, he increased the speed. The V-8 engine tore a long white rip in the dark water.

He had never been so buried in work for so long. Nor had he ever shown much interest in boating or fishing. On occasion he invited her along, but not in a way that meant he really wanted her to go. Maybe it was his way of relieving stress. Why else would he spend so much of his scarce free time in the boat?

She had few spare hours herself. It was impossible to get everything done during the day, so studies and church work always stretched into evenings. They were both under pressure, but that wasn't all of it. There was something else.

She looked out over the lake. A thought. Her breath caught in her throat. *Don't start imagining things, El. Phil would never. He's not that kind of man.* She turned, drew her white cotton sweater around her and hurried to the house. The breeze was chilly. There was work to do. Never again would she take on the Spring Bazaar. When she had her degree, they were going to become a couple again. Nothing was more important.

David sat in the Lund bass boat along the shoreline, just a cast away from the west shore of Spirit Island. He had found a school of bluegills and was pulling them in with every cast. Most were fries, but every eighth or ninth one was a keeper.

He was taking a nice one off the hook when he heard a boat scream around the point. Glancing over his shoulder, he saw the red and white Interceptor. He twisted in his seat and started to shout but didn't because of the distance and noise of the motor. His dad never ran the boat that fast. Something had to be wrong. David slipped the fish off his hook and tossed it overboard. He pulled in the stringer of fish, started the Johnson outboard and followed the dissipating wake of the Interceptor.

The Interceptor angled toward Robinson Bay, went straight to shore and disappeared. David goosed the throttle to catch up. The Interceptor curled into a small cove virtually hidden from view by a sliver of land that ran parallel with the shoreline. Dense lily pads lined the cove. It looked like a dynamite fishing spot.

His dad lashed the boat to a short pier two hundred yards into the cove, ran ashore and disappeared into the heavy foliage. Glimpses of a white building showed through the trees and bushes. Houses lined the cove, all isolated by trees, hedges and undergrowth.

There must be some emergency.

David dropped anchor. He stripped to his shorts and dove into the water. Two minutes later, he pulled himself onto the pier and lay on his back until he got his breath.

A set of steps went up toward the white house behind the trees. A sandy path to the right of the steps looked like a shortcut through the shrubbery. He started up the path.

A door opened. David froze. Voices. His dad's and another. The second voice sounded familiar, but he couldn't quite place it. They came into view and David stopped breathing. His temples pounded. His throat constricted. When he finally inhaled, his breath came in shallow drafts. He bit his lip and tried to control his quivering face.

She's none of his business. What's he doing here? What's going on? Does Mom know about her, too?

Was he the only one left out, so he'd had to find her on his own while they knew about her all along? Why would they deceive him like that?

What in hell is going on?

David stepped back to the path, his knees buckled and he nearly fell. He scrambled to the pier. He dove into the water, swam to the boat and climbed in. He lay exhausted and shivering for nearly an hour. The setting sun left the cove in shadow. Finally, he peeled off his briefs and yanked his dry clothes on. He brought the anchor up and started the electric trolling motor. The boat began to move quietly toward open water.

Two figures appeared on the path. They stood out against the dark background like two marble statues in a dimly lighted church. David flicked off the motor and uncased his binoculars.

His father and birth mother walked hand in hand to the end of the pier near the moored Interceptor. They embraced and kissed. His father's hands dropped down over the back of the woman's white slacks and pulled her to him. She turned slightly, reached down to the front of his pants and unzipped him. David set aside his binoculars and snapped on the electric motor.

As he drew near the mouth of the cove, he noticed a dark green flat-bottomed fishing boat lying next to a pile of brush against the opposite shore. A black tarp stretched across the boat, and a long, black barrel protruded from beneath it. A gun? Guns weren't allowed on the lake. Why would some idiot have one? It wasn't even hunting season. David looked over his shoulder. A loon with three chicks floated on the rippling water of the cove, safe from most predators in the gathering shadows of dusk. The breeze quickened. Thunder rolled in the distance.

The crash was part of a dream Phil would never remember. Ellen must have been partially awake, for she cried out and shoved him.

"Wake up! It's David! Something's wrong!"

Phil rolled off the bed. The digital alarm glowed two-thirty. Lightning flashed through the windows. Phil raced down the stairs and out the front door into a driving rain. He stopped. The Camaro had struck a garage stall partition. David was in no danger from the impact. That wasn't the problem, not even close.

Ellen came out in her robe.

"Wait there, honey," Phil said.

He opened the door of the Camaro and turned off the ignition and headlights. David sprawled across the console. Vomit covered the steering wheel and dash. Phil slid an arm around David and pulled him from the car.

"Can you stand, son?"

David's head rolled. At first, his arm hooked reflexively around Phil's neck. Then he pushed away. "Get away from me!" He staggered back and fell. Ellen bent over him and helped him to his feet.

"Oh, Mom, Mom. I'm so sorry!" He began to sob, quietly at first, trying to suppress it, then uncontrollably.

"It's all right, David. Let's go in."

She helped him to the downstairs bathroom where she cleaned him up. In his bedroom she undressed him down to his shorts, and put a clean T-shirt on him. He began to cry again when she helped him into bed, and reached out to her.

"Mom, I'm so, so sorry!"

Phil looked on while Ellen held David on the edge of the bed until he calmed down, then stayed with him until he fell asleep.

Later, she dried her eyes in the kitchen. "Why, after all this time? Why tonight? Why? Why?"

"Honey, it can happen after twenty years."

"I know that! But *why?* What happened? Something must have happened."

Phil leaned against the counter next to the fridge, wanting to reassure her but not knowing how. "We may never know, El. We might not want to know. Let's hope it's a one-time episode. I'll talk to him in the morning."

"How? Tell me how. You leave in the middle of the god damn night, Phil! All you do is work, work, work! This family is falling apart, and you don't even know it!"

"It won't be forever."

"Why do you deceive yourself? If it's not Borglund, it'll be some other big project. And if you go to the university, you'll bury yourself in work there, too. At least be honest about it. I'll teach, we'll go our separate ways and maybe, just maybe, we'll have a little time each summer to get reacquainted. But I doubt it."

"We'll have all summer every year. And more time during the year."

"I don't believe it anymore. I did for a long time, but not anymore. I'd chuck it all for two eight-to-five jobs. We could live in a smaller house, sell the boats—"

"We can't decide these things tonight. Let's go to bed. I'll stay in the morning and spend time with David."

He put his arms around her. She shoved him away.

"Don't patronize me! Damn it, don't you dare patronize me! Nothing makes sense anymore. How can we have so much and have nothing? David is drinking, Jessica is losing weight again, you're never around, we never make love anymore. What's happening to us?"

Her cry came in a high-pitched wail. She spun in a tight circle in the center of the room until he threw his arms around her. Her body went limp. Her crying trailed off. She wrapped her arms around his neck and held on as if begging him to protect her from the snapping jaws of unspeakable demons.

"All I want is for us to be together and happy. I don't need fancy cars and a country club. You know that, don't you?"

"I've always known that, El." Over Ellen's shoulder, in the shadows of the stairwell, Jessica shrank from the light of the kitchen. Phil released Ellen and hurried to the stairwell. He embraced Jessica. "Everything will be fine, honey. Please don't worry." Jessica offered no resistance, nor did she hug him back. She seemed distant and detached, catatonic. Ellen also threw her arms around her daughter. They remained in their awkward huddle for several long moments until Jessica said, "I want to go to bed now," in a flat, lifeless voice. Phil did not want to let her go. He did so only when Ellen did. Jessica climbed the stairs without another word.

Phil stayed awake deep into the night. The onslaught of self-recriminations would not permit sleep. They came at him in slashes and torrents, as though he were adrift in the North Atlantic surrounded by mountainous rogue waves. His stomach burned and perspiration beaded his forehead. He finally arose, put on a fresh T-shirt and went to the kitchen for a glass of milk and an apple. The storm thundered outside. He returned to bed and was hovering at the edge of sleep when something brought him to full wakefulness. He listened intently. What had made him alert? A sound? A smell? A flash of lightning? He knew only that it had occurred earlier, perhaps when he had dozed or had been lost in thought. Whatever it was, it wouldn't let go of him. Alighting from bed, he made his way to David's room and quietly opened the door. The lightning revealed David asleep in his bed.

A moment later, Phil stood over Jessica's empty bed. He checked the bathrooms, then every room in the house before hurrying to the garage, where he yanked on a pair of rubber boots and a rain coat.

The cold rain pummeled him when he closed the front door and leaned into the wind. Reaching the city sidewalk, he turned left and strode through the rain. There were no side streets on this stretch of road. After continuing for some ten blocks, he retraced his steps and proceeded in the opposite direction. How could he find her? She could be anywhere, and she probably had run rather than walked, so she could be miles away. Phil sloshed through the downpour block after block for more than three miles before he saw a dark form lying on the sidewalk in the dim light of a street lamp.

Chapter Forty-One

Phil ran as fast as he could in the heavy boots. When he got close enough, he recognized Jessica's royal blue and white jogging outfit.

"Jessica!" She didn't move. He got down on his hands and knees and cradled her in his arms. "Jessica? Talk to me! Please, honey!" Jessica's eyes rolled. Her whole body shook. "It's me, Jess. Daddy. Let's go home."

He gathered her up, but when she tried to stand, she buckled and fell to the ground with a cry of pain.

"What is it? What's wrong, baby?"

"My ankle, Daddy. I think my ankle's broken. It hurts really bad."

Cursing himself for not bringing his cell phone, Phil gathered her up in his arms and carried her to the nearest house. He laid Jessica on the stoop and rang the door bell again and again until the entry light came on.

In the emergency room, a young doctor swung the door open to the waiting area. Phil and Ellen jumped to their feet.

"It's a bad sprain. She'll be fine." The doctor paused. "How is her health in general?"

"Why?" Phil asked.

"She seems underweight and rather frail for a girl her age."

"She's anorexic," Ellen said.

"Please be seated," the young doctor said, motioning them to chairs. "Why was she out running at this hour in this weather?"

"She was upset," Phil said. "Her brother has some issues right now that she reacted to."

"I think you'd better stay on top of this. Start with your family physician, but have him refer you to a specialist. Have you worked with one before?"

They both nodded.

"Good. Her sprain will take some time to heal. She could become despondent, so don't wait. She became thoroughly chilled tonight. Her body temp was down, but that's fine now. The anorexia is a serious threat. I know you know that, but I can't emphasize it enough. Her life is in danger."

In the morning, Phil showered and shaved but instead of leaving right away for the office, he woke David.

"Let's talk about last night, son."

David buried his face in his pillow.

"Time to face the music, David. What happened last night?"

"I got trashed. So what?"

"Isn't that a big deal?"

"Let me sleep."

"Not until we talk about it."

David pulled the covers over his head. Phil touched David's shoulder. David jerked away.

"Don't touch me!"

Phil took a deep breath. "I want to know what's going on."

"No, you don't."

"David, let me help you."

"Oh, man, that's a good one. Right."

"Not the time to be a smart-ass, son. At least talk man-to-man."

David sat up. "Okay, Dad. Man-to-man, I don't want to talk right now. I can't. And you don't want me to. Take my word for it. Now let me alone." David twisted away and pulled the covers over his head once again.

What the devil was he talking about? Well, badgering would do no good. There was no sense pushing things into complete ugliness. Phil backed through the doorway and closed the door behind him.

* * *

"It's okay, Jess. It's okay. Things'll work out." David held Jessica in his arms on the floor of the family room. She wasn't crying, but tears still streaked her face. She rubbed her nose and swept the hair from her eyes.

"I don't think so," she said. "I did. I don't any more. I wish I knew what was going on. Do you know?"

"Just hang in there. That's all we can do. We have to stick together. You, me and Mom. Dad's crazy right now. Maybe he'll always be crazy. Who knows?"

"I wish it could be like it used to be, when we were all happy."

"Me, too, Jess. Me, too."

At the office, Marty was on the phone but waved Phil in.

"That's right, we'll have it for you by Monday. I received the agent-of-record letter yesterday. Okay. *Adios."* He hung up. *"Felipe,* my friend, we have good luck. *Tenemos suerte.* We are this close to making it official on Varspand. Nice account for us."

Phil winked.

Marty studied him. "What's up?"

"Just dropping in."

"You'll tell me sooner or later."

"Later, wetback. Congratulations on Varspand."

Phil left the office and drove downtown. It would feel good to get to the city for an hour without rushing to an appointment. On impulse he went to St. Olaf's. Father Wark was out. His thirtyish assistant had a manner that was too smarmy by half.

"I used to attend St. Olaf," Phil said. "I wanted to see Father Wark."

"Would you like to wait in his office? He should return shortly."

"No. No, thanks."

The priest drummed his fingers on his desk twice before catching himself.

"Thanks for your time, Father. I have an appointment." The last thing he needed was to spend time with an assistant pastor who probably didn't quite know the inning, let alone the score.

He drove to Flying Cloud, rolled the plane from the hangar, preflighted and taxied to the hold line. He flew over Lake Minnetonka and banked sharply to get an unobstructed view of the sailboats that reminded him of ivory arrowheads. Contrails of powerboats fanned out in all directions among the sailboats.

He headed south, cross-checked the heading indicator with the compass and flew to New Prague, where he turned south by southeast to race along the outer edge of the Minneapolis-St. Paul TCA to Northfield. From Northfield he looped around Cannon Falls and retraced his flight path to New Prague, tuned in his VOR to Flying Cloud and enjoyed the scenery.

That's what he liked about flying. You went by the numbers. You learned to fly that way, and you kept doing it. Instruments measured what had to be measured, you used good judgment on weather and you flew with confidence in the outcome. You kept the excitement while neutralizing much of the risk. You kept it as uncomplicated as possible.

When he approached Flying Cloud later, the tower cleared him for a straight-in approach for a touch and go. He stayed in the pattern for five more touch and go's before taxiing back to the hangar.

Instead of returning directly to the office, he went to the Foshay Tower. He flipped through an old Newsweek magazine while Lester finished shining the shoes of an old man in an outdated suit. Lester always signaled the end of a shine by pulling a cloth across the toe of each shoe and releasing one end to make the cloth crack like a whip. The old man paid Lester the exact amount of the shine and then gave him an extra quarter.

"Thank you very much, sir," Lester said, with no hint of irony. "You have a wonderful day now."

Phil climbed into the chair. "Louie said to say hello."

"Good morning, Mr. Tag. I saw the man myself Sunday. Why didn't he say hello his ownself?" Lester asked with a laugh.

Phil settled into the chair and relaxed. They made small talk while Lester applied saddle soap.

"How long have you been married, Lester?"

"Long time. Forty-one years next month."

"She must be a good woman."

"Oh, yeah. We're like a sweat suit. Comfortable."

"Ever loved another woman?"

Lester slapped his hand on the tin of black wax. He smudged the wax on the toes of Phil's shoes, along the sides and across the backs. "Thing about of it is, I didn't get married till I was thirty-nine. I loved lots of women before I married Janetta. None after that. Oh, some of them looked mighty sweet. But ol' Lester didn't need problems like that. No, sir. Bad enough, one woman mad at you." He chuckled and shook his head. "I don't understand how them Mormons and Muslims do it. Like the old song says, 'Is you is or is you ain't my baby?'"

Phil couldn't help laughing with Lester. He was better than having a psychiatrist. And the twenty dollars he handed the man was cheap at twice the cost.

Greta Pederson leaned across her desk.

"So what do you think you should do," she said, "now that you've called them both every name in the book?"

"I'd like to strangle them," David said.

"Not an option."

David kicked the front of her desk and grunted. He slumped into a chair.

"What can you do?" Greta asked.

"That's why I'm here! Why do you keep asking me questions? I don't know what to do. I hate them!"

"Okay, let me jump in. Number one, you can't let it knock you off the wagon. You okay there?"

David shrugged.

"Listen, young man: you've got to take care of yourself before anything else. No alcohol. End of lecture. Second, you don't want to hurt your mom. Third, you need to talk to your dad. And maybe your birth mother."

"My mom can't find out, know what I mean? Jeez, it'd kill her."

“What about the other two?”

David gripped the arms of the chair. “I don’t think I could talk to my dad. I can’t stand being around him, can’t stand the sight of him, know what I mean? No way could I talk to his … my … whatever. Jesus, she didn’t want me, now she wants the guy who did. I mean, is this crazy or what?”

“Things happen. Look at you and me. How do—”

“That was different!”

“Don’t you think everyone says that?”

David rose from the chair and shoved his hands in his pockets. “I can’t handle it. I want to yell at them and tell them what I think, but I can’t. God, my head hurts.”

“If you can’t talk to your dad right away, stay away from him. You’re liable to say something in front of your mom.” She came around the desk and put her hands on his shoulders. “What about your birth mother? Think you could talk with her?”

He stared at her for a long moment before shaking his head. “I couldn’t face her. Don’t ever want to see her.”

“Just let it rest for now. Call me anytime, David. Take care of yourself, okay? One more thing,” she said as he neared the door. “Try to be generous. Your dad’s been pretty forgiving, hasn’t he?”

He swept his hand across his face. “Everyone’s doing it with everyone. Wagner’s old man. My old man and my whatever. Like a big game of love tag or something. One person’s it, and then another. Just like the underwater tag we used to play in the pool. Un-bitching-believable. I feel like I’m underwater all the time.”

Ellen had always liked Dr. Patrick Fleming, an intense but affable man of sixty who had been the Tag family doctor for over twenty years and belonged to the same club.

“I’m referring you to Dr. Corvadd. He’s the best for this. Be sure Jessica maintains her intake. Balanced nutrition is ideal, but right now I don’t care if she eats nothing but pizza and potato chips for the time being. I exaggerate, of course. But you get the idea. Do you have any questions?”

"No. Thank you, Patrick."

"Say hello to Phil and David for me."

Ellen drove to the rectory after dropping Jessica off at home. Father Banning was with a parishioner, so she spoke with the secretary.

"I want a mass said for my daughter."

Just as she and the secretary finished up and were chit-chatting, the door to the priest's private office opened to reveal an elderly woman and Father Banning, who saw the woman off gracefully and insisted that Ellen come into his office. She told him about Jessica. "You know all about David. Now this. I don't know where it's going to end."

She didn't resist when he held her, but when she felt his lips on her forehead, she backed away. "I have to go home and take care of Jessica."

"Why did you come?"

"I'm having a mass said for her."

"You could have handled that by phone."

"I know."

"Let me hold you."

Ellen closed her eyes for a moment when he embraced her. Her shoulders sagged. "God knows I need holding right now, Father. But I have to get home to take care of my daughter." She gave him a hug. "Thank you." She squeezed his hand and made a hurried departure with the realization that she really didn't want to leave.

Chapter Forty-Two

"The phone's been ringing off the hook. Everyone's looking for you," Ruth said. "You have an appointment with Dean Aagard in forty-five minutes. I called and said you had a small emergency. You can still make it if you hurry."

Eleven phone messages littered Phil's desk. Ruth had probably handled three times that many in his absence. He didn't want to return calls or dig into the heap of papers on his desk. Nor was he crazy about seeing Aagard at the law school. He wanted to see Nora, wanted to make love to her until he was exhausted and then just look at her and touch her and hold her.

He paced around his office. Normandale Lake had changed from its midday glitter into a more formal late afternoon blue. In the distance Hyland Hills lay green and dappled. The flow of southbound traffic had begun to congeal on Normandale Avenue. The office would close within the hour. Phil turned from the window and went to Ruth's desk.

"Call Aagard and tell him I'm on my way. Thanks."

A stocky, balding man in his late fifties, Dean Robert Aagard had a national reputation for his knowledge of constitutional law. Behind the scenes locally, his tough-mindedness was legendary. He waved Phil to a chair.

"It was unfortunate to keep you in a state of, ah, suspension after my phone call, but I thought it best that we meet in person. Now then, we foresee increased demand in all areas of taxation, with particular emphasis on income, gift and testamentary taxes. It is the belief of our tax experts that the federal estate tax will reappear full force in 2011. With that in mind, I have every reason to believe that this position will be approved expeditiously. The entire situation arose and has developed somewhat beyond the parameters of conventional procedure, but that is neither here nor there. Suffice it to say that this expansion is, if you will, part of a pilot program that both the University and the School of Law will monitor closely as it progresses.

"Let me briefly describe the program. The ultimate incumbent will hold the rank of assistant professor. Promotion and tenure procedures will follow normal policies. The position will emphasize both research and teaching. It will further require that the incumbent devote twenty percent of his or her time to nonacademic activities—private practice, if you will, according to clearly defined parameters, which have not yet been I delineated and I therefore see no reason to speculate upon at this time." He waited for Phil's reaction.

"Would I keep any fees generated by 'nonacademic activities'?"

"That is correct." Aagard seemed to have something on his mind. "There is one other aspect of the arrangement that is, ah, unconventional. Our president naturally knows many, shall we say, influential people, not only regionally and nationally, but also locally. If and when the incumbent were to be promoted to Associate Professor, he or she would receive a nomination for membership in a country or other club of his choice. Acceptance, of course, would be at the discretion of the club itself. The University would bear none of the expense of membership, including any initiation fee, should the incumbent be accepted as a member."

"How does this entire arrangement go down with other faculty?"

Aagard slipped off his glasses, fogged them with his breath and wiped each lens with his handkerchief. "They may view the incumbent as somewhat removed from the academic mainstream, if you will. It would be up to him or her to overcome any, ah, animosities that might possibly develop in the perceptions of his or her peers."

"What are your feelings, Robert?"

Aagard resumed his lens polishing. When he finished, he held the glasses up to the light and squinted at them. He blew on each lens before putting them on.

"It is an arrangement which I believe could be very productive and bring credit to the institution, which after all, has been a leader in community activism since its founding. It certainly would be inappropriate for me to be, ah, unsupportive in any way. So long, of course, as no conflict of interest or other ethical problem were to arise.

"In accordance with University and public policy, we shall announce the new position and interview numerous candidates. This procedure will be rigorous, fair and nondiscriminatory. In light of previous conversations you and I have had, however, and in view of your publications and the fact that you are a valued and supportive alumnus, your viability became immediately apparent when this expansion began to appear necessary. Shall we keep in touch?"

"By all means."

Aagard was even more full of himself than Borglund was. Phil left the dean's office and ran to his car, where he immediately grabbed his cell phone. Nora answered on the third ring.

"May I see you early in the morning?" he said.

"Come now."

"Can't. Five-thirty tomorrow?"

"Come at five. We'll have more time."

David wasn't home when Phil got there. He still had not come home by eleven when Phil said he was going to bed. Ellen was working on a term paper and said she'd come up later. He knew she was waiting up for David, but David didn't come home.

A hint of autumn laced the air when Phil backed onto the street at a quarter to five and left for Nora's.

Ellen had been pleased when he told her about his meeting with Aagard. More pleased and responsive than he had expected, what with summer school finals and her concern for Jessica, who had been turned down by Northwestern and was working out and running constantly. Everything would get back on track again. It had to. He looked forward to fall, his favorite time of year, and even to winter. Maybe David's lapse wouldn't be repeated.

Nora stood barefoot in the wet grass waiting for him, wearing a sheer white negligee that swirled in the early morning breeze. She felt as light as a child when he swept her into his arms and carried her inside.

"Love me!" she said.

They made love urgently and intensely. Barry White's music permeated the room, the air, the bed.

"You shouldn't tell me you love me," she said afterwards.

"But I do." *And you gave me my son.*

She put her fingers to his lips. "Please don't.

He leaned on his elbow, his face close to hers. "I love the way you look, the way you laugh, your touch, your taste, your voice, your teasing, your everything. When I think of you, I don't care about anything else in the world. I want to tell the world!"

"Ellen, too?"

He fell back on the pillow.

"Sorry about that," she said. "Definitely bad taste." She leaned over him. "Let's be sinful, truly wicked: vanilla ice cream and Frangelico for breakfast."

Virtually every time he came to her she surprised him with something different to eat, typically an ethnic hors d'oeuvre. She never repeated what she had made previously, even if he requested that she do so. Whether oriental or European or Mediterranean, her choice was always delicious, and she prepared just enough to tantalize him and make him want more. He realized for the first time that the mounting, nearly unbearable anticipation he felt each time he went to her was an exquisite admixture of desire, hunger and curiosity.

While she prepared the liqueur and ice cream, he told her about the meeting with Aagard.

"Darling, that's wonderful! It's working out just as you wanted. What a coincidence."

"No, it's not coincidence. Not by a long shot. Know the best part? Remember Lankar? He'll be green with envy. Not just over the prestige of the law school or the Borglund money. He never wanted me in the world he grew up in. To him I was a blue collar Polack, and that's what he wanted me to remain. I wish my father were still alive. Not that he'd take pleasure in the situation, but I'd feel more vindicated."

"I've heard Lankar is still looking for work. And his wife is divorcing him."

"Couldn't happen to anyone more deserving. He was making more in kickbacks than he was in salary. Borglund figured that out."

"How does Ellen feel about the law school opportunity?"

His head jerked up. "Fine."

"I'm sorry. That wasn't fair."

"This is delicious."

A frown dented her face. "Lovers do strange things to each other," she said. "For a time after we met, you disliked me and acted tough and abrasive. Now that you have feelings for me, I see a vulnerable side."

"Nora, please."

"I'm trying to think it through. I've had dual involvements, but I've never been in a deep, caring relationship with two people at the same time. So it's hard for me to understand your situation. I want to." She took a spoonful of ice cream and kept the upside-down spoon to her lips. "I've always found the term 'mistress' detestable. I despise the idea of mistress, paramour—whatever."

"You're not my mistress."

"What am I?"

"You're a beautiful, passionate woman."

"I'm the other woman."

Phil dropped his spoon to the table and rose out of his chair. "Damn it, this isn't the nineteenth century! Another thing: you've got to stop sending me gifts."

"I think of you when I see things."

"Look, the cards were bad enough. They made Ruth suspicious even before the packages began arriving. And every time I see you lately, you have another present."

"But you give me gifts, too."

"That's different."

They both laughed. She sat on his lap and kissed him. The kiss left a smear of ice cream on his mouth.

"Don't get upset with me, darling." A smile tugged at the corners of her mouth. "Aren't we setting a record of firsts today? You said 'I love you' and here I am calling you 'darling.' Sounds nice, but we mustn't. Don't tell me you love me. I love it when you do, but don't. I don't want you to leave Ellen. If you did, would it be as good with us? Would it ever be the same? I've come close a dozen times to calling this whole thing off. For more than one reason. But I like us the way we are."

She reached inside his robe, the one she had bought for him. She rubbed his nipples with a finger, then nibbled them.

"One of us has to make a decision," he said.

"Not today." She massaged his chest and loosened the belt of the robe. They lowered themselves off the couch to the deep pile carpet.

"Wait," she said.

She left the room and returned moments later with a sheepskin. Barry White continued singing and talking in the background. Phil never knew the names of the songs, but White's voice was unmistakable.

"Remember this, when you came back that first morning? I put it away afterward. It's only for special occasions."

After spreading it on the carpet, she stood erect and shrugged her shoulders. Her robe fell to the floor. Her tanned body glowed like stained alabaster.

He held her face in his hands and kissed her while she undid his robe.

"Like a private cloud," she whispered.

He didn't hurry to the sweetness that would signal the beginning of the end of their passion. He couldn't touch her enough, or inhale as much of her scent or taste her as deeply as he desired.

"There!" she said. "Stay right there! Don't ever stop! Never! Oh, God!"

Afterwards, he braced on an elbow and cupped her face in

his hand.

"There's something I need to tell you."

"Well?" she said when he hesitated.

He toppled over on his back. "On second thought, it's nothing."

She arched over him. "Something is nothing?"

"It was personal, nothing I should burden you with. Please don't press me."

"Why won't you confide in me?" She lay back and folded her arms behind her head. "Does it have something to do with me? With us?"

"I move to strike it from the record as inadmissible."

"If you need to tell me, counselor, then tell me. Why not? Is it about your family? Ellen? The kids?"

"It was only a thought."

"Followed by second thoughts. You've done this so many times, and I hate it. I always have the feeling something's on your mind, something you want to share with me, but you always end up pulling back. Your version of *coitus interruptus*. Don't you trust me? Isn't it time you did?"

"More than I trust myself. Nora, please. Let it be for now."

"Okay, fine!" She rolled away from him and went silent for several moments before turning to him and kissing him on the cheek. "Know one of the things I found attractive about you right off? This scar under your eye. It looked like a fresh wound when we first met. How did you get it?"

"Just a little accident."

"Tell me."

He cupped his hand under her breast. "My son did it. We nearly drowned last year. He dug into my face trying to hang on. Then he ended up saving my life."

Nora sat upright and gazed intently into his eyes.

"What's wrong?" he asked.

She touched his cheek with a finger and traced a circle around it. She hovered over him and kissed the scar.

"Nothing. The thought of you drowning … such a lovely mark." She snuggled up to him, her breath warm on his throat. "Your son saved you?"

"He sure did." He closed his eyes. *If only I could tell her ... no, it would only make things worse. But I must. It's all so dishonest otherwise.*

Chapter Forty-Three

A determined night wind swirled and tugged at the sheers, billowing them into the room like sheets on a clothes line, then drawing them to the screen like a trailing breeze blowing a summer skirt against a woman's body.

Phil draped his arm over his eyes to shield them from the light of Ellen's reading lamp. Ellen dropped her book to the floor at the side of the bed.

"It's midnight. If he comes home drunk again, I don't know if I can handle it."

"Let's wait and see."

"We've done that for too long. We have to do something!"

Phil removed his arm from his eyes. "He's twenty years old, El. We can't do it for him. He won't even talk about it. I've tried a dozen times to get him to open up. When I force the issue, he gets belligerent. It's his deal, remember?"

Ellen swung her feet to the floor and went into the closet. She came out wearing her beige robe.

"I know he has to do it. I don't need you to tell me that. Why do you take it out on me?"

"What's that supposed to mean?"

"Don't you realize how critical you've been? Not just the last three weeks. All summer. It just gets worse when one of the kids has a problem."

Phil covered his eyes with his arm again.

"For over three years David put us through hell," Ellen said, "but we weathered it together. When he seemed to come out of it, we began to fill the vacuum by going at each other. Then everything was great for awhile after the two of you survived on the lake. As if new bonds had been forged, a new lease on life for all of us. But this summer has been awful, whether you want to admit it or not."

"Come on, El."

"Oh, let me count the ways. Let's start with your irritability and preoccupation—when you're here, which isn't often. You're always working, or out on the lake. You're not even here when you are here. You and David have turned into enemies. He won't stay in the same room with you. And what about Jessica? The poor kid can't figure out what's going on. She was on the verge of crying again tonight at the dinner table. Did you even notice? She's fussier than ever, eating like a canary and losing weight. You're blind if you don't see it. She's tied up in knots. And we never make love anymore. I feel so useless. Like an old, worn-out bitch!"

Their age difference. Once a point of gentle kidding, now an unwelcome topic.

"You know that makes no diff—Listen! It's David."

The sound of the Camaro came through the open windows.

"You go down," she said. "I can't."

Phil closed the bedroom door behind him and went downstairs. He intercepted David in the kitchen. David reeked of alcohol.

"Son—"

"Get away from me!"

Phil stopped short.

"I don't want you in my life!"

Phil grabbed him and pushed him against the fridge. "Listen up, mister! You know what you're doing to your mother, coming in like this?"

"What I'm doing? Oh, man, give me a break! What'll you do when the lake freezes over, use one of the snowmobiles?"

"What are you talking about?"

"As if you didn't know, you double motherfucker!"

"David! Watch your language!" Jessica cried from the doorway.

Phil froze. He released David.

"Why'd you do it, Dad? Why? Oh, God, I feel so sick!" He

began to vomit. Dropping to his knees, hands flat on the floor, he retched and cried.

"What are you talking about, David?" Jessica asked. "Daddy, what's going on?"

She sounded panicky, almost hysterical.

"Jessica, please go upstairs."

"But Daddy—"

"Right now, Jessica! Thank you."

Jessica ran up the stairs.

Phil braced himself over the sink. His legs wobbled beneath him. He reached for the paper towel dispenser, unrolled seven or eight sections and ripped them off. Crouching beside David, he wiped his son's face and helped him up.

"Go to bed, David. We'll talk tomorrow when you feel better."

David stumbled to the foot of the staircase. "Man, you just don't get it, do you?" He climbed the stairs on all fours.

After cleaning up the vomit, Phil sat at the kitchen table and tried to think. His hands wouldn't stop shaking when he held them out. He'd never had a loaded gun aimed at him intentionally, but it had to feel something like this, with one huge difference: right now he wanted the gun to fire and put a bullet into him. Calling off the affair was no longer the simple solution it once might have been. Would David tell Ellen? No. He'd protect her. But this shared knowledge would pervade their lives. He dragged himself out of the chair and groped his way to the bedroom.

"How bad was he?"

"Bad."

"What's causing this? Why now? What if he can't kick it? He was such a happy toddler. Sometimes I see him as an older man…." She began to cry.

Phil held her. "Don't start thinking like that. We'll work it out, El."

"We can't work anything out. He has to. He's an adult. If only I knew what demons were chasing him!"

Oh, yes. That would solve everything.

Her remark about David as an older man alluded to a warm,

bright day in St. Paul during the time of David's treatment. After eating ice cream cones in Rice Park, Ellen and Phil had strolled to the ribbon of city park that ran along the Mississippi just off downtown across from the Radisson. They had talked and laughed and enjoyed the radiant sun, stealing a few moments of lightness that didn't exist in their lives but which they so desperately needed.

When they leaned over the concrete railing, Phil happened to glance directly down and saw two middle-aged men lying on a narrow strip of grass below. They wore rags, and their movements were those of men in a stupor. Phil immediately backed away from the railing and suggested that they drive to Summit Avenue to walk the bluffs near the seminary, but he was too late. Ellen had also seen the men. They both knew they would never forget the sight of the two winos, two lost souls who were once young like David.

"Do you love me, Phil?"

Their hands met and locked under the covers.

"Of course I do."

He did love her, didn't he? It had to be true. It had always been true. He squeezed her hand and blinked rapidly in the dark. He would break off the affair. He had to. He couldn't have it both ways.

"I love you, too," she said. "I need you so much. We need each other. More than ever."

She curled next to him. Did she want to make love? No, thank goodness. "When things get so bad they can't get any worse," his father had always said, "they've got to get better." The convoluted optimism of the cliché had always appealed to Phil, but it provided no comfort now.

Much later, still awake, he turned to look at the alarm. Feeling him shift his weight, Ellen rolled away in her fitful sleep. The quickening wind blew through the windows, twisting and tangling the sheers. A distant, hollow cordon of thunder pitted the smooth silence of the night. He got up to close the windows. Boat lights glowed on the lake like scattered embers.

Chapter Forty-Four

"Borglund's secretary just called," Ruth said.

"And?"

"He wants you to cancel any appointments and meet him in forty-five minutes."

"I'm open. Ruth, what's wrong?"

"He wants to meet you … at the corner of Nicollet and Seventh. On the street."

Phil sat motionless at his desk, a fly-buzz alarm deep in his brain. Well, with nine hundred million, a man could call a meeting in a swimming pool if he wanted to.

He drove downtown and walked the three blocks from the parking garage to Nicollet and Seventh. Borglund was waiting. He motioned Phil to follow him across the street to where a man was jackhammering concrete.

"You will receive a letter from my counsel later today by courier," Borglund said over the noise of the jackhammer. "Effective immediately, you are no longer associated in any manner with Borglund Enterprises."

He turned away. Phil grabbed his arm.

"Why? Tell me why!"

Borglund cocked his head and pulled back, as if trying to avoid inhaling stench. "I choose not to provide a reason. However, you knew my standards from the outset. I genuinely wish your wife and children well. They don't deserve to have a—they deserve better than you."

Borglund crossed the street and disappeared into the crowd on the far sidewalk. Phil turned and collided with a young man.

"Watch where you're going, asshole!" the man said.

People and buildings swirled. Everything blurred. He leaned against the IDS Tower. He had to tell Marty what had happened.

And he had to see Nora.

The letter said it was "a corporate decision made after full and complete consideration of all relevant facts and circumstances." It went on to cite two broad provisions of their contract. One sentence referred to "potential conflicts of interest," a piece of boilerplate lawyers couldn't resist, and with good reason. They could almost always find a potential conflict somewhere and build a case, no matter the stretch.

It was all moot, of course. It would be sheer idiocy to challenge Borglund's power and money. There was no upside. The affair with Nora would be headlined. Ellen and the kids would have to suffer through a messy business. Was Nora's consulting work for companies owned by Borglund the conflict of interest they could point to? A legal case and a bucket of mud all mixed together?

"So it was the impossible dream," Marty said. "I feel bad for you, *amigo.*"

"Marty, I blew it."

"Maybe it wasn't you. Maybe I screwed up."

"No, it was me. He didn't get into any details, but he made it clear."

Marty ran his hand over his face and through his hair. He came alongside and threw his arm across Phil's shoulders.

"He got what he wanted from us. He doesn't need us anymore, and he doesn't need a reason. Know what? We did great for a long time without Borglund. We'll do it again. Let's go play tennis and drink beer."

"Not today, Marty. Not today. Give me a rain check."

For three days Phil said nothing to Ellen about losing the Borglund account. A myriad of problems had arisen with other clients while his attention had been on Borglund. Several good accounts had been lost. The loss of Borglund's monthly retainer delivered a crushing blow. He had to get back to doing what he had done for years, like it or not, and he had to do it in a hurry.

His mind wandered. He called Robert Aagard. The secretary told him the dean wasn't in. Phil asked that he return the call at his convenience.

In the morning Phil called Aagard again. Did he imagine it, or was the secretary's voice a hair too cordial when she told him Aagard was out of the office? In mid-afternoon he phoned the law school once more. In the same saccharin voice the woman said the dean was unavailable.

"When will he be available?"

"He's in meetings all day."

"What's his schedule like tomorrow?"

"The dean is very busy, Mr. Tag."

"So am I, dear. Tell him that if he doesn't have the courtesy—or the balls—to return my call, I'll come over there and break his door down!"

Aagard called two minutes later.

"I would appreciate your not speaking to my secretary in that manner, Tag."

"You've been ducking me."

"You're imagining things."

"What's our status, Robert?"

"We, ah, have run into problems. We are on hold."

"What kinds of problems?"

"Problems, Tag, problems. I'll have to get back to you at a later date."

"Funding problems, as in Borglund?"

"I see no reason to continue this conversation."

"Neither do I."

Chapter Forty-Five

He went home early and told Ellen about Borglund's letter and the lost law school opportunity.

"I know how much it meant to you. But don't expect me to be sad because I'm not." She put her arms around him. "You're too much your own man to be controlled by Borglund. That's what he wanted, to have you split your time between the university and him, so he could hold you hostage every minute. That's why he cut you off. He knew he couldn't own you."

Her loyalty brought a lump to his throat. He held her tightly. "We don't know that, El."

"I do. Maybe now we can get back to normal. You and David haven't said ten words to each other since I don't know when. It's like a feud. When are you going to tell me what's going on? You must know. He won't give me a hint, no matter how much I pressure him."

They talked for two hours, not about David, but about Jessica and about changes they needed to make now that the Borglund retainer was gone. Her support gave him strength. By the time she proposed pizza and beer for dinner, he had nearly begun to believe things would work out.

At the Pizza Hut, Ellen had two glasses of beer. A seductive look came into her face. Her shoeless foot slid up the calf of Phil's leg. "If Jessica's not home when we get there, we're jumping in the sack, Tagarooski."

A bite of pizza caught in Phil's throat. He ran to the rest room and dislodged it into the toilet. He bent over the toilet choking in long, wheezing gasps. Ellen burst in. She pounded on his back.

"I'm okay! I'm okay! Please leave me!"

He stayed in the restroom for five minutes after Ellen left, working up the courage to face her again.

They returned home to find Jessica and three of her friends.

"Wait till later," Ellen said with a lascivious smile.

Phil stepped out to the patio. The lake was calm. Shadows at water's edge across the bay were lengthening and an autumn smell of ripeness and decay hung in the air. Soon the leaves would turn and begin to fall, and the smell of burning leaves and wood smoke would waft through the air during the merciful, preparatory interlude before winter. Sailboats glided across the water with just enough wind in their sails to keep them underway. He returned to the house and told Ellen he was going out on the lake. He caught her look.

"Don't worry. I'll be right back."

At Gray's Marina he realized for the first time how obvious he must have been all summer long: rushing to the pay phone, talking in a hushed voice, roaring across the lake. Now he recognized the over-politeness of the employees, their ingratiating smiles, their knowing looks. Some stupidities have no bounds.

Nora waited for him on the path that led down to the lake. The sun behind her silhouetted her legs through the gauzy white skirt. After a long embrace, she tilted her head for a kiss.

"Let's go inside," he said.

"What's wrong? Why won't you kiss me?"

He picked her up and carried her through the sunroom door. The aroma of herbal tea and the remarkable voice of Whitney Houston filled the air.

"Sit here," he said, motioning to one end of the sofa and going to the other. "It's over. I'd have to be a poet to tell you how much I love you. I'll never stop loving you. But it's over."

"Why now? Why at this very instant?"

"For all the reasons that existed from the beginning."

She threw a stuffed pillow at the wall. A painting fell to the floor.

“Don’t come waltzing in here like a martyr.”

“Don’t make this tougher than it already is.”

“Did Ellen find out?”

“It’s only a matter of time.”

She stood bathed in late afternoon sunlight, a radiant, defiant flower against a barren moonscape of possibilities.

“Love me,” she said.

Her lips crushed his, her breasts pressed against him, her warm breath caressed his face. Her clean, delicate scent enveloped him. He scooped her up and headed for the bedroom.

“No,” she said. “Outside.”

They removed each article of clothing slowly and deliberately, as if by so doing they could slow the rush of time, and when they made love they did all the things they had done before, the touches and whispers and reassurances that gave each other pleasure while consummation followed consummation until at last their concupiscence lay quiet.

“Now can we talk?” she asked.

“There’s nothing to talk about. We just have to end it.”

“You’re not telling me everything.”

“Why are you pressing me like this? We both knew this time would come.”

“You’re being evasive.”

“I need to go.”

“Of course. You always have to go. I give you a hundred opportunities to be intimate—I mean, truly intimate—with me, and you refuse or leave. I don’t think there’s much honesty in this relationship. Maybe it’s one big mistake. Maybe it should never have happened.”

He embraced her. “Don’t ever say that.”

She returned his embrace and they lay still for several moments. It was time to tell her everything. He took a deep breath and—

“Will I see you again?” she asked.

Would he see her again? Christ, it was one thing to break it off, but never see her again? He couldn’t imagine it. Nor could he bring himself to tell her about David. Not now.

“Yes.”

The horizon had eclipsed the cooling sun when he made his way to the boat and pushed off the dock into the twilight.

Nora watched the wake of Phil's slow-moving boat spread into a wide inverted V on the dark, calm surface of the lake. For months she had pondered over the effect of his arrivals and departures, often watching for him through the trees or from the pier, the commotion in her chest signaling her anticipation, the constriction in her throat as telling an indication of her desire as the insistence below.

She hurried inside to a phone.

Phil nosed the Interceptor into open water. It had gotten dark. He'd have to keep a sharp lookout for other boats. His gaze, though, was inward.

Ellen had always been his safe harbor. They knew each other so well. Or did they? Did she really know him? Did he know himself? With half a life yet to live, must he live it the same as the first half? Did he want to?

And the kids. They were probably better off without him in the stream. If the flow were cut, Ellen had said, they'd all dry up. He was the blockage. Maybe it was time for him to leave the stream so their flow could continue.

Almost too late he saw the fishing boat lying low in the water. Its lone occupant, a squat man wearing a black jacket and a blue Twins baseball cap, waved wildly. Phil turned sharply left.

"Watch where you're going, you stupid prick!" the man said in a raspy voice.

When had the world become so hostile?

Nora. Fascinating and nourishing Nora. Endless variety, at once younger and older than her years, she refracted the morning sun and distilled it into endless beauty and wonderment. Could she paradoxically be the catalyst for a fresh start for him as well as his family?

By the time he approached his pier, the slight breeze had

quickened into a wind punching its way over menacing water. Thunder erupted in the distance, and the air had the feel of a storm coming. Only his long familiarity with the pattern of lights on shore enabled him to dock the boat on the first try.

"Want my advice?" Connie's voice came through the receiver. "Don't answer, I'm giving it anyway. Tell him you know who he is. Tell him you know he knows who you are. There's no downside."

"I came within a heartbeat a while ago. He's nearly told me several times. What would it accomplish?"

"Depends. What do you want it to accomplish? Do you want him to leave his wife?"

"Do you realize he's never said one negative word about her? She sounds like a nice person. A lovely person, in fact. Their sex life might be in the pits—not that he's ever said anything about it—but he probably loves her. I'm sure he does."

"How would you feel if he told you with no prompting that he was David's adoptive father? How would you react?"

Nora didn't answer.

"Good morning, anybody home?" Connie said.

"I'd be a goner. I like being with him and I love him in bed. If he'd level with me, I think I'd fall head over heels."

"Nora, it's not going to stay the same, no matter what you do. You worry me on this one. Your head always read the chart before. Now your heart needs bifocals."

"Somehow, the off-center symmetry of the whole crazy thing appealed to me from the start, in spite of my rule against married men. It seemed different this time."

"It happens to all of us, one time or another. Better lay your cards on the table. It's read 'em and weep time."

"Connie, you are so remarkably supportive. Remind me not to call you next time. But that's all beside the point. The real issue is David. Can you imagine what knowing about this could do to him? No kid needs that."

"What would you do if he did know?"

"I'm not sure. It grinds me that Phil hasn't come clean with me. I won't if he won't. He has to make the first move. I'm not giving on that. It would be like forcing his hand, and I'm not going to do that. There's the principle of it. He started all this."

"Want to have coffee in the morning and really get into it?"

"The Little Apple at seven?"

"See you there."

She hung up and leaned on the counter. Maybe it was time to pawn David and go for checkmate.

Chapter Forty-Six

The phone rang at two in the morning. Phil picked up the receiver, said hello and listened.

"Yes, he lives here. I'm his father."

The voice at the other end was clinical and dispassionate. It was probably one of many calls she had to make this night and many nights. No despair, no hope; just facts and directions.

"I understand. I'll be there in thirty minutes."

Ellen was quietly frantic.

"It's David," Phil said. "At a detox center downtown. I'll be back in a while."

"I'm going, too."

"There's no need, El. Try to—"

"I'm going. After I tell Jessica we have to be gone a while."

Jessica watched Phil and Ellen drive off. Then she put on a running outfit and started running. The ankle was still tender, but she would take good long run anyway.

David was unconscious under a sheet on a gurney.

"His blood alcohol is more than three times the legal limit," the paramedic said. Her nametag said she was M. Thayer. "We'll keep him here until tomorrow."

A sigh came from David. As they all watched, liquid dripped down the sides of the gurney. In a moment it became a flood. The paramedic caught the look on their faces.

"He's lost control of his bladder. We'll call you when he's

ready to leave."

She reached for some towels on a shelf, and drew a curtain between them and David.

Jessica wasn't home when they returned from the detox center, so Ellen waited up for her. When Jessica returned an hour later, she was utterly exhausted and having difficulty breathing. Ellen made her some herbal tea, helped her dry off, tucked her into bed and decided to stay up until Phil came down to go to work. But when he came down, neither of them said a word about what had happened. Phil kissed her and left.

Chapter Forty-Seven

On Saturday a gusting wind woke Phil before the alarm went off. He went downstairs, made a pot of coffee and showered while it brewed. He poured coffee into a Styrofoam cup and put on a jacket. Outside in the gray light of predawn, the horizon showed no sign of sunrise through the cloud cover.

He walked across the wet grass to the end of the pier and sat on the bench with the southwest wind in his face. He leaned forward and hunched his shoulders. Raggedy gray-bellied clouds raced toward him low against an even grayer sky. It would get warm later, one of the few good days left before the hard weather blew in.

A few fishing boats marked the choppy water of the bay. One large cabin cruiser plowed toward the points. There were no sailboats. It was a gray scene that would turn into a beautiful waterscape when the sun rose high enough to add some color. If only the mind were incapable of dulling such beauty. But then, beauty in its turn had ample power to dull the mind. He had learned that. Oh yes, how extremely well he had learned all about that.

A pair of Canada geese pitched about in the rolling water near shore. He had read somewhere that geese mate for life. Was this pair old, young or middle age? Had they survived the hazards of a lifetime? Or were they just beginning?

The water looked rough enough that he didn't relish the thought of going out on it. He emptied the cold coffee into the lake, returned to the house and woke David, who had come home the previous afternoon.

"What do you want?"

"Son, we'll talk more in a day or two. Right now, I want you to know how sorry I am for hurting you, and for what's to come."

David rolled over and pulled the covers over his head. Phil proceeded to Jessica's bedroom. "Honey, Mother and I have to go to the cabin for a day or two. You and David be careful." She didn't question him, didn't say a word. He hugged her. "I love you, Jess. Love you with all my heart."

Returning to the master bedroom, he gently shook Ellen awake.

"Get some things together. Please don't ask any questions now. We have to leave in an hour."

She sat upright. "What's wrong? Is it the kids?"

He put his finger to his lips and shook his head. "Please get ready."

She looked fearful and bewildered.

"I'll be back shortly."

He left her and strode to the pier where he untied the Interceptor and started the motor. Twenty minutes later, while climbing the steps to Nora's, he heard a car start and drive off. Nora came to the door fully dressed.

"May I come in?"

She looked over his shoulder toward the driveway and nodded. Inside, she didn't respond when he held her.

"I'm going to tell Ellen everything."

"I wish you well."

"You wish me—That's all you have to say?"

He smelled, then saw, the sliver of smoke rising from the counter. On a saucer there were two long cigarette butts, one of which still smoldered. He crossed over to the counter. Unfiltered Pall Malls. The pounding in his ears deafened him.

"Why was Lankar here?"

Her expression provided no answer.

"Have you—"

"You disappoint me. Totally disappoint me."

"What the hell's going on?"

She touched her right temple with her fingertips. "He called last night. Said he had to see me first thing this morning, very early. Wouldn't tell me why. Said he had something I'd be most interested in seeing. Pictures. God, did he have pictures."

"I'll kill the bastard!"

"He's already got you. I'm next if I don't stop seeing you. Borglund alone could ruin me."

"We can't just cave in, can't let him get away with this."

"There is no we. That's over. Go to Ellen. I'll deal with Lankar. I need some time to figure it out, but I will."

He wrapped his arms around her. She returned his embrace for a moment before pulling back.

"Let me tell you some things," he said.

"No. Please don't. It's too late."

"Is it?"

"You know it is."

Unprepared for this finality, he said, "Are you all right?"

"I'm a survivor."

He drew her to him. She neither resisted nor returned the embrace. Her breasts against his chest took his breath. He released her and stepped back with a feeling of incalculable loss. He had to leave. When he opened the door, he turned to her.

"If I were leaving Ellen, would you stay with me?"

Her face told him nothing and everything. He gazed at her for a long, terrible moment before he backed through the doorway and hurried away with long strides. The wind flowing over his face rustled through the trees that lined the path to the pier. Golden popple and birch leaves rained to the ground and scraped over the asphalt driveway. His father had died on a day like this, a day that would never blur in his memory.

The flight to Rag Tag Point took forever. With anger flanking Ellen's apprehension, she by turn questioned Phil, went silent and shouted at him because he wouldn't tell her anything. It was cruel but the best way to prepare her. Better that she be spitting mad and full of fight when he told her what he had to tell her. The weather turned cold and wet fifty miles from the landing strip. Later, at the cabin, Phil built a fire while Ellen made tea.

"Now, damn it, what's this all about?"

He closed the fireplace screen and took a deep breath. "I've been unfaithful."

He started from the beginning and rained down blow after blow on her. She listened alertly, never interrupting, never questioning. She visibly fought back her emotions only once. When he finished she remained motionless for a few moments before getting up and pouring herself a cup of tea.

"I want to be alone now."

"El, I—"

"Get out!" She wheeled around to face him. "Damn you to hell! Get out! Get out! Get out!" With a long, gasping inhalation, she drew back from the edge of hysteria. Her crying, if she cried, would be private. She might pace the cabin ranting, talking it out with herself, or even trashing the place. Whatever she did she would do alone, and Phil knew there wouldn't be a trace when he returned.

He went to a nearby tavern where he drank soft drinks and shot pool for two hours before going back to the cabin. He found her sitting on the dock. The rising wind swirled mist over the lake, which had the color of a blackboard covered with chalk dust.

"Is this how it looked when you and David were on the lake?" she said.

"It was worse."

She shuddered.

"Did you love her?"

He nodded.

"Did you tell her?"

He didn't answer.

"Did you?"

"Yes."

She pushed her hands into her coat pockets and gazed across the dark water.

"Do you still love her?"

"It's over, El. Completely."

"That's not what I asked you."

"I still do."

"She broke it off, no doubt."

He spread his hands before him and said nothing. She closed her eyes. "Does David know? Is that what happened?"

The one part he hadn't told her.

"He knows."

Her breath caught in her throat. She dabbed at her nose with a tissue.

"How could you, Phil? How could you?" She shoved the tissue into her jacket pocket. "Does she know you raised her child?"

"She has no idea."

"Thank God for that. She has far more decency than you."

Ellen rose from the bench. The wind off the lake blew her hair.

"When did you stop loving me?"

"I never did."

"Don't you think the time for lying is over?"

"It's true, El. God help me, it's true. And I'm so very sorry."

She dropped the empty teacup, an old Victorian one she had found at a flea market in Wisconsin on the day they were notified they had been approved to adopt Jessica, into the lake at the edge of the pier.

"Interesting that you invoke God. I'm going to bed. Alone."

Phil took her place on the bench. The water was kicking up; the mist had changed to rain; whitecaps attacked the pier pilings; nightfall would come early. Staring at the water, he decided to retrieve the cup. Ellen had to have been totally dazed to discard it.

He went inside to put on old clothes and a pair of sneakers, returned to the pier and slipped into the water, which was only three or four feet deep, but frigid. He took a deep breath and ducked under the surface. At that moment, he wished he were at the bottom of the lake, sucking water into his lungs, with no chance of reaching the surface. Brief cowardice before oblivion would be preferable to the pain of living the days ahead. It took six submersions to feel the cup among the rocks.

Ellen stayed in bed all afternoon and through the night. Phil slept on the couch after a long hot shower. In the morning he heard her in the kitchen when the incipient sunrise had only begun to dilute the darkness. He decided to stay on the couch a few minutes longer to give her a chance to settle in with a cup of coffee. In the best of times she never liked to talk before her morning coffee.

How the kids had always loved coming to Rag Tag Point! Even during his worst days, David had found refuge here for short periods. And Ellen, too, always seemed to loosen up at the cabin. She even adopted the elderly couple down the road as stand-in parents. She gloried in the lazy afternoons of reading and cheerfully entered into the nighttime games of cards, Tripoli and Monopoly. Not surprisingly, some of their best lovemaking occurred while the kids were out boating or cycling with summer friends. As much for that as for anything else, Phil had engineered long weekends at the cabin whenever possible.

He dressed and went to the kitchen. The teacup was on the table where he had put it last night.

"Good morning," she said. "Coffee's on the counter. I want to leave right away. How soon can you be ready?"

"I thought we might stay a while."

"I can't stand the sight of you."

He stood in the doorway, unable to think of anything that would change her mind.

"I'll go over to Lunken's to fuel the plane. We can leave in an hour."

"Fine. Thanks for getting my cup."

Her surface civility would continue. It often did when they argued and was more punishing than anything else she could do. It wasn't a tactic this time, if it ever was. It was her way of holding herself together.

They reached altitude and got on a heading for Flying Cloud.

"We need to discuss what to say to the kids," he said.

Ellen shot him a stern, incredulous look. "I'll handle that. You're moving out as soon as we get home. And I don't want to talk about it."

Minutes later, she turned in her seat to look directly at him.

"You are despicable beyond words. A simple affair would be

be inexcusable. With David's birth mother, barbaric. Sick. That part I'll never understand—and never forgive you for. You should be ashamed of yourself right down to your stupid penis. Whatever possessed you? Did you give any thought to David's feelings? To the fact you're destroying him and Jessica? If you don't get to a good psychiatrist, you're even more cold and insane than I think you are. Now don't say a word to me, not a damn word. I don't want to hear anything you could possibly say."

Chapter Forty-Eight

The congealing remains of a TV dinner stuck to the flimsy plastic container on the scuffed coffee table. Phil glanced up periodically from his paperwork to catch Jay Leno mugging and cavorting through his monologue. Files were stacked on the floor and on the only other chair in the room. Marty and Ruth also took files home nightly. There seemed to be no end to the work. It was only January and already the meteorologists daily proclaimed that the Twin-Cities winter was closing in on the record for subzero days.

Upon returning from the cabin, Phil had rented a cheap efficiency apartment a mile from the office and had bought some second-hand furniture. He and Marty had gone to a hotel room for two days to begin mapping out a strategy for saving and rebuilding their business. That's when he told Marty about Nora.

"That's why Borglund dropped us. Lankar had the goods on me. Pictures, the whole nine yards."

Marty threw his pen into a wastebasket with force. He slumped into a chair and closed his eyes. Arising from the chair, he went to the window and looked out. "You don't need me to tell you you're a complete rotten son of a bitch," he said, "for what you've done to your family and mine. I hope your religion is right, that there's a purgatory, and that it lasts a long time. No parole for you for about three fucking centuries. Now let's get to work."

A week later Marty gave him a handmade plaque with the inscription, *Estamos pasando muchos apuros, pero volamos con nuestras propias alas.* "We're having a hard time of it, but we stand on our own two feet." It brought tears to Phil's eyes. He knew he would treasure it for life.

At least the punitive winter, by taking away most recreational distractions, enabled them to attack business like two galley slaves with a promise of freedom if they worked themselves just short of death. For three months they worked fourteen-hour days, six days a week and a partial day on Sunday, as well. In the meantime, they took barely enough money from the business to cover the most basic of personal expenses. With luck, in a couple of years they'd be able to squeeze out more income.

The loss of Borglund's retainer had forced them into a large bank loan at outrageous interest to cover the cost of the computer system. Though they felt lucky to get the money at any price, the debt loomed over them. The monthly payments absorbed nearly everything they could scrape together. They had to cut salaries, but they hadn't yet laid anybody off, though five employees had quit. Their airplanes were gone, as were their country club memberships and meager savings. The Cadillac, boats, and Rag Tag Point had been sold. Marty also had sold everything but his home.

Phil pulled himself up from the lumpy sofa he had purchased at a salvage store and went to the stairs that led to the ground floor. With another two hours of work ahead, he needed a breath of air to stay awake. He stood on the concrete landing just outside the common foyer in the frigid Minnesota night. Some people, probably teenagers, were drinking in a car parked next to a dumpster in the parking lot. Their empties littered the icy asphalt. Returning to his apartment, he drew the curtains, ugly green things with the texture of burlap, across the ice-covered window of the living room. There was work to do. He went to the kitchen and swung the fridge door open. A lone apple huddled in the corner. He decided to save it for tomorrow. Apples were so expensive this time of year.

He stretched out on the sofa and covered his eyes with his hands. After a while he sat up, found the remote and tuned in the weather channel. A few minutes later the local forecast came on: a predicted thirty-four below tonight, eighteen below for a high tomorrow. He flicked off the TV. The stack of paperwork on the kitchen table wouldn't get done with the TV on.

He phoned Ellen once a week to make sure the furnace was working and the car was running okay, those kinds of things. She always answered his questions tersely and never volunteered any information. She never called him. It had taken three weeks of calls and notes to get her to discuss a second mortgage on the house, which they would finalize in a week. He would do everything in his power to spare them the humiliation of having to move out.

She hurt him most by telling him nothing about the kids. He knew she would inform him if one of them were seriously ill, but otherwise she refused to offer information or to answer even his most direct questions. Craters of silence pocked their phone conversations. A week ago David had stayed on the line for a few minutes until Ellen could get to the phone. Before that, neither David nor Jessica had spoken to him. Nothing could have prepared him for this kind of excommunication.

He saw Nora twice, once as she sat in her car at a stoplight. She did not see him on that occasion. The second time, they nearly ran into each other on the sidewalk on a cold, windy day. She was with a handsome man about her age, possibly younger, in front of the Norwest Bank building. When he said hi, she said, "Hello, Mr. Tag," resumed her animated conversation with her escort and strode past without a second glance. The encounter saddened him beyond words.

Chapter Forty-Nine

The office of Lyle Shoemaker, a mortgage loan officer for Minnesota Pioneer Mercantile Bank, was tidy, small and very corporate. Phil and Ellen had just begun signing the paperwork when the phone rang. After a word or two into the phone, Shoemaker excused himself. Ellen was reading the mortgage papers and acting as if Phil weren't there. The door opened. Wade Lankar entered.

"Hello, folks. Lyle got called away, so I'll handle your transaction for you."

He sat in Shoemaker's chair behind the desk.

"Let's see here … mortgage, right? Oh, I see. *Second* mortgage. Well, this won't take long. Everything is approved. What's the problem? Business setbacks? Personal problems? Or do you have a new business opportunity and need some cash? Regardless, we're glad to help here at MPMB."

Ellen's face reddened.

"None of that is pertinent," Phil said. "The loan is approved. Let's get this over with."

"Haste makes waste, so we'll take our time." Lankar shuffled the papers on the desk. A slight smile played at the corners of his mouth. "Hard to understand why a second mortgage is necessary, given our relatively strong local economy and all. Business profits are holding up quite well."

Phil bit his tongue. There was no sense in showing anger or frustration. That's what Lankar wanted. It was one of those times to hunker down and take a whipping.

"Let's just take a minute to review the paperwork. By the way, do you still occupy the house?" he said to Phil.

"It's occupied."

"Who are the occupants?"

"My wife, our son, and our daughter."

"I take it you will be living elsewhere?"

"That's correct."

"Interesting. Very interesting. How long will you remain in different quarters, Mr. Tag?"

"Indefinitely."

"But I assume you will continue to be responsible for the payments?"

Phil nodded.

"Very well," Lankar said as he continued to peruse the paperwork. His unbuttoned suit coat revealed his huge belly. "I'm sure it's noted here somewhere, but are you employed, Mrs. Tag?"

Lips pursed, Ellen nodded.

"May I ask where?"

"Abbott Northwestern Hospital."

"May I ask in what capacity?"

"I'm a nurse."

"Been there long?"

"Three months."

"And I believe you were a homemaker before that, right?"

Ellen nodded.

"I understand nurses returning to the workforce are given cruddy hours and duties. Are you finding that the case?"

Phil rose up off his chair. Ellen grabbed his arm. "I'm working nights, weekends and holidays," she said, "and enjoying every minute of it. Do you have any further questions?"

Her retort flustered Lankar for only a moment. "Well, no. Not right now. I'm glad you like your work. Hope you get a lot of it. Just in case your husband can't make the payments."

Lankar proceeded to stretch the twenty-minute transaction into an hour. Every few minutes he fixed Phil in his cold gaze and smiled a tight smile that wasn't a smile at all. What hurt Phil most was Ellen's total humiliation.

Finally, it was over. As Phil and Ellen got up to leave, Lankar extended his hand to Phil, who stared at the man in disbelief before turning his back on him and leading Ellen from the room. Lankar laughed loudly. His laughter followed them down the corridor and into the lobby.

"Jo, it was just awful," Ellen said into the phone. "He's the most despicable human being I've ever met. Phil wanted to kill him. How depressing. I'm brewing a pot of tea, and I'm going to kick back and do nothing for an hour while I have the place to myself. Hold on a second. Someone's at the door."

"I have to run, too. Call me later."

Ellen hung up and went to the door. "Hello, Ellen," Father Banning said when she opened the door.

Ellen glanced at her watch. "Were we to get together? Have I forgotten something?"

"No, no. Nothing like that. I was in the neighborhood and thought I'd drop by."

"Please come in."

"Thank you." The priest entered and Ellen closed the door behind him. "Are you alone?"

"Until Jessica gets home from school, yes. May I take your coat?"

She hung his coat in the foyer closet. "Would you like a cup of tea, Father?"

"Love one. Do you think this weather will ever moderate?"

"Just another January in Minnesota." She went about preparing the tea and wondering why the priest had come, although she thought she knew.

"Are you and the kids all right?"

She turned from the counter to face him. "Yes. Why do you ask?"

"Well, there's been talk—that is, I've heard you've perhaps fallen on hard times."

"My husband's business has problems right now, but things have a way of working out. I appreciate your concern."

Father Banning moved closer to her. He placed his hands on her shoulders close to her neck. "Ellen, if there's any way I can help, if there's anything I can do for you…." He drew her to him.

"Father, I'm so glad you came." She pushed him away. "So I can tell you what I should have told you a long time ago."

"Ellen, what—"

"I'm sure I gave you the wrong impression. I didn't mean to, but I did. It was wrong, and you know it. All your innuendoes and touching."

"You can't tell me you don't have feelings for me. You need me, and I need you. I know all about Phil's escapade. How could he do that to you? You should be cherished. I do cherish you." He advanced toward her.

She cocked her arm to slap him if he came closer. "Stop it, Father! Enough is enough! I should have drawn the line a long time ago. Now you waltz in here and try to take advantage of a situation. You were hoping I'd be vulnerable. Well, I'm not. My family needs me more than ever. Please leave."

The priest grasped her wrist. She jerked it free.

"Let me rephrase that: get the *hell* out, Father Gerard Banning! And don't come back." She stomped to the foyer closet, ripped his coat from the hanger and flung it at him. She yanked the door open. "As of right now, I am no longer involved with any parish committees. None. Go say your prayers!"

"But—"

"Go to hell!"

Father Banning stepped across the threshold barely ahead of the door slamming behind him.

That night, just as Phil was getting ready for bed, the phone rang.

"Hello, Tag. This isWade."

"I know who it is."

"How's it going?"

"Just fine."

"Sure it is. By the way, I'm a senior VP at MPMB. Don't normally handle petty mortgages, but I wanted to provide a little extra service for an old friend today. I enjoyed our visit, didn't you? I know you're happy for me. Making damn good money. And I'm porking the cutest little thing that ever put on panties."

"Yeah, but you still have the class of a barnyard boar, and

your kickback income has dried up."

A moment of silence before Lankar laughed.

"That's your theory, Tag. I don't care what you think. Why should I? You're nothing but a tits-up insurance agent. You don't have a pot to piss in, your marriage is on the rocks and your kids are fucked up. You were always a loser, always will be. Have a nice life, loser."

The receiver clicked in Phil's ear. His breath catching high in his chest, he laid the phone on the cradle and stood over it for several long moments before turning out the light. He recalled one of his father's favorite expressions: "You can't beat a man at his own game." He retreated to his bedroom and waited for the merciful oblivion of sleep.

Chapter Fifty

"Marty, when we get back up to speed, I'm walking."

"Whoa. Talk to me."

"Arizona. Warm climate, fresh start. I've got, what, twenty good years left? No more winters."

Lines furrowed Marty's face. "You can't eat sunshine."

"I'll open an agency. Personal sales. Just me, maybe a part-time secretary. The big money was nice when we were hot, but I don't need it anymore. I'll work at a decent pace and make enough to live comfortably. With a good woman, if I have any luck in that department.

"Know something? As much as I wanted to be a big shot and belong to the right clubs and all the other stuff, I was never really comfortable in that world. Borglund, Aagard, all the rest—deep down, I didn't fit in. I think I wanted to show them I was as good, but I always felt like an outsider. Ellen never lost sight of who she is; I give her that. I was the one who had to get back to reality. A new start in Arizona with a new attitude is just the ticket."

"You've thought it through?"

"Fifty times. I'll give you plenty of lead time. We'll work out the details."

Marty clapped him on the shoulder.

"Keep an open mind, my friend. Whatever you decide, *buena suerte, mi amigo.* Good luck."

Chapter Fifty-One

Winter dissolved into spring. Phil visited Father Wark at St. Olaf's. He told the priest about Nora and all that had happened.

"I remember the day you came to see me," Wark said. "You were agitated and hostile, a fuse waiting for a match. Is this a confession?"

"No. I haven't forgiven myself yet. I need more time, Father."

The priest stroked his chin. "The sacrament gives strength. So does communion."

"Not yet."

The priest contemplated him and said nothing.

"Besides, my wife and I aren't going to get back together."

Summer turned to autumn. Life solidified again into ice and snow, the second winter of estrangement and work without end. Arizona beckoned by the minute, even more so, ironically, following a phone call from David in November. The conversation rambled in fits and starts. David wanted to know how Phil was doing. Things were okay at home. He hadn't touched any alcohol for over a year. Jessica was doing fine at the U. In addition to her nursing job, Ellen had taken a part-time job with Carlson Travel. As strong and effective as ever with the kids, she had them on the right track without him. The conversation initially renewed Phil's hope of reuniting with his family. But upon reflection, he recognized the profound flaw in his thinking.

"I'll always make sure she's comfortable, Marty. But it's

senseless to stick around. I'm a reminder of what went wrong. Ellen has the kids on the right track. They're better off with me completely out of the picture. A blow to my ego? Sure. And I miss them all more than I can put into words. But, hell, I need to be honest about it. Honest and realistic. As to the business, I don't want much. A small stake to get me started in Arizona, and it's yours. "

"I don't want you to give it away, now that it's coming back. We'll strike a fair deal."

"Ellen always had her head on right. Oh, she had her traits, but she knew what was important. Ironically, sex with her was always great. I had no complaints whatever. With Nora, now that I've analyzed it a hundred times, it was the intrigue and clandestine excitement. She was an artist in more ways than one. Not only an artist, but an architect; an architect of sensuality. Did she wear me out in bed? Totally. Emptied me and turned me inside-out. But energized me, too, and made me ready to take on the world and every creep like Lankar in it."

Marty's look said he understood.

"Enough of that," Phil said. "It's over with. If I meet a good woman, I won't make the same mistakes again. More time with friends, intellectual pursuits, work to live, not live to work, doing things together. One thing's certain, I need a woman in my life.

"Know what I really miss? Intimacy. I had it with Nora on a certain level. Next time I want it at every level, like it used to be with Ellen. If I get a chance, I won't let other things get in the way. Make any sense?"

"All the sense in the world."

"Maybe I'll teach part-time at a junior college. Might even hook up with another teacher, who knows? We could take summers off together."

For the time being, his recovery plan included making one extra sales call a day, one more than he really had energy for, one more than he really wanted to make: an exercise in discipline, an exertion of will. He had done it now for fifty-seven straight weeks with two tangible results. The additional commissions enabled him to provide Ellen and the kids with sufficient income to maintain a more than decent standard of living. And it had gotten him back into the family life insurance market. Because he had worked exclusively with wealthy clients, most of them business owners, for more than ten years, it was a difficult adjustment at first. The cases were far smaller and generated lower commissions. But instead of taking months and sometimes years to close, they took only days or weeks.

"I like working with families, Marty, and helping them with their financial planning. They're young, their hopes are intact. I'm going to concentrate on the family market in Arizona. We think of Arizona as border-to-border retirees. Not true. People work there, too. People with loved ones and retirement dreams."

"Ellen and the kids still doing okay?"

"Doing great. Would you believe it? Ellen dropped all her committee work and goes to mass only on Sunday. David told me. Never thought I'd see the day."

Chapter Fifty-Two

Phil burst into Marty's office, smiling broadly. "Guess what I did last night. Never mind, I'll tell you. Went to a Little League organizational meeting. I'm going to coach a team this summer."

Marty smiled and nodded. "You sure it's Little League? You're acting like the Twins drafted you."

"It's going to be great, Marty. Funny thing, I used to hate Little League games. The kids' ineptitude drove me crazy. Ellen would tell me to take a walk to calm down. I know that most of the kids will be athletically challenged, some will be okay and one or two will have the skills and attitude to be standouts. All they need is discipline and someone to teach them. That's what I'm going to do. Teach them and lead them. And the first thing I'm going to do when I get to Arizona is get involved in Little League there."

David called a second time, and a third. Before they knew it, the calls had become part of their routine, although the conversations were short and kind of bumped and rattled along. Phil called on a night when the forecasters predicted an overnight low of minus thirty-seven. He wanted to make certain Ellen had had the furnace inspected and that things in general were okay. Jessica answered.

"It's Dad, Jess. How are you?"

"Did Mom tell you? I'm going to the University of Wisconsin at Madison in the fall. With reciprocity, it'll cost the same as Minnesota. Madison is a great college town. Daddy, I'm so happy!"

"Matter of fact, your mother did mention it. I'm happy for you, honey."

"How have you been, Dad? I wish you were here. It's not the same without you."

Phil swallowed hard. "I do, too, Jess. Sometimes things don't work out exactly the way we'd like."

"I'll keep hoping. Did you want to speak with Mom?"

"If she's handy."

Chapter Fifty-Three

The second winter finally passed. Phil attended mass every Sunday and occasionally during the week. He saw Father Wark regularly. He liked the old guy, and over the months they forged a respectful friendship. The sacrament of reconciliation beckoned, but something stronger repelled it. What was the point? If he remarried he would simply and completely adopt another faith as his own and practice it with the woman he loved.

Women. There seemed to be no shortage. Several single and divorced women in the office, including Karen, the lovely, libidinous administrative assistant, came on to him.

"They don't realize how poor I am, Marty," he said with a laugh. "It's great for the ego, and tempting, but sleeping around somehow doesn't square up with everything else. Maybe I'm crazy not to lead a single life. What do you think, *amigo?"*

"You're not crazy, my friend."

Chapter Fifty-Four

It would take only a few more days of warm weather to melt the remaining patches of snow on the Hyland Hills ski slopes south of the office. The trees would bud and the grass would turn green. With ice no longer covering it, the water of Lake Normandale would shimmer in the sun.

Phil turned to the mound of work on his desk. A rap on his open door accompanied *"¿Qué tal, Felipe?"* as Marty strode in. He carried a manila folder and a flying magazine. "I've found this Cessna with low hours. A beaut. Only a 152, but you have to start someplace."

"Buy two. We'll fly to the poorhouse together."

They both laughed. Marty could no more afford an airplane than he could jump over the IDS Tower.

"¿Adónde irá el buey que no are? 'Where can an ox go that he won't have to plow?' Nothing is easy, my friend, but we'll fly again. It's a go on the Trotter case. Nice bowl of guacamole."

"They need a wetback like you taking care of their stuff."

"Exactly what I told them."

Marty's daughter Sarah had won the drug battle. His son Steve, with the help of student loans, had developed into an outstanding student at the university. Marty and Liz had done a great job of holding everything together. Phil was happy for them.

After Marty left, Phil picked up the phone and dialed.

"May I speak with David Tag, please?" Knowing from previous calls how UPS disliked pulling employees off the floor, he added, "It's an emergency."

David came on the line.

"David? Dad. How about a bite of lunch?"

"Mom packed mine."

"I could pick up a burger and come there."

"I only get a half hour."

"There's something I need to tell you."

"Cool your pipes! I'm talking to my dad," David said to someone. "It's pretty warm out. I guess we could eat on the loading dock."

"Twelve-thirty?"

"Okay."

The hamburger from Wendy's was stuck to the bun and rigid by the time Phil parked in the UPS lot, but it didn't matter. He proceeded around the sprawling brown building to the loading dock and sat on a wooden crate. Perspiring, he took off his suit coat and loosened his tie. David joined him.

They said hi and took out their lunches. In addition to three sandwiches, Ellen had packed Doritos, cookies, tapioca pudding and an apple.

Most of the docks had brown trucks backed up to them. Loaders and drivers read manifests and shouted orders as they climbed in and out of trucks.

"Looks like business is good."

"Yeah, we're swamped. Never changes."

"Talked to Wagner lately?"

"Uh-huh. He was home from school last weekend. We went to a movie."

"You guys'll be golfing before you know it. Is he doing okay?"

"Yeah. His folks' divorce is final. I think he's worked through it." He shrugged. "Who knows?"

David finished his sandwiches, pudding and cookies. Reaching into his lunch bucket, he brought out a large Fuji apple. Handing it to Phil, he said, "Here, Dad, you take it. Mom always packs so much. I still owe you one from the lake. Remember?"

Phil reached for the apple. David held onto it for a thin second before letting it drop into Phil's hand.

"What'd you want to tell me, Dad?"

Phil polished the apple on his sleeve. For two days he had held back from telling David. Now the indecision returned. He pushed it aside.

"Your mother and I are going to dinner tonight. Nothing fancy, maybe a pizza. Might be a one-time deal, y'know? I really had to sell hard to get her to go."

David squinted out across the parking lot. He raised his feet up level with the loading dock and twisted them in little circles.

"Hey, Tag! You taking two lunch breaks?" someone yelled from inside.

"Why not? I work twice as hard!" David said over his shoulder. "I gotta get back to work, Dad."

"Sure."

Phil gathered up his coat and jumped off the dock to the asphalt below.

"Dad, can I ask you something?"

"Fire away."

"Did she know you're my dad?"

Phil shook his head. "She had no idea, son. I wanted to keep an eye on her because I was afraid she'd cause trouble. One thing led to another, but she never had any reason to link me with you."

David nodded and headed to an open loading door. Just before he disappeared, he turned and flashed thumbs up. Phil's chest heaved. He swallowed hard against the constriction in his throat. With a wisp of breeze flowing over his face, he threw his coat over his shoulder, gripped the apple and strode toward his car.

Two young women in UPS uniforms were watching him. He smiled at them and waved. Then he ran the remaining distance to his five-year-old blue Ford with the ding in the door and drove away with the windows down and the radio blasting.

Peter Shianna grew up in Red Oak, a farming village of 100, in northwestern Illinois near the city of Freeport. His father worked for the Illinois Central Railroad; his mother was a homemaker and an artist. In addition to farm work, Peter dug graves, pumped gas, poured cement, soda jerked, worked in a slaughter house and in a wire mill. He received his B.A. in economics from Loras College in Dubuque, Iowa and his M.A. in English from Northern Illinois University in DeKalb, Illinois. He taught briefly at NIU before moving on to the University of Cincinnati, and subsequently entered the insurance and financial services field as an agent. Following a move to the Home Office, he served in a variety of executive positions, including Vice President, Field Operations.

A licensed private pilot, Shianna enjoys the arts, travel and playing cards, especially poker and bridge. He's also an avid golfer and pickleball player. He and his wife, the former Loretta "Lori" Johnson of Freeport, Illinois, live in Florida. They have two grown sons, Eric and Kevin, and one grandson.

Love Tag is Shianna's second novel. His writing has appeared in the Rockhurst Review, the Kansas City Star and the Creative Writers' Journal. His fiction has been included in three anthologies.

You are invited to visit his web site at:
www.petershianna.com

We hope you have enjoyed reading *LOVE TAG.*

We'd love to hear your comments.

Please email us or the author at:
firesidepubs@comcast.net

www.firesidepubs.com
www.petershianna.com